## What readers have said about previous Collins & Clark books

*'My husband and I read this book on holiday and both found it a great page-turner. I loved the relationships in the book as well as the plot. The characters fit well within the location and time and there was a delicious sense of humour running along a serious story. An easy but clever read what's not to like? Would make a great TV series.'*

Polly

★★★★★

*'This was a very good enjoyable read. The banter between colleagues is very funny and fits well into this book between the serious parts.'*

Neil Mullins

★★★★★

*'What a joy this novel is to read. There is non-stop action and intrigue to keep you turning the pages and two very likeable protagonists with some good repartee to keep you warm and amused.'*

Elaine Tomasso

★★★★★

*'Clive, Michael, and Agnes make a great team in this British procedural. It's sometimes easy to forget what it was like for police in the days before CSI, DNA, and surveillance cameras everywhere but McGrath has written a cracking good mystery story that reminds you of the basics.'*

Kathleen Grey

★★★★★

A Death in Autumn: 1968

A Collins & Clark Story

Jim McGrath

ISBN-10: 1-91-260567-8
ISBN-13: 978-1-912605-67-5

Published by j-views Publishing, 2020



Body set in 11pt Brioso Pro, chapter titles and headings in Motorway

www.j-views.biz

publish@j-views.biz

j-views Publishing, 26 Lombard Street, Lichfield, UK, WS13 6DR

# A DEATH IN AUTUMN: 1968

Dear Steve,

Thank you for your thoughtful words,

Best Wishes.

Eija, Helen & Michael

## Dedication

For Martina Cole, who does not know me from Adam but whose work, especially *The Ladykiller,* inspired me to write.

# 1968 Police Attitudes, Terminology and Equipment

## Terminology

Separate forensic teams did not exist in the 1960s. Usually a single officer in each division was designated as a Scenes of Crime Officer (SOCO) and he (it was nearly always a he) could enlist the help of other officers as and when required. The same officer was also responsible for photographing the crime scene.

## Geography, dialect and poetic licence

Birmingham lies to the south of the Black Country and Handsworth marks the border. Although they are neighbours the differences in attitude, accents and customs remain significantly different. Simply put, if you want to insult someone from the Black Country you call them a Brummie.

The Black Country has no clearly defined borders, but it is usually defined as "the area where the South Staffordshire coal seam comes to the surface". This includes Brierley Hill, West Bromwich, Oldbury, Blackheath, Cradley Heath, Old Hill, Bilston, Dudley, Tipton and Walsall but not Wolverhampton. However, using other criteria it is accepted by many people in the region that Wolverhampton is part of the Black Country. If they didn't, we would be unable to have the Black Country derby match between West Brom and Wolves.

Each town has its own version of the Black Country dialect and none of them share any resemblance to the typical "Brummie" accent. The following few words are used by Clark and other characters throughout the book to give a poor impression of how a person from West Bromwich might sound.

| | |
|---|---|
| Ain't = will not | Wi = we |
| Bostin = good/great | Wiek = week |
| Dain't = did not | Wem = we are |
| Kidda/Matte = friend | Yow = you |
| Summut = something | Yowm = you are |
| Tarrar or tarrar a bit = goodbye | Yam Yam = person from the Black Country |

Many readers have remarked on the accuracy of the Birmingham locations used. So as not to mislead anyone, I need to say that while most of the streets, locations and buildings referred to in my books do/did exist, I have also invented a few of my own when the story required it.

## Acknowledgements

Once more I must acknowledge a huge debt of gratitude to David Brown. David served in the West Bromwich and Lichfield forces for ten years during the 1960s and early 70s before becoming a social worker. He has acted as technical advisor, grammarian and critical friend. As a painter of considerable talent David understands the creative process and is a constant source of encouragement and support. It is his painting which adorns the cover of this book.

I would also like to thank my nephew Stephen McGrath, who served in the Staffordshire Police for over twenty-five years. Stephen has given me a rare insight into the attitudes of police officers which has helped me to create the characters found in this book.

Thanks again are due to my publisher and fellow Lichfield Writer, Hugh Ashton, who is a constant source of encouragement. He is also responsible for the design and layout of this book. How he does all this and still manages to turn out his own thrillers and Sherlock Homes stories is beyond me.

# Contents

# A DEATH IN AUTUMN: 1968

JIM McGRATH

A COLLINS & CLARK STORY

J-VIEWS PUBLISHING, LICHFIELD, ENGLAND

# Part One

## Prologue

### Monday 3rd June 1968

### Birmingham, 11.30hrs

Sir Charles Endbury was fifty, looked forty and had the energy of a thirty-year-old. He prided himself on being able to work harder and longer than anyone in his engineering company, but today he was finding it difficult to concentrate. He had read the Council reports twice for the meeting he was due to attend at two pm, but nothing had registered. His thoughts kept returning to the previous Saturday night.

He had been introduced to Christina Murray by Councillor Hill at a Council reception for a Saudi prince, who was interested in investing in Birmingham. After a few drinks they had retired to her flat in Moseley where they had both enjoyed a night of energetic sex. Now he found it impossible to get her out of his mind. Such smooth skin, beautiful long blonde hair, a lovely smile and the best arse and legs he had encountered in the last ten years. Wonderful.

*Thank God Claire's away,* he thought. *I have plenty of time in the next three weeks to discover all of Christina's many charms.* He felt himself grow hard at the thought of what was in store. Of course, he realised that when his wife returned from holiday his meetings with Christina would have to be less frequent. But he would ensure that she had plenty of spending money and would be only too happy to have her describe in glorious detail her experiences with her other special friends. A smile of expectation spread across his lips. Christina's other encounters would provide the perfect excuse for why she should be soundly punished.

He was still thinking of the wonderful description she had

given him of how she had lost her virginity to an oily biker who had bent her over his beloved BSA, when his secretary knocked and entered. 'I know you don't wish to be disturbed Sir Charles, but this parcel has just been delivered by courier. It is marked private and urgent. So, I thought I should bring it straight in.'

'Thank you, Sylvia. It might be concerned with today's Council meeting. I'll look at it in a moment. Could you make me a cup of coffee please?'

'Of course.'

Endbury started to open the package. It was very securely wrapped, with almost as much Sellotape wound around it as paper. Irritated, he took the scissors from his desk and cut away the packaging. Inside was a small plastic box and a pack of photographs wrapped in a typed note. Laying the letter aside, he turned over the first photo already fearing the worst. It was a poor-quality picture of Christina on her knees, eyes closed, her face buried in his crotch, while he beat her with a short black leather whip. *Blackmail. The little bitch,* he thought. *She will not get away with this.* The next nine photos showed how the evening had progressed to the point where he was shown having intercourse with Christina while restricting her breathing with his hands over her mouth and nose.

The last three photos were solo shots of Christina. The first showed her badly bruised and beaten. In the second, she was naked, spread-eagled and tied to the four corners of the bed. The fear in her eyes was real and pitiful. The third picture showed Christina hanging by a noose. Her eyes were bulging, and it was obvious that she was near the point of death.

His secretary knocked on the door, and as she entered Sir Charles quickly turned the pack of photos over.

'Are you all right, Sir Charles? You look as if you've seen a ghost.'

Fighting to control himself, Sir Charles said, 'I'm fine. You were right to bring the parcel in. It is from the Clerk's Office.

Some additional information and photos about the new development we're looking at.'

Sylvia placed the coffee on her boss's desk and left. With a shaking hand Sir Charles picked up the letter. It simply read, *Change your vote or else.*

Twenty minutes later Endbury left his office and walked down the road to the Queen Victoria pub where he ordered a large gin and tonic. He drank half of the colourless liquid, then, with glass in hand, walked to the back of the pub and into the telephone box that was housed beneath the stairs. Closing the door, he took out a scrap of paper on which he had written a telephone number. With a trembling hand he picked up the receiver and started to call the man whom he thought had ordered Christina's death.

## Friday 20th September 1968

### Handsworth, 09.20hrs

Clark bustled into the CID room and dropped a file on his desk before asking Collins, 'Are yow all set for our meeting with the Super this morning?'

'Yeah,' said Collins without any enthusiasm.

Like most coppers Collins hated sitting in the office. He wanted to be out on the streets, but he was not looking forward to visiting Superintendent Wallace. The Super had been off work since the last week in July and everyone knew that he would never return. The stomach and bowel cancer had raced through him and had already eaten away a third of his body weight and was spreading fast. But he had always been a fighter and he was still fighting.

Every officer in the station including Collins and Clark had visited him regularly, but today's visit was different. He had contacted Collins and asked if he and Clark would see him about a case he had been investigating on the side for nearly two years. He stressed that he did not want anyone else to know the reason for their visit.

'Are you ready for it?' asked Collins, standing up.

'Yeah, I suppose so. But it's bloody terrible to see a good man go out this way. If I were him, I'd finish it.'

'Well, we'll all get the chance to make that decision in time.'

'And what will yow do?'

'I'm with you. I think we all have the right to end it. But I don't want anyone else making the decision for me or helping me do it.'

'Not even me?' asked Clark.

'Especially you.'

## Streetly, 11.50hrs

Mrs Wallace showed Collins and Clark into the lounge where a single bed had been set up for the Super. He looked even worse than Collins remembered. In just two weeks he had lost another stone. His skin was gossamer thin, stretched over the bones of his face and hands it had assumed a dirty yellow hue. *It's eating him alive,* thought Collins. *Poor bastard.*

'Thanks for coming, lads. I appreciate it.'

'Can I get you a cup of tea?' asked Mrs Wallace.

'No, wem fine,' said Clark, remembering what an atrocious brew the lovely lady made.

'Well, I'll leave you to it then,' she said and gave her husband a shadow of a smile.

'I know you're busy, so I'll make this quick, lads,' said Wallace. 'Give me that file on the chair and I'll explain what it's all about.'

Collins picked up a heavy black lever arch file from the fireside chair and handed it to his boss.

Tapping the file with a bony finger the Superintendent said, 'This is something I've been working on. It's my secret. My last case.' His voice for a moment sounded melancholy. 'It's about corruption, blackmail and murder and I've got virtually nowhere with it because I couldn't investigate it officially.'

'Why not?' asked Collins, even though he already knew the answer.

'It involves councillors, local government officials, and men who could buy and sell the three of us with the change in their pocket. There's probably a few MPs in there as well. I knew I'd be crushed if I went public. I collected what information I could on the QT. It doesn't amount to much. The best stuff came from that Irish lass who you sent down for conspiracy last spring. It's sparse at best. Mostly it's innuendo, hearsay and a few names but no real proof.' He lay back and closed his eyes. The pain was etched on his face. For thirty seconds he fought down the enemy. Then it was gone. But he knew it would return soon, stronger than ever. Then, eventually it would stay and not leave until the darkness came.

Both Collins and Clark could see the effort that the dying man was making, and it was Clark who stepped in first. 'So wem here because yow want a couple of loony bastards to go through the file and start shaking a few trees and see what wi can find. Is that about it, Sir?'

The Superintendent smiled for the first time since Collins and Clark had arrived. It was the smile of a skeleton. But his eyes were still bright, alive and combative. 'Aye, that's it. I wanted the best pair of bright, obstinate bastards I could find but you two will have to do. See what you can find out. See what you can do before I go. Please.'

## Handsworth, 13.56hrs

When Collins and Clark returned to the station, they found Chief Inspector Hicks getting ready to go to court, 'How was the Super?' he asked.

'Slipping fast, Sir,' said Collins

'That's a damn shame. What did he want you for?'

Collins quickly outlined the Super's request and when he finished Hicks nodded and said, 'Fine. Have a dig around but do it on the quiet. I don't want the powers that be giving me a good kicking with their clodhoppers. But remember you've still got four unsolved burglaries on the patch to look at.'

'Will do, Sir,' said Collins as Hicks walked out the door.

Left alone, Clark asked, 'Have yow still got the burglary file?'

'Yeah,' and rummaging in his desk drawers Collins pulled out and handed over a blue manila file.

'What did yow make of it?' asked Clark.

'Very professional. In and out with the minimum mess or fuss. Same MO on all four. Small window at the back of the house removed or hole cut in it and catch released. If that didn't work, the window pane was removed, allowing a smallish guy to wriggle through and open the door. All break-ins done at night with people sleeping in the house. In every case the owners were old age pensioners and there were no kids or dogs on the premises. They're taking a risk with the owners in the house but they're so bloody quiet no one's heard a thing. From your long and illustrious career, covering many years, does it ring any bells?'

'From the way yow talk yow'd think I were bloody ancient.'

'If the shoe…'

'Don't, I'm warning yow.' Collins smiled but said nothing. 'I've got a couple of guys wi should look at" said Clark. 'Alf's checking the records to see if them's out at the moment and where them staying.'

'When will you get the list?'

'Probably Monday or Tuesday.'

'OK.'

'Anyways, are yow heading off early tonight?'

'No. Agnes is at a meeting in London and won't be back until around seven. She's agreed I can pick up some fish and chips for our supper.'

'Yam starting to pull her down to yowr level. Next she'll be after faggots and peas in thick brown gravy.'

'Up yours.'

'I don't know how a lady like Agnes puts up with yow. Are you sure she's still going to marry you in February?'

'Why the interest?'

'If it's still on I'll need to visit Burtons and be measured for me suit. Anyways what yow going to do this late in the day?'

'As soon as you piss off and give me some peace and quiet, I'm going to have a look at the Super's file.'

'OK. Call me if yow find anything interesting.'

As the door closed Collins opened the Super's lever arch file and started reading. The Super had been right when he said that the file was long on speculation and hearsay and short on facts and proof. Collins quickly identified why; no interviews had been undertaken with the suspects. All the Super had been able to do was compile intelligence on local builders and councillors who were connected to a range of council committees. To move the investigation forward Collins knew that he and Clark would have to rattle a few trees and annoy several people who belonged to that august British club known as "the great British upper class."

Collins extracted a foolscap notepad from his desk, found his favourite pen and started to make some notes.

## Handsworth, 20.15hrs

Agnes dried the last plate and put it away in the cupboard while Collins rinsed the sink clean of Fairy Liquid soap bubbles, then dried his hands.

'That was nice,' said Agnes and brushed a stray strand of auburn hair away from her face. The action caused Collin's heart to miss a beat. 'It's a while since we had real fish and chips.'

'Clark thinks I'm pulling you down to my social level.'

'That's the thing about being upper class my dear, you don't have to care what the hoi polloi thinks,' said Agnes and laughed. 'Anyway, are you going to tell me what's in your Superintendent's file?'

'I will as soon as I've made us a cup of tea. Go and sit down now.'

'Yes, O great master, your wish is my command,' laughed Agnes.

With Agnes sitting in her favourite armchair, her feet tucked under her, Collins picked up his notes and said, 'The Super's got a lot of speculation, a few names and a couple of odd decisions at various council meetings. However, he has no hard evidence that anything significant is going on in the Council. But something feels wrong. I'm not sure what it is, but my gut tells me that the Boss is onto something.'

'What are you going to do?'

'What Clark and I usually do. Go blundering about until we annoy someone enough for them to show their hand.'

'Where will you start?'

'Well there are a few characters mentioned more than once. I think we start with them.'

'Anyone I know?'

'I don't know,' said Collins looking at his notes. 'I have John Reece, a friend of his called Chris Thorne, Martin Cunningham, and a couple of councillors by the names of Hill and Robbins. Do you know any of them?'

'I know Hill and Robbins. I wouldn't trust them to help me cross the road. Some people are in politics for the power, a surprising number because they want to help people and a few for the money they can make. Robbins and Hill definitely fall into the last category.'

'Why haven't they been drummed out if it's so obvious that they're on the make?'

'Because they are very clever. They look after the people in their wards, are never too greedy, and cover their tracks wherever they go.'

'What about the others?'

'I've met Martin Cunningham. He's a builder with a reputation for treating people fairly. No one has a bad word to say about him. I'd be surprised if he were involved in anything illegal.'

'And the other two?'

'I've never met either Reece or Thorne but there are stories about them.'

'Such as?'

'The usual. Nothing specific. Just rumours of strange decisions made by councillors and committees. But that's all they are, just stories. No one has any proof.'

'From what you say I should probably start with Martin Cunningham. It sounds like he might be willing to point me in the right direction. When I take Sheba for a walk tomorrow, I'll call in on Clarkee, see if he fancies a drive out to Solihull on Sunday.'

'Why Sunday? We're having dinner with them.'

'Guess.'

'He's going to a football match tomorrow.'

'Not just any old football match,' said Collins. 'It's Wolves at the Hawthorns.'

'Well, give little Mickey a kiss from me.'

'Will do.'

## Saturday 21st September 1968

### Handsworth, 09.30hrs

Collins and Agnes were tidying up after breakfast when the telephone rang. Picking it up, Collins just about got his name out before Clark's familiar voice interrupted him. 'Had a call from O'Driscoll earlier. There was another burglary last night, but this time the owner came down and got hit over the head with a poker.'

'How bad?'

'He's in hospital with a cracked skull. He should be OK, but he were hit hard.'

'Did the wife see anything?'

'No. The bastards had scarpered before she made it downstairs.'

'OK, are you at the scene now?'

'Yeah.'

'Give me the address.'

'It's 3 Endwood Avenue. Just before you get to the island.'

'I know it. I'll be there in ten minutes.'

Endwood Avenue was the last turning off Hamstead Road before it crossed the roundabout at Church Lane and continued on to Hockley Hill two miles away. It took Collins less than five minutes to reach the house. Clark's green Morris 1100 and the van of the new Scenes of Crime Officer (SOCO), Gary Dobbs, was parked outside.

The SOCO was dusting the interior kitchen window for prints when Collins walked in. Clark was in the dining room talking to a woman in her late sixties. It was easy to see that the forty-year-old woman beside her was her daughter. The family resemblance was unmistakeable, both had green eyes, long slim noses and thin small mouths.

Clark stood up when Collins walked in. 'Ladies, this is Detective Sergeant Collins, he'll oversee the day-to-day investigation. Sarge, this is Mrs Robinson and her daughter Mrs Monroe. I'm just taking Mrs Robinson's statement.'

'Ladies, I'd like to say how sorry I am that this happened to you. A violent burglary in your own home is a terrible shock to the system.'

'Thank you, Sargent,' said Mrs Monroe. 'My mother is very shaken. I'm going to stay the weekend and my husband is coming over later.'

'Good. If you don't mind, I'd like to look about the house and garden while Detective Constable Clark finishes taking your statement. Is that all right, Mrs. Robinson?'

'Yes, of course,' came the whispered reply.

The semi-detached house had a single flat-roofed garage that extended to next door's fence. The rear garage door was about six feet from the kitchen window that the thieves had climbed through. Collins noticed gravel on the pavement between the kitchen door and garage. Moving one of the dustbins, he stood on it and inspected the garage roof. The gravel near the edge had been disturbed where someone had slipped or had lowered themselves over the edge before dropping into the garden.

Stepping down, he inspected the kitchen window. It opened in the middle and each side was divided into two rows of three panels, each about a foot square. The central panel on the left had been removed entirely but the window lock had not been damaged. *Either a kid or a very skinny lad got through that,* thought Collins.

He was about to move to the back of the house when he spotted a slip of paper lying on the drain grating under the window. Using his handkerchief, he picked up the ticket and examined it. It was a 10/6 ticket stub for a concert by the

Beach Boys at the Birmingham Odeon, dated Saturday, the fourteenth September.

Collins tapped the window and Dobbs looked up. 'Have you done outside yet?'

'No.'

'Well, I've just found this. Can you dust it for prints pronto and run anything you find against the records?' said Collins handing the stub to Dobbs through the pane less window.

'Will do.'

'Ta.' Collins continued around to the back of the house where he examined the French windows. They had been opened from the inside by whoever had crawled through the kitchen window. Clark had finished taking Mrs Robinson's statement and she and her daughter were waiting for the SOCO to finish in the kitchen so that they could make another pot of tea.

Standing by the door, Collins asked, 'Mrs Robinson, did you or your husband attend a concert at the Odeon last Saturday?'

Mrs Robinson appeared confused by the question and shaking her head said, 'No.'

'Has anyone visited you in the last week?'

'No. Just my daughter and her children.'

'No young callers at the door?'

'No.'

'What's this all about, Sergeant?' asked the woman's daughter.

'I'm just looking to eliminate some possibilities.'

Clark waited until they were both outside before he asked, 'How do yow want to handle this?'

'The sods crossed a line when they hit the old man with a poker. Next time they could kill someone. Why don't I go to the station and write up the report and you can push off to your match? Who are you playing?'

'I've already bloody told yow.'

'Yeah, you did. It's Birmingham, isn't it?'

'God help me from prats and Irishmen. It's the bloody Wolves.'

'Are they the ones who play in claret and blue?'

'Now I know yam just trying to piss me off.'

Collins smiled and said, 'Afterwards, I'll go to Dudley Road and see if Mr Robinson saw anything.'

'That sounds good to me. I'll chase up Alf for the info I asked for. See if wi can get it first thing Monday.'

'Now seeing as I've done you a favour, I have one of me own to ask. I'd like to go and see a bloke called Cunningham tomorrow. He's a builder in Birmingham and is mentioned in the Super's file. Lives in Solihull.'

'Fair enough. Pick me up around 11.'

Collins collected his car from home and drove to the station. Sergeant Ridley was coming out of the CID office just as Collins rounded the corner. 'Morning, Jim,' said Collins. 'Looking for someone?'

'I was looking for O'Driscoll but he's not in.'

'What do you want him for?'

'I've got a Mrs Lafferty in reception reporting a missing daughter. I think the girl is on the game but the woman is worried.'

'OK, show her into Interview Room 1 and I'll be with her in five minutes.'

'Thanks, Mickey. Appreciate it.'

Collins made it to the interview room long before Mrs Lafferty did. Breathing hard, her gait unsteady, she was led by Sergeant Ridley into the Interview Room. She sat down heavily and said nothing as she tried to bring her breathing under control.

'Would you like a cup of tea, Mrs Lafferty?' asked Sergeant Ridley.

'No, I'll be fine, thank you, Sergeant,' came a hoarse whispered reply.

Mrs Lafferty was a small woman just a little over five foot, with very little weight on her. She had high cheekbones, an aquiline nose and dark blue eyes. If she had weighed another two stone, she would have been very attractive. As it was, she looked seriously ill.

Collins rose and shook her hand. He was surprised at how cold her hand felt, 'I'm DS Collins. Sergeant Ridley tells me your daughter has gone missing. Would you like to tell me about it?'

'Are you from Dublin?' she asked.

''Yes. And yourself?'

'Drumcondra. You've lost some of the accent but it's still there,' she said with a smile which lit up her entire face. 'Well I'm a bit more hopeful now.'

'What do you mean?'

'Well you're young, you're Irish and you're a Detective Sergeant. You must be good.' Collins felt his face turn red. Mrs Lafferty saw the effect her words had on him and immediately apologised. 'Here's me running off at the mouth. I'm a terrible one for saying whatever comes into me mind.'

'It's all right. Why don't you tell me what's happened, Mrs Lafferty?'

'My daughter Claire is missing since May time. She moved to Birmingham about two year ago. At first, she wrote to me regular like. Late last year she told me that she'd been signed up by some modelling agency, which was what she'd always wanted. Really excited about it she was. But then her letters got fewer and fewer. When I didn't get a letter in May or June I came up and went to see her. But she'd gone from the flat which she'd shared with another girl, Christina. I don't know her surname.'

'Where did this Christina say she'd gone?' asked Collins.

'Well that was the problem, she was gone too. Both just vanished into thin air.'

'What did you do?'

'I went to the landlord, but he had no address for them. He

tried to stiff me for a month's rent, cheeky sod. I didn't want to bring the police into it, so I went to a private detective.'

'Why didn't you want to bring the police into it?'

'I was afraid that she was into something illegal.'

Collins didn't ask what the something might be. Instead he asked, 'Did your private eye find anything?'

'Yes, he did. He said that he'd made enquiries and was sorry to tell me that my daughter had been working as a prostitute for over a year before she disappeared. He suggested that the most likely cause of her disappearance was that she had moved to London. He said a girl could earn a lot more there than in Birmingham. He also said that a lot of girls, when they get involved in the business, cut off contact with their families. Like they were ashamed of what they were doing and afraid that the family would find out.'

'I'm sorry but that is often the case,' said Collins. 'Sometimes it's the girl's pimp that forces her to cut contact. It gives him greater control over her.'

'I don't believe it. I'm not daft. Claire was always a bit wild. But she was intelligent. She had her head screwed on and knew the value of a pound. A grand little businesswoman, she was. I've heard it said that prostitution is the only job where the young start at the top and work their way down. Well, if my Claire did become a prostitute, she'd have had too much sense to start at the bottom working for some slimy pimp.'

Collins realised that the woman in front of him was not your usual worried parent. Whether it was the proximity of her death or just her nature she had few illusions about her daughter or what she might be willing to do to earn good money. 'Do you know when they left the flat?' he asked.

'Well that's what convinced him that the pair of them had gone off willingly. You see, when they didn't pay the rent on the thirty-first of May the landlord went around.'

Collins interrupted the woman's flow and asked, 'When did the landlord go around?'

'Two weeks later, I think. He found they'd done a moonlight flit and taken everything they owned with them. Me PI— you know, I've always wanted to say that,' she said with a sad smile. 'Anyways, he said he didn't have the resources to investigate beyond Birmingham and gave me the number of another private detective in London, but he was too expensive for me. That's why I'm here.'

'Did your PI find out when they were last seen?

'No. But he told me that Claire and her friend had been to some do at the Council House on June first for some Saudi Arabian prince. I think that might be the last time she was seen. He sort of implied that she might have gone off with him.'

'When was the last time that her friend was seen?' asked Collins.

'I don't know.'

'I'll be honest with you Mrs Lafferty. I think that your PI was probably right. If Claire and her friend were on the game they may well have gone to London. And if she had signed up to a model agency it might be the kind that deals in pornography. Now the centres for such work are London, Amsterdam and Hamburg. She could easily be in any of those cities and if she is, it will be extremely hard to find her.'

'But you'll look into it for me, won't you?' The woman's voice was low and pleading and Collins could see the desperation in her eyes. 'You'll look for her, Sergeant Collins, I have to know what's happened to my little girl before I...'

Collins asked,' How long do you have?'

'The doctors told me last Thursday that I have a month or two at most.'

'Look, Mrs Lafferty, if she has gone off with her pimp or girlfriend and doesn't want to be found we could be looking at a long investigation. I may not be able to find her within a month.'

'But you'll try, won't you? Please.'

'For a fellow Dub I will. I'll do everything I can to find her. But what about her father? Is he still alive?'

'I don't know. We split up fourteen years ago. I've not seen him for twelve years. Even if he is alive he won't be interested. All he's interested in is where he'll get the next drink from.'

Picking up his pen Collins turned to the missing person report form he had in front of him and said, 'All right Mrs Lafferty, let's take down some details. Can we start with your contact details, the address of Claire's flat and a recent photo of your daughter, please?' Mrs Lafferty gave her address near Coventry and Claire's address on King Edward's Road, off Grove Lane, Handsworth.

After Mrs Lafferty had left, Collins examined the small black and white photo of Claire Lafferty. She was certainly a beautiful young woman. Small and slim, with a face undamaged by age or illness. She reminded Collins of Audrey Hepburn, with the same dark silky hair and mischievous eyes. She was standing by the monkey house at Dudley Zoo and was laughing as she tried to control her skirt from being blown up over her waist. Rising he headed back to his office and wrote up the missing person report. Only then did he turn his attention to the report on the burglary.

It was nearly 3pm when he called Dudley Road Hospital and asked for Mr Robinson's ward number.

## Handsworth, 16.19hrs

Crick Lane ran from Holly Road, across Broughton Road and up towards Ivy Road. It was something of an oddity in Handsworth, a named road with no house frontages. Plenty of back garden fences and garages abutted onto the lane but no front windows overlooked it. Although it was a recognised shortcut, few adults used it after dark, which made it a perfect place for teenagers to hang about in.

Sixteen-year-old June Gregg sat with her back against a

garage door playing with a six week old black and white kitten. The little fella was busy chasing a piece of wood tied to a length of dirty string she was holding. Every time the kitten got near the lure the girl pulled it away and laughed.

A noise at the end of the alley made her look up. It was one of the lads who worked at the HP Factory in Aston. He was new to the area, but her mates reckoned he was 17. They also thought he looked great; with his collar-length black hair he was the spitting image of John Lennon. As she watched him walk closer, she forgot the kitten and the lure which was now resting in her lap.

The kitten took its chance and jumped at the sliver of wood. One set of tiny claws grabbed the lure. The other set sank into the back of June's hand. She screeched at the sudden pain and backhanded the tiny cat away. It flew across the alley and landed in the middle of the lane. Looking down. June saw four claw marks, each less than an inch in length, which had barely broken the skin. 'Fucking cat,' she said and sucked the back of her hand.

'You OK?' asked the boy.

It was the first time she had seen him up close and she really liked what she saw. 'Yeah, I'm fine, but that fucking cat scratched me.'

The boy picked up the kitten. 'This little bastard?'

'Yeah,' she said.

'It shouldn't be allowed,' he said. 'They should have a law against scraggy cats scratching beautiful girls.'

She smiled at the compliment and pushed her light brown hair away from her sea green eyes. 'Yeah they should. They should fucking hang 'em,' and laughed.

'But you gotta have a trial first. It's gotta be legal, ain't it?'

'Yeah. What's your name?'

'Andy Dewar.'

'OK. Judge Dewar, I want that cat tried for scratching me.'

'Did this kitten viciously attack you today and scar your hand for life?'

'Yes, me Lud, it did.'

Holding the cat level with his face, he asked, in a poor imitation of Michael Dennison's posh accent in the TV series *Boyd QC*, 'What have you got to say in your defence, pussycat?' Then he looked at June. 'It seems the accused has no defence. As the victim of this crime, what do you think should be done to this vicious wild animal?'

June was smiling widely, a bright shiny look in her eyes. She placed her left index finger across her chin and started to chew on the second knuckle. All the time her eyes were locked on Andy's face. *Would he do it, really?* He was just standing there. Confident. Gorgeous. 'I want to see the fucker hang,' she whispered.

'I'm sorry, I dain't hear that.'

'I want you to hang the cat.'

Looking at the kitten, Andy said, 'Sentence has been passed. You will be hung by the neck until you are dead. Here, hold the mangy shit while I make a noose.'

June took the cat and held it tight against her breast. It tried to squirm free, but she held it tighter. Her eyes locked on Andy as he fashioned a noose from the piece of string that moments earlier, she had been playing with. Her heart was beating fast and the blood was pulsing in her temples. Everything in the alley seemed clearer, sharper. The colours. The smells. Even the feel of the paving slab beneath her backside. For the first time since Andy had spoken to her she noticed a wetness between her legs. *He's going to do it.*

Noose complete, Andy slipped it over the kitten's head and wrenched the kitten from Marie's grasp. Holding the cat at arm's length, he started to laugh as he watched the cat jerk and thrash about in the air.

'Spin it round,' said June.

'Yes, me lady,' he said and started to whirl the cat faster and faster around his head. After half a dozen revolutions he stopped. The cat hung lifeless from the string. 'Sentence complete, milady,' he said and spinning the cat again he let go of the string and sent the lifeless body crashing into the brick wall of number 14.

June could hardly breathe or take her eyes off him. She licked her lips and waited.

'A workman deserves to be paid don't he, milady?'

'Yes,' she whispered and stood up. 'What do you want?'

'You.'

June felt a flood of hot liquid cascade through her body. Silent. Smiling. Still watching Andy, she undid her jeans and pulled down her white cotton knickers. Andy did not smile. He grabbed her by the shoulder and turned her round. 'Put your hands on the wall and stick your arse out.'

She did as she was told and cried out in pain and joy as without any foreplay, he thrust his penis into her. It took less than thirty seconds for both to come.

## Sunday 22nd September 1968

### Solihull, 11.10hrs

Clark yawned loudly as he slipped into the passenger seat of Collins' new two litre Ford Capri.

'Late night?' asked Collins.

'Na. Little Mickey were kicking up a fuss. He can be a right sod at times. Don't know where he gets it from.'

'How come you call him Bram most of the time but Mickey when he's a problem?'

'His name is Michael Abraham. Now his grandfather Abraham dain't never cause me a problem.'

'That's because he was dead when you met his daughter.'

'That don't make it any less true. But a certain guy called Mickey has caused me more problems in the last five and a bit years than any bloke I've ever met.'

'Fair enough. As long as there's a logical reason.'

'Anyway, did yow get anything out of old man Robinson?'

'No. They were waiting for him in the dining room and thumped him before he had turned the light on.'

'Vicious little sods then. Ready to break someone's head rather than be seen.'

'That's what I was thinking.'

Closing his eyes, Clark laid his head against the doorpost and was asleep before they drove past the Birmingham City ground and out towards Elmdom Airport, which saved Collins having to listen to Clark's report on the nil-nil draw between Albion and Wolves the previous day. Or his explanation for about the twelfth time, as they passed St Andrews, as to why Birmingham City were a second-rate club that had never won anything in their history.

In his six years in England Collins had begun to learn about Brum and how the people felt about it. Birmingham was never a city that the rich wanted to live in. No, Birmingham was where the rich made their money and the poor worked, lived and died under 30,000 factory chimneys. Agnes had told him that in Edwardian times the well-to-do lived in Handsworth and the Royal Town of Sutton Coldfield. By the end of the mid-1950s the middleclass had deserted Handsworth, and Sutton Coldfield had become the premier address for every executive in Birmingham. But by 1968 Solihull was coming up fast on the rails as the most desirable place to live in the Second City. As for the working classes, most of those still lived within a four-mile radius of the city centre.

Martin Cunningham was one of the rich. He lived on Lady Byron Lane in a five-bedroom detached house that had been designed to his specification and boasted a snooker room, an indoor swimming pool and a triple garage.

He had left Ireland in 1949 with five pounds in his pocket and caught the mail boat to Holyhead and the train to Birmingham. When he exited New Street station, he'd had a decision to make. Should he turn left, or right? He had enough self-awareness to realise that his entire future might depend on which direction he took. He decided to turn left and head for Sparkbrook. He was nineteen years old and did not have a single friend in this new and frightening country.

For the next four years he lived in the cheapest room he could find. He worked over sixty hours a week on the rebuilding of Birmingham, said little, and observed everything that was going on and saved as much money as he could. By 1953, he was ready to make his move. His escape ark was ready and like the animals of old he asked two of the best brickies, chippies, sparks, plumbers and plasterers he knew to join him as his partners in Tricolour Construction. By 1964 the partnership was recognised as one of the top ten independent house builders in England and there it had remained. Tricolour had an unrivalled reputation for workmanship and civility and no one; not his workers, customers, suppliers, or even his competitors, had a bad word to say about Martin Cunningham.

Clark rang the bell and a cheery, bright-eyed, bottle blonde in her late thirties answered the door, wearing a quilted blue house coat and slippers. She didn't look like a millionaire's wife. 'Good day. Can I help ya?' Her Dublin accent was strong and unmistakable.

Collins decided to play the Irish card. 'Good morning to yourself. Would you be Mrs Cunningham?'

'I would. And who are you?'

'I'm Detective Sergeant Collins and this is Detective Constable Clark. I'm sorry to disturb you on this fine Sunday morning but could we have a word with Mr Cunningham?'

'Well you could. But he's at Mass with the kids.' Looking over her shoulder at the hall clock, she added, 'But he'll be back in a quarter of an hour. Do you want to come in and wait?'

'That would be grand,' said Collins.

As Mrs Cunningham led them into the house, Clark leaned over and whispered in Collins ear, 'That would be grand, Mrs Cunningham. Wanker!' Collins grinned and said nothing.

The lounge was large and expensively furnished, but it was a family room, not a showpiece. Kids' toys were scattered on the floor. School books lay on the sideboard. Furniture from Lee Longlands which would have cost Collins six months' salary was scratched and scuffed. It had a lived-in look and Collins immediately felt comfortable in it.

'You'll have a cup of tea?'

'That would be bostin,' said Clark.

Ten minutes later, Mrs Cunningham returned with an ebony tray on which were three mugs of strong, dark tea, side plates, some plain Irish soda bread, sweet soda bread with currents and raisins, a sliced brack, a selection of Jacob's biscuits from Dublin and a full butter dish.

As she placed the mugs on the table she said, 'I didn't think you'd want a cup. A mug keeps the tay warmer.' Unbidden

Collins remembered his mother asking if wanted a cup of tay after his first communion. 'Help yourselves to a bit of me home-made soda bread. Now, tell me, what can I do for the Garda?'

Collins filled his plate with two slices of sweet soda bread and a piece of brack. After spreading a large dollop of butter on each he sat back and said, 'Well, I think it would be better if we spoke to Mr Cunningham. It's about his work.'

Mrs Cunningham sat up straight and looked at Collins, clearly appraising him. She took her time, but eventually said, 'I was the first person Martin employed when he started up. I was his secretary and bookkeeper. I still keep an eye on things. These eejit Chartered Accountants, with all the letters after their name, know feck all about the business or building sites. They've never been on a site in their lives. But me, well there's not much I don't know about the business.'

*I bet there isn't,* thought Collins, as for the first time he saw behind the façade that Mrs Cunningham had created for herself. He decided to dive in. 'We're looking into possible corruption in Birmingham City Council ...'

'Well, I can assure you Martin has nothing to do with that rubbish.'

'No, we're not suggesting he has.' Collins' heavy Irish accent had disappeared. 'But we think he can point us in the right direction.'

'Others have tried and got nowhere. Some of them lost their jobs. Some had accidents. Why are you doing this now?'

Both men exchanged looks. It was Clark who spoke. 'Our boss, Superintendent Wallace, has been doing some digging for nearly two years. He ain't got very far and asked us to take a look at it on the side.'

'Why doesn't he do it himself?'

'Because he's got about two weeks to live. Stomach cancer,' said Clark.

'God help the poor man,' said Mrs Cunningham and made the sign of the cross. 'That's an awful way to go. Me Mammy went the same way. All right then. You might as well take your jackets off; you'll be here for a bit. Martin and me have a lot to tell you.' Before Mrs Cunningham could launch into her story, they heard a key in the front door and three young girls, ranging in age from six to twelve, rushed screaming into the hall pursued by the their father. Knees bent, knuckles dragging on the floor grunting like a gorilla, he chased them into the lounge. All four stopped and stood still at the sight of the two strangers.

Standing up, Mrs Cunningham said, 'Martin, girls, these men are from the police.'

Collins stood up and introduced himself and Clark. After a round of handshakes, Mrs Cunningham shooed the girls upstairs and made a fresh mug of tea for her husband. Martin Cunningham was not tall, five foot ten at most, but his build resembled that of the gorilla he'd been imitating moments earlier. His legs were short and heavily muscled, straining the seams of his expensive suit. His arms looked like a series of coiled steel wires beneath the rolled-up sleeves of his shirt. His hands were big, calloused, hard, and looked like they could crush a coconut. Somewhere along the line he had picked up a broken nose. It should have made him look frightening but with his gentle brown eyes and the laugh lines around his mouth it just made his face look lived in.

After a quick recap from Mrs Cunningham, her husband leaned forward, selected two Jacob's biscuits, and said in a slow deliberate voice that gave him plenty of time to think, 'So someone is finally doing something about the bastards.'

'You'll help?'

'I will. But I'll only go on the record after you get some evidence to back up what I say. And that'll be hard to find.'

'Fair enough,' said Collins.

'Have you ever heard of John Reece?' Collins and Clark both nodded. 'Well he owns Birmingham. I don't know who he's got in his pocket, but he gets about eighty per cent of all Council building work and wins most of the bids he puts in for Council land. Back in the late fifties anyone who bid against him would find they had a strike on their hands, or their yard would burn down or their suppliers would suddenly ask for cash up front. He put a lot of good men out of business. Ruthless bastard. Nowadays, if he's bidding very few go up against him.'

'Have yow had any run-ins with him?' asked Clark.

'A couple. But we don't do much Council work.'

'Had any recently?' asked Clark.

'Well, now that you mention it. Yolande and me were at this Council shindig for some fecking Arab or something back in May or June. Reece was there. He came waddling over, all friendly like, and asked me if I was bidding on a piece of land off the Birchfield Road. Well the bastard knew full well I was. Anyway, he wished me luck and wandered off grinning like a twenty stone evil leprechaun.

'Now that made me suspicious. I'd spoken to Sir Charles Endbury, the chairman of the sub-committee earlier in the week and he as much as told me that my application was going to win. Well Endbury was over in the far corner talking to this bit of skirt. Nice looking woman. Just his type. Tall, long blonde hair, about thirty. We wandered over and I asked him if Reece had put a bid in. He didn't say yes or no. But he did say, "Martin, we need cheap houses for newlyweds more than another office block and a few shops." It's not often that you get such a big nod and a wink from a councillor, so I thought that Reece was just trying to get a rise out of me. Anyway, we fecked off to The La Dolce Vita and had a cracking night. Dave Allen was on.'

'He worked for us for a while in the fifties when he was still Dave Mahoney,' said Yolande. 'We went backstage after the show. He came home with us and the next morning I cooked him breakfast. He had the girls in fits with his vampire stories. They loved the one about the part-time vampire hunter who was a chef. His last words to Dracula were "How do you like your stake?" as he hammered it into his heart.'

'What happened over the land?'

'The sub-committee had a meeting the following Monday. Out of the fecking blue Endbury changed his vote and took three of his cronies with him.'

'Yow think he were bribed?' asked Clark.

'Na.' said Martin. 'He's always been fair and straight with me. He's an old Tory. He believes in helping people get on. For feck sake, the houses were his idea in the first place. It was him who came to me. That's why I bid.'

At that moment there was a crash from upstairs and a series of shrieks and screams from the girls. Martin stood up and went to the bottom of the stairs and boomed, 'Are you girls behaving yourselves? Or do I have to come up there and thump the lot of ya?'

In response there was a chorus of laughter and giggles and a single voice said, 'You and whose army?'

'That'll be Patricia. The middle one. Got a gob on her like a Moore Street trader. I don't know where she gets it from,' said Yolande.

When Martin resumed his seat, he was smiling. Clark asked, 'Did yow ever ask Endbury why he changed his vote?'

'I did. But he wouldn't say. That bastard Reece or more likely his pet gangster, Thorne, had scared the poor bastard shitless.'

'Thorne?' asked Collins as if he had never heard the name before.

'Yeah. A big Geordie gobshite of the first order,' said Yolande.

As if to emphasise the point Martin added, 'A right vicious bastard.'

'Have you ever heard of him,' Collins asked Clark.

'Na, strange that. I thought I knew all the muscle for hire in Brum.'

'Ah, he's muscle all right but not the sort you'd come across. Thorne runs his own business, Thorne Security. Has about twelve full–time blokes and a load of casual workers on the books. He says he specialises in personal and commercial security, but I wouldn't want him to fit a burglar alarm in my house. My bet is that he spends most of his time sorting out problems for Reece,' said Martin.

'Problems, such as what?' asked Collins.

'An upstart of a union rep or worker on site, a slow paying customer, an overzealous planner or architect. The word is he will have a chat with them, make them an offer and settle things all friendly if he can. He doesn't mind spending a bit of money if it makes him a new friend.'

'And if that don't work?' asked Clark.

'He, or more likely a couple of his lads, drop by and persuades them to change their mind. Rumour has it he starts slow and builds up. First, it's threats, then your dog might get killed or your house burgled. Or maybe a strange man calls on your wife while you are at work or he's seen talking to your kids or taking their picture. After that there might be an accident or a serious problem at work. If all that fails, you get a going over.'

'Anyone ever been killed?'

'Only rumours Sergeant, only rumours. No evidence. Just like the stories of blackmail?'

'Blackmail?' queried Clark.

'Sure, you can't go round beating up councillors or knights of the realm. It gets noticed. This isn't America, oh no. Thorne finds a weakness and goes for it. Drink, gambling, a liking for the girls or boys, even drugs. Those drugs you know, they're starting to become awful popular these days.'

Collins saw Clark glance at his watch. It was nearly two o'clock. Ruth had planned dinner for Agnes and Collins at three and she would not be best pleased if he was late. Shifting forward on the chair Collins said, 'Well, Mr Cunningham, Mrs Cunningham, we've taken up enough of your time. You've given us some great information. When we've done a bit of digging I'd like to come back and ask you a few more questions.'

'Happy to help anytime. And in future it's Martin and Yolande,' said the big man.

Holding the door open, Martin scratched his nose with his index finger and said, 'You know who you should talk to in the Corporation, Harry Freeman. An Australian fella. Works in the Housing Department now. But he knows more about what's going on in the Corporation than any man I know. But don't go after lunch. He's terrible with the booze.'

As the men walked back to Collins' new car, Clark returned to a familiar refrain. 'Look at that load of yellow shit, would yow? It's a fucking embarrassment.'

'How can a Ford be embarrassing?'

'A two litre, canary yellow Capri, with a black hood and a bonnet as long as a bloody E-type. It's the sort of car a pimp would buy, or someone who's been short-changed in the meat and two veg department.'

'Bollocks. You're just jealous.'

Collins slipped into the car and quickly accelerated away before Clark had settled himself. The acceleration slammed the small man into his seat and Collins grinned.

'Bastard. Anyhows, where do wi go from here?'

'Reece's in the file so he's already on our list. But Thorne is only mentioned in passing. We need to move him up the table. Sir Charles Endbury is new and so is this Harry Freeman character. I think we should collect some more info before we visit Reece or Thorne.'

'I agree,' said Clark. 'Wi should start with the Freeman geezer.'

'There is just one other thing,' said Collins and told him of his interview with Mrs Lafferty on Saturday.

'What's that got to do with corruption in Brum?' asked Clark.

'Well the last time Claire Lafferty was seen alive was at a Council do for some Saudi Arabian prince.'

'Bloody hell. Now ain't that a coincidence?'

'I thought you didn't believe in coincidences?'

'I don't. Especially, when they happen to me. Now a little less chat and a bit more speed. We've got a date with Sunday dinner and *High Noon* is on the box at three thirty.'

'Why don't you watch a real cowboy film like *A Fistful of Dollars?*'

'Na. Italian rubbish. Besides, Eastwood's a middleweight. He'll never be as good as Wayne, Cooper or Stewart. Them's real heavyweights.'

They were still arguing the merits of the four stars when Collins drew up outside Clark's house. They were met at the front door by Ruth, standing beside Sheba and Sailor, whose tails were wagging at the sight of their respective masters. Behind Ruth stood Agnes, holding Bram who was busy pulling her hair. Collins smiled. *Life is good,* he thought.

## Monday 23rd September 1968

### Birmingham, 11.40hrs

Collins and Clark trotted up the steps to Bush House on Broad Street, showed their warrant cards at reception and asked to see Mr Henry Freeman, Estates Department.

Five minutes later a dishevelled giant of a man lumbered into reception. He was wearing a pair of beer-stained trousers, an off-white shirt with a frayed collar, and a yellow and green Australian cricket tie that had seen far too many Test Match celebrations. His shirt sleeves had been rolled up, and there were multiple scars on both forearms. Moving slowly, he approached Collins and Clark. 'You the rozzers looking for me?'

'If yow're Mr Freeman, wem looking for yow,' said Clark.

'What did I do this time? I don't remember doing anything,' the big man sighed.

'Nowt,' said Clark. 'Wem just here for information.'

'Oh, why didn't you say so? Tell you what, mate,' he said, looking at his watch, 'why don't we continue this conversation in my office?'

Collins and Clark expected to follow the big man into the bowels of the Housing Department. Instead he headed for the front door. They caught up with him at the traffic lights. When they turned green Freeman marched smartly across the road and into the Granville Pub. 'Take a corner seat and I'll get the drinks in. Pint of bitter each OK?'

'I don't drink,' said Collins.

'Never mind, we can't all be perfect. I'll get you a lemonade. That all right, mate?'

'Fine. Thanks.'

It was before lunchtime and the pub was deserted. A thick carpet that had seen better days, with flowers and a purple thistle design, covered the floor. The four captain's chairs around each table were wood and leather were old but still comfortable. The smell of stale beer and old cigarette smoke oozed out of every crevice of the pub.

Minutes later Freeman laid the tray of drinks on the table and flopped down into one of the padded armchairs. In addition to the three pints and one lemonade there were two double whiskeys. Picking up a whiskey, Freeman emptied it into his pint and lifting his drink, emptied a third of it in two swallows. Banging the glass down, he wiped the foam from his lips and said, 'First of the day. Best of the lot.' His Australian accent was unmistakable. 'So, what do you want to know?'

Collins briefly explained the purpose of their visit and ended by saying, 'Martin Cunningham said we should talk to you.'

'That sanctimonious shite. You should watch him.'

'Why?' asked Collins.

'No one gets to be as big as him in the building trade without having a few skeletons buried somewhere.'

'Such as?' asked Collins.

'Well that's it. He's a clever bastard. Him and the wife. They don't leave any fingerprints. Leastways, none that I ever found. But there's something not right about them.'

'Let me get this straight, yow don't like him 'cause he's clean?' asked Clark.

'No one in the building trade is clean, mate. And if you believe they are, you're a mug.'

'What do you think he might be up to?' asked Collins.

'No idea. But don't trust him. That's my advice.'

'What about Sir Charles Endbury?' asked Collins.

'Lover boy. Who's he been screwing this time?'

'No one that we know of,' said Collins. 'Other than the women, what's he like?'

'For a politician he's almost human. Of course, he looks after himself but he doesn't screw the public doing it.'

'Yow don't think he's on the take, then?' asked Clark.

'Na. He's got more fucking money than Fort Knox. As I say, his weakness is the ladies. He'll fuck anything in a skirt provided its halfways decent.'

'What if the bribe were some tart?' asked Clark.

'He doesn't need to pay for it. He gets plenty free. Besides, I've seen him operate. He likes the thrill of the hunt.'

'If he's so clean, why do you think he changed his position on the Birchfield deal?'

'You heard about that? I don't know. What's more surprising is that the Committee Clerk doesn't know either.' Freeman took another long swig from his pint followed by a sip of whiskey and eased back in his chair. A loud fart that sounded like a starched cotton sheet being ripped in two caused the barman to look accusingly in their direction. Freeman ignored him.

'Yow don't think he was nobbled, then?' asked Clark.

'Na. He's clean.'

'What about blackmail?' asked Clark, 'A young girl maybe?'

'Na. He likes them mature. Woman who know the rules. Women in their late twenties or early thirties with big tits, long legs and an arse he can hang onto.'

'If pressure was applied on him who do you think was behind it?' asked Collins.

'Reece gained from the decision, so he'd be number one in the runners and riders. But Ronny Charlton was also bidding on that bit of land.'

Clark jotted the name down before asking, 'What's his story?'

'Came to Birmingham in the mid-fifties from Liverpool. He's a right scally. His family are dockers and the story goes that his father and brothers are responsible for organising most of the pilfering that goes on at the docks. Charlton would steal the pennies off a dead man's eyes, then screw the widow before evicting the kids if it would make him a few quid. But he's not known for violence. He prefers to lie and cheat. My guess is that he'd be happy to use blackmail to get what he wants.'

'But in this case, he dain't get what he wanted,' said Clark.

'Are you sure of that? He'd be happy to make a deal with Old Nick himself if it gained him a few quid. Maybe he got a fixer's fee.'

'You're saying he may have blackmailed Endbury for Reece?' said Collins.

'It's possible.'

'But why?'

'You'd have to ask him that.'

'What's Reece like?' asked Collins.

'He's like a fucking fat shark off Bondi Beach. Always swimming. Always looking for a kill. Always needs to win. All in all a right dangerous bastard and his mate, Thorne, is a vicious sod too.'

'Has he been involved in anything like the Birchfield deal before?' asked Collins and sipped his lemonade.

'Nothing proven but there have been stories. A lot of stories. He's got a lot of friends on the council including Councillors Hill and Robbins. Now those fuckers are worth having a look at. Bent as a pair of hair pins and bosom pals even though one's Labour and the other Conservative.'

'If we were to start digging into Reece, where do you think we should start?'

'Take a look at the planning application for Trent Tower. There was a young auditor, I think his name was John Simpson, who kept asking for more information. Ended up killing himself when he found out his wife was shagging some bloke. The wife denied it, but there were photos.' Finishing his pint, Freeman leaned back and looked expectantly at Clark.

Collins nodded and Clark moved to the bar.

'You've been a big help, Mr Freeman. Just one more thing. There was a Council reception for a Saudi prince a few months back. Could you get us a copy of the guest list and any photos that were taken?'

'Sure, what are you looking for?'

'Not sure yet. But I would like to trace a tall blonde woman aged about thirty who was seen at the party talking to Sir Charles.'

Freeman smiled, 'No problem. Give me your number and I'll call as soon as I get them.'

Collins scribbled down his number on the back of a beer mat that Freeman handed him.

Just then Clark reappeared with two pints and matching whiskey chasers and laid them on the table.

Freeman looked at the drinks and smiled. 'That's very generous of you, mate. You can definitely come again.'

Collins had parked at the side of Lee Longlands and waited until he was in the car before asking, 'What did you make of that?'

'Well Charlton is a new name on the list, and he confirmed that Hill and Robbins are dirty. He's also right about Cunningham. Wi both liked him, but that don't mean wi should treat him as if he's clean.'

'I agree,' said Collins as he put the car in gear and pulled away. 'I wonder where Freeman got the scars on his arms from.'

'Torture.'

'How do you know that?'

'Because I've seen 'em before. Some Jap guard tied his arms to a table, palms down and beat the shit out of them with a bamboo cane.'

'Bloody hell.'

'Exactly,' said Clark. 'Where to now?'

'Let's go see Marie,' said Collins looking at his watch.

## Birmingham, 13.05hrs

Collins and Clark found WPC Marie Bolding in the same office that Katie O'Neil had occupied just a few months earlier. But now, instead of files covering every chair, desk, and square inch of floor space, it was neat and orderly. A row of filing cabinets had been installed along one wall and three rows of built-in pigeonholes had been erected opposite. Katie's oak desk had been replaced with a modern monstrosity made of teak and chrome. Marie, head bent, was reading a file laid flat on the pristine surface, her back to the frosted window overlooking Steelhouse Lane.

Collins knocked on the open door and said, 'Have you got time to see a couple of old friends, or are you too grand to speak to us now?'

Marie's head snapped up and a broad smile spread across her face. 'I've always got time to see my two favourite coppers. Come in.'

'Ta,' said Clark. 'But what's this about yowr two favourite coppers? I thought I were yowr favourite?'

'You're my favourite on Tuesdays, Thursdays and Saturdays. Collins is my favourite on Monday, Wednesdays and Fridays.'

'What about Sundays?' asked Clark.

'That's my secret. Grab a chair. Can I get you a cuppa?'

'We'll buy you one in a bit, if that's OK,' said Collins closing the door and sitting down. 'How's the arm?'

'Fine. Nothing that another three operations won't put right.'

'Do yow get much pain?'

'Na. Only when I move it or bang it or try to bend it. Other than that, it's painless.'

'Well yam lucky. Some people who get shot in the elbow are in constant pain,' said Clark.

Marie smiled and gingerly placed her left forearm on the desk. 'Anyway, what brings you here and why the closed door?'

'You heard about the Super?' asked Collins. Marie nodded

her head. 'He's been looking into a case on the side for the last couple of years. To quote Marcellus, of Hamlet fame, he thinks there is something rotten in the state of Denmark. For Denmark read Birmingham. He's asked us to look into it?'

'Corruption?'

'Yeah. Big time if he and Martin Cunningham are right.'

'Who's Martin Cunningham?' Marie asked.

'One of the good guys, wi think,' said Clark.

'Who do you want info on?'

Collins withdrew the notes he had made on the file and added Simpson and Charlton's names to the list. As an afterthought he added, *plus any rumours about Trent Tower* and handed them over. 'That's my summary of the info the Super has collected. I've highlighted six names I'd like you to look into. But I have to warn you we could be dealing with some pretty important people, so this is strictly off the books and—.'

'Hush-hush. I get it. Tell you what. I'll copy the notes and see you in the canteen. Mine's a coffee and a ham and cheese sandwich, please.'

Twenty minutes later Marie sat down beside Clark. A saucer covered her teacup and a ham and a cheese sandwich sat beside the mug.

Passing Collins his notes, she said, 'That photocopier's crap. You only have to look at it and it goes doolally. When do you want the info?'

'As soon as you can manage it.'

'OK. Give me forty-eight hours.'

'Anything else?'

'Nope,' said Collins, then hesitated. 'Well, when you look at Martin Cunningham see if the Garda have anything on him in Ireland, but I doubt you'll find much,' and picked up his egg sandwich.

## Birmingham, 14.30hrs

As they walked from the car, Clark asked, 'Where to now?'

'I think we should have a chat with Mr Endbury and discover why he changed his vote.'

'OK, but how do yow want to play it, seeing as wi have nowt on him?'

'The usual. I'll start easy and then if you think he's holding back you go for him.'

'How come I'm always the hard bastard?'

'Because at your best you can be a really irritating little sod that gets under people's skin and would try the patience of Job.'

'Fair enough. As long as yow ain't taking me for granted. It can ruin a relationship if yow start to take someone close to yow for granted.'

'Have you been reading *Woman's Own* again?'

'Na. Ruth read it to me. I dozed off halfway through.'

Albert Endbury had established The Foreign and Empire Engineering Company in 1899. No one seemed to mind that his most distant customer was located just thirteen miles away in Wolverhampton. Expansion was helped by the First World War when the factory was put on a war footing and produced munitions for the duration. The Company's most profitable years had been 1917 and 1918 when Winston Churchill had been put in charge of munitions by the new Prime Minister, Lloyd George. The profits generated in those two years alone had been enough to provide the capital required to move into the production of plating plant equipment and the sale of anodising chemicals post war.

Charles Endbury joined the family firm in 1937 at the height of the depression and was almost resigned to the firm closing until war came to the factory's rescue. Foreign and Empire dusted down the old machines, bought some new ones and quickly started selling both munitions and machine parts for military vehicles. By 1945 they were supplying parts for everything from bicycles to tanks and Charles had plans for further diversification. For the next twenty years profits increased year on year and Charles Endbury became the darling of the Stock Exchange and in 1961 a knight of the realm.

Collins and Clark pushed their way thought the revolving doors and found themselves in the main reception area which was heavy on marble, oak panelling, and tradition. On the wall were two large plaques. The first listed the employees of Foreign and Empire who had died in the Great War, the second those killed fighting for Britain's survival in the Second World War. The top of each was adorned with a carved relief showing a battlefield altar of drums draped with Union Flags. The centre of the reception area was dominated by a fountain with a statue of a naked woman standing in the centre, water pouring from a jug balanced on her shoulder.

Five minutes later Collins and Clark were seated in Sir Endbury's office, his secretary fussing around them with tea and a plate of biscuits. 'That will be all, Sylvia, thank you,' said Sir Charles, his voice tinged with irritation. He waited until his secretary had closed the door before asking, 'So gentlemen, how can I help you?'

'We're investigating possible corruption in Birmingham City Council. We're particularly interested in approval of land sales and planning permissions,' said Collins.

'Well you certainly don't beat about the bush, Sergeant Collins. As the chairman of the Sub-Committee on land disposals am I to assume that I'm a suspect?'

'Yow got nothing to worry about,' said Clark. 'Wem just here for background information.'

'Well, that's good to hear. What do you want to know?'

'Has any architect or builder ever offered you or any of your fellow councillors an inducement to vote in a particular way?'

'You mean a bribe? Money?'

'It may not have been money. It might have involved gifts, holidays, entertainment, or a place on someone's board. It could be a range of things,' said Collins.

Sir Charles stroked his chin and took his time replying. 'There are always rumours. Whispers. But I've never been presented with any evidence that suggests anything is amiss in Birmingham. I'm sure small-scale stuff goes on all the time but nothing like what's going on in some places. Now take Newcastle for example...'

Collins cut off Endury's digression, 'So no-one has ever offered you a bribe, sir?'

'No, never.'

'Are yow sure?' asked Clark.

Sir Charles gave Clark the stare he used when he wanted to put some upstart of an employee in their place. It had no effect on the small man, who held Sir Charles' eyes and waited for an answer. 'Yes, I'm quite sure.'

'Of course, me old dad always used to say that if yow had a political scandal yow could bet your bottom dollar, that if it were a Labour politician it would be about money. But if it concerned a Conservative, it would be about sex. Any rumours about yowr mates on the Council shagging the hired help?' asked Clark.

'No!' A blush of anger appeared on Sir Charles cheeks and his eyes narrowed.

'What about yow?'

'How dare you, Constable? I'm a respectable married man.'

'So are most of the punters who visit prozzies.'

'Really Sergeant, this is outrageous. Can't you control your man?'

'I'm sorry, Sir. Normally I would but you see, he's not my man. Were you at the council reception for a Saudi prince on Saturday, June the first?'

'Yes, I was.'

'I believe that you spoke to a Mr Martin Cunningham and gave him the impression that you and your fellow Conservatives were going to approve his bid for a parcel of land on Birchfield Road. But when it came to the vote the following Monday you voted in favour of Mr Reece's proposal. Why did you change your mind?'

'Is that what this is all this is about? Has Martin Cunningham been throwing accusations about?'

'If you could just answer the question, Sir,' said Collins.

Sir Charles took a couple of breaths. When he spoke, his voice was low and he emphasised each word as if he was speaking to a particularly stupid child who was trying his patience. 'I did not give Mr Cunningham any cause to think that I favoured his plan over Mr Reece's. The truth is that I did favour building just houses on the site rather than the mixed development of houses, shops and offices. However, Cunningham's plans were poorly prepared and presented. Reece's proposals were simply more professional.'

'But yow dain't tell him that at the do?' said Clark.

'Of course I bloody didn't. It would have been unethical, and besides, it was an important social event and I didn't want a scene.'

'And why did you think there would be a scene?' asked Collins.

'Because Cunningham is---.'

'Irish and might blow his top. Would that be it, sir?' suggested Collins.

Sir Charles did not reply.

'Well, we won't take up any more of your time, Sir Charles.

Thank you for your hospitality,' said Collins and rising he held out his hand. Sir Charles took it but remained seated.

Clark stood up but didn't offer to shake hands. 'Just one last question, Sir. What time did yow leave the council do that night?'

'About ten fifteen. Why?'

'No reason. Did yow leave with anyone?'

'No.'

'So yow dain't leave with a good looking blonde woman that yow were seen talking to that night?'

Sir Charles wet his lips with the tip of his tongue before he replied. A slight tremor in his voice. 'I left alone.'

'I wonder why I don't believe yow.'

Endbury's face turned bright red with anger but he said nothing.

Outside on the pavement both men looked at each other and nodded. 'He's hiding sommut,' said Clark.

'Yep.'

'Where to now? The nick or Reece's?'

Collins looked at the sky, where heavy black rain clouds were moving slowly across the sky. They were in for another downpour. 'The nick. Let's see if Alf has turned up the info on those burglary suspects of yours.'

The rain was pouring down by the time Collins parked in the station yard and he and Clark made a dash for the door. 'Yow get a couple of teas in, Mickey, and I'll see what Alf's got.'

After purchasing tea and doughnuts for two Collins slid into a chair by the canteen's central window. The rain was now coming down in stair rods and bouncing off the concrete yard. But the wind was pushing the clouds along at a fair old lick and Collins knew it would soon clear. His reverie was broken by Clark dropping into the chair opposite.

'Well, me three suspects are down to two.'

'How so?'

'The esteemed Mr Leggott of this parish popped his clogs six months ago. Heart attack. Which surprises me – I never thought the bastard had a heart.'

'He's not going to be much of a loss to the community. What about the other two?'

'Peter Quine's been out two years. No problems with him since release. And then the master himself, Sid Williams. Released from prison on health grounds three months ago.'

'What's wrong with him?'

'Don't know but if he can walk, I wouldn't rule the git out.'

'Who do you want to see first?'

'Quine is nearest. Antrobus Road.'

'OK.'

Antrobus Road was off Grove Lane and only yards from the bottom of Holly Road. Quine's house was at the bottom of the dip, a big Victorian townhouse that had seen better days. With its peeling black and white paint and an untended front garden it looked forlorn and unloved, and was typical of most of the houses in the area. However, it still looked better than the monstrosity next door where the owner had decided to paint the bricks bright red and the mortar between the bricks white. It might have worked if he had had patience, a steady hand, and if the cheap paint hadn't run. As it was it looked bad enough to reduce the value of every house in the road.

Clark used the heavy iron knocker and moments later a woman in her early forties opened the door. Despite the rose-decorated pinafore, the grey in her hair, and the worn look that women get when their men have served serious time, she was still a good-looking woman.

'Hello Anne. Is he in?' asked Clark.

'Back room. He's just got home from work. Whatever you think he's done he ain't. He's been clean since he got out. Honest.'

Clark looked at Anne Quine. He'd known her for nearly fifteen years, and she'd never lied to him, which was unique in his experience. It was rare to find a crook married to such an honest woman. If Quine was doing jobs again, she didn't know about it. Seeing the fear in her eyes, he said, 'It's just routine, love, honest.'

She nodded and led the men down the hall. Peter Quine was at the table tucking into a couple of pork chops. His shirt off, it was clear to see he had been working all day His arms were covered in soot, with only his hands and face washed clean. He looked fit without an ounce of fat on his five-foot nine frame and his biceps and shoulders were well developed.

'Yow put on a bit of muscle since I saw you last,' said Clark.

'I ain't done nothing,' said Quine.'

'I ain't told yow what it's about yet.'

'It don't matter. I've been clean since I got out.'

'How come yow've become a reformed character at yowr age?'

Quine put his knife and fork down. 'After the last time I ain't never going back to prison again. I'll top meself first. So, help me God.'

'What happened to change your mind?' asked Collins.

'I ain't saying.'

'OK. Where were yow last Friday night between about eleven o'clock and six in the morning on Saturday?'

A smile of relief spread across Anne's face. Quine looked at her and returned the smile. 'We was in London. Brother's wedding in Tottenham. Went down Friday, came back Sunday. Dozens of witnesses. Do you want their names and addresses?'

'Maybe later,' said Clark. 'We'll get out of yowr hair and let yow eat your dinner in peace.'

As Anne walked them back to the front door Clark asked, 'What happened to him?'

'It weren't him. It was his cell mate. Four or five queers grabbed him in one of the workshops and raped him. Pete tried to help but got beat up for his trouble. They threatened to come after him if he said anything.'

'What happened to his mate?' asked Clark.

'Weeks in hospital. Pete knew that there were plenty of queers inside, but he'd never seen anything like that. Still has nightmares about it.'

As they walked back to the car Clark said, 'I think wi can strike him off our list. Something got broken during his last stretch. His nerve's gone.'

'I agree. On to Williams, methinks.'

Sid Williams had lived on Radnor Road, just yards from Villa Road, for as long as Clark could remember. It was easy to judge how well he was doing as a professional burglar, as he had a weakness for large cars. He liked to buy a new one whenever he made a big score. Clark had recognised this early on and had kept a regular check on Sid's cars. Whenever a real beauty appeared, he'd drop by for a few words. But this time was different – there was no car outside the house.

Clark rang the doorbell and it was answered almost immediately by a tall, well-built lad with blond hair.

'Hi Mitch, is your Grandad in?'

'He ain't well. Can't yow let him be?'

'We just want a quick chat. That's all.'

Knowing it was futile to argue, Mitch stepped back. 'He's in the front room,' he said as he closed the door. The front room had been converted into a downstairs bedroom. Williams was sitting by the gas fire in his pyjamas with a blanket draped around his shoulders – a mere husk of the man Clark had once known.

Clark exchanged looks with Collins. Sid was not their man.

'What do you fuckers want? Can't you let a man die in peace?' asked Williams, who had to take a deep breath after every couple of words.

'We were just checking where you were last Friday night from eleven until six on Saturday morning?'

'I ain't moved out of this room since I was released from prison. I just moved from one cell to another and I'll die in this 'un.'

'What is it you've got?' asked Collins.

'Emphysema. I'll be gone within three month.'

'I'm sorry to hear that, but I have to ask, do you know anything about the recent spate of burglaries in Handsworth and Handsworth Wood?'

'Na. None of the old lads visit. I've heard nothing.'

'How about you, Mitch? Have you heard anything?'

'Na, sorry. I'm not into that caper. I got a job with the gas board. Is this about the old geezer who got hit on the head with the poker?'

'How do you know about that?' asked Collins.

'It were in the *Sunday Mercury*, I get it for the football reports.'

'Yow don't say. Who do yow support?' asked Clark.

'Villa.'

'Not doing great, are they?'

Mitch didn't reply.

'What else do you like?' asked Collins.

'Rock and roll.'

'You mean the Beatles and the Beach Boys?'

'Fuck no. I'm a rocker.'

The rain had stopped but there was a strong wind blowing down Radnor Street which sent the fallen leaves into a swirl that piled them up against walls, fences and tree trunks and blocked the gratings on drains. 'I take it yow picked up on that?'

'Yeah,' said Collins.

'So, what wi going to do?'

'Watch him. See if he's got a skinny mate who likes the Beach Boys. I'll have a word with Ridley tomorrow. I'll come back tonight, around 10. Fancy joining me. You can sleep the whole time if you like. I promise not to start crying.'

'OK, but I'm heading home now. See yow later.'

Collins settled down to read the crime reports from the weekend, when the phone broke the silence and he picked it up.

'Mickey, it's me, Ridley. I was wondering, can you help me out if you ain't busy?'

'I will if I can.'

'I've got a woman on Broughton Road says she found a dead kitten nailed to her back gate this morning. It gave her a right turn.'

'Can't one of uniform look after it?'

'I'm short-handed. I've got two down with summer flu.'

Collins knew that summer flu was shorthand for a copper taking a few days off with the wife and kids when the weather was particularly nice, or in this case it was their last chance to get to the sea before winter set in. 'OK. What's the name and address?'

Mrs McCann, a mother and grandmother, lived on Broughton Road. When she opened the door and heard Collins introduce himself, she smiled. 'From Dublin, are you?'

'And here's me thinking I'd lost me accent.'

'Sure, it's going but it's still there. How long have you been here?'

'Just coming up to seven years.'

'Ah, you're just a babie. Forty-three years for me next

October. But I go home every year for me holidays and for all the weddings, funerals and baptisms. Jesus, I'm always there. Anyways you're not here to talk about me. I just want ya to know that I've worked in hospitals as a cleaner, nurse and ward sister, and I've never seen anything like that poor kitten. Whoever did it is sick in the head. That's why I called you. I reckon there's some sick bastard around here and next time it could be a dog or, God forbid, a babie.'

Collins agreed that a cat killer could easily move from killing a cat to slaughtering a dog. However, he thought Mrs McCann was going too far to suggest that they might progress to murdering a baby. But he said nothing except, 'Can you show me where you found the cat?'

In the back garden Mrs McCann stopped by the coal shed and opened the door. Picking up a shoe box, she handed it to Collins. 'I put the poor thing in that.'

Collins was not prepared for what he found in the box. The piece of string was still around the kitten's neck and it had bitten deep into the poor cat's fur and skin. But worse – each of its front paws had been pierced by a two-inch steel nail.

'They nailed the poor thing to me back gate by its paws.'

Collins shook his head. He'd been on the job six years and had seen his fair share of beatings, suicides, murders and decomposing bodies. Those he could understand. But this seemed as if pain had been inflicted on the kitten for the sheer love of it.

Opening the back gate Mrs McCann pointed at the blood smear where the cat had hung. 'I left it on till you'd seen it.'

A back gate to one of the houses on the opposite side of the lane opened, and a young girl and her boyfriend emerged holding hands. 'Afternoon, Mrs McCann. How are you today?'

'I'm all right I suppose, June. But some fecker killed a poor innocent cat and nailed it to me gate last night. That's why I've got the police here.'

'You from the police then?' the boyfriend asked.

'Yes.'

'Think you'll catch him?'

Collins thought he heard an edge of mockery in the lad's voice and looked at him closely. The youth's eyes were bright, sparkling and alive. There was something wrong about him, but Collins wasn't sure what. He decided to put it down to the arrogance of young men, who think they know everything because they have not lived long enough to realise that they know nothing.

Holding the boy's stare, Collins said, 'If he does it again, I'll catch him.'

June, who was still holding the boy's hand, said, 'Come on Andy, we'll be late. Bye, Mrs McCann.'

Andy reluctantly followed his girlfriend down the lane. Just before they turned onto Broughton Road he looked back and waved at Collins.

Collins ignored the gesture and wrote out his number on the back of a piece of paper and handed it to Mrs McCann. 'Call me if anything else happens around here. You can be sure I'll keep an eye out for any other reports of small animals being killed on the patch.'

## Handsworth, 21.40hrs

Collins arrived at Clark's house at nine forty. All was silent, so Collins tapped on the front window instead of using the bell or knocker. A few moments later Clark opened the door and whispered, 'Keep it down. Ruth's just got him off. You wake him, she'll duff yow and me up.'

In silence Collins watched as Clark sat on the stairs and put on his shoes before taking an old tweed overcoat down from the stand and slipping it on. As gently as possible Clark closed the door. They were halfway down the path when they heard little Mickey start crying. Clark didn't hesitate. 'Scarper. She'll blame me for sure. We'll use my car.'

The roads were virtually deserted, and it only took a few minutes to reach Radnor Road. Clark parked four houses down from Williams' on the opposite side of the road. It was a couple of minutes to ten and the night sky didn't show the moon or a single star. Thick rolling rain clouds had blacked out all celestial light, leaving just the underpowered street-lights, the odd headlights and any light escaping from behind pulled curtains to breach the blackness. Within two minutes of parking Clark was asleep. Collins hunkered down in his seat and pulled his collar up. Nothing happened in the next hour, other than it started to rain again. Then at ten past eleven Mitch opened the front door and a tall skinny kid came out, pulled his collar up, and started to jog up the street.

Collins nudged Clark in the ribs. He was immediately awake. 'We've got a fish.'

Clark started the car and followed the lad up the street. Turning right at the corner, Skinny ran down the hill before turning right onto Wellesbourne Road. Clark accelerated and passed the boy as he opened the door to number 23B.

'Home James, and don't spare the horses,' said Collins with a grin. 'We'll get a warrant tomorrow.'

Fully awake now, Clark asked, 'Anything interesting happen after I left?'

'Not really. Ridley asked me to check out a dead cat which had been nailed to an OAP's back gate.'

'Bloody hell. Yow don't get that every day.'

'No you don't.'

'I had a case of a young kid in the fifties, no more than about sixteen, who went around killing family pets. He'd done seven of them before I caught him.'

'What did he get?'

'Fourteen months in an approved school.'

'You think he should have got more?'

'When he came out he disappeared. Seven years later he was arrested in London for killing three kiddies all under the age of eight. So yeah, I think he should have got more. Kids can be vicious little bastards, they'll pull the legs of a daddy-long-legs but they stop short of killing animals of any size. Those that don't, those that like it, are dangerous. Whoever did the puss needs to be caught.'

'What happened to your lad?'

'He tried to plead insanity but the press were after his blood. He were hanged.'

## Tuesday 24th September, 1968

### Handsworth, 11.00hrs

Collins had thought about applying for a warrant to search the houses on Radnor Road and Wellesbourne Road but decided that they were not required. If necessary, he'd wave his warrant card at anyone demanding one, ensuring that he held his finger over the word "Card". He was reading the Superintendent's file again and checking for anything he had missed earlier, and Clark was talking to the gas board when Chief Inspector Hicks returned from his meeting with the Chief Constable. Most of the station believed that it had been about who was going to take over from Jock Wallace, but no one was going to ask the question. Hearing the end of Clark's conversation, he asked, 'What's up?'

'We got lucky on the burglaries, Sir,' said Collins. 'We were checking known burglars on the patch and Sid Williams was on the list. Well, Sid has emphysema and can't stand up. But his grandson Mitch asked if the old man who got hit with a poker was all right. Said he'd read about it in the *Mercury*, but we never told the press what the old man was hit with.'

'He also told us he worked for the gas board. I were just checking if any of his gas visits were to houses burgled,' said Clark. 'Wi'll get an answer back later today.'

'On top of that Mitch has a skinny mate who would be perfect at squeezing through small windows.'

'Sounds hopeful. When are you going to search the properties?'

'We'll leave it until Mitch is back from work. Say six tomorrow.'

'Do you think the old man knows what his grandson is up to?'

'A pound to a brass farthing he bloody trained the pair,' said Clark.

'Do you want me to clear the warrants?'

'Na, that won't be necessary,' said Collins.

Hicks looked at Collins and said, 'OK, but be careful. In the meantime, what have you got on for the rest of the day?'

'We were planning on seeing a guy called Reece about land purchases.'

'OK. But remember what I said about the Super's investigation. I don't want a load of grief from upstanding citizens because you pair have trampled all over their finer feelings.'

## Birmingham, 12.10hrs

John Reece's office was situated at Five Ways, Edgbaston. A concrete and steel tower block, it was what architects described as "an exceptionally fine example of Brutalist architecture". The locals described it as "bloody awful". Reece's office could not have been more different from Sir Charles' wood panelled walls and Edwardian chairs. Here everything was black leather and polished chrome. The paintings on the wall reflected the modernist look with expensive signed prints by Roy Lichtenstein and Andy Warhol adorning two of the walls.

The office was oblong, and Reece's desk rested on a nine-inch raised dais positioned directly opposite the door. This meant that anyone entering had to navigate twelve yards of bare carpet before they reached his desk. Collins was impressed. As a way to unnerve and intimidate staff it was very effective. The walk would embarrass the little people and leave them in no doubt as to who was in charge. But it had no effect on Collins. Nor on Clark, who ignored Reece and decided to examine the Pop Art that adorned the walls as if he was in a public art gallery.

Collins walked casually to the desk and held out his hand,

'Mr Reece, I'm Detective Sergeant Collins and the gentleman admiring your paintings is Detective Constable Clark.'

Clark turned and waved at Reece, 'Morning.'

Reece rose. He was a couple of inches taller than Collins and was at least twenty stone. Rolls of fat moved as he stood up and his handshake felt soft and sticky. His blond hair had been carefully combed forward to cover the signs of a rapidly receding hair line. The front of his hair had been shaped into a V and extended an inch past his forehead and all held in place by hair lacquer. The shape reminded Collins of the end of the runway on aircraft carriers and made Reece look like a narcissistic fool. His eyes, hidden behind folds of fat, were pale blue and his tanned skin looked as if it was out of a bottle. 'Nice to meet you, Mr Collins. What can I do for you?'

Collins ignored Reece's failure to recognise his official status. He knew what he was dealing with, a bully. A man who had to have his own way or else he would stand in the corner and scream, shout and stamp his little feet until everyone did what he wanted. 'We think you might be able to help us with our enquiries. We're investigating corruption in Birmingham City Council and your name has been mentioned as someone we should talk to.'

'Are you saying someone has accused me of corruption?' demanded Reece, his voice rising. 'If so, I want to know who they are.'

*Thin-skinned or just acting,* thought Collins, 'I'm sorry. I didn't mean to imply that you have been accused of corruption. It's just that you do a lot of work with the Council and you might have seen or heard something.'

Reece sat back in his chair, the anger in his watery eyes receding. He ran a hand across his chin and said, 'You should watch how you phrase things, Mr Collins. In my game if you say the wrong thing you can end up in court.'

Collins recognised the implied threat. 'Oh, I'm used to being in court, Mr Reece. It has never bothered me. Now, if you could tell me have you ever been asked for money or other favours by a Council official?'

'And why would they ask me for money?'

'As payment for ensuring that your quotation for work or planning application was approved.'

'I've already told you I'm not aware of any corruption in the council.'

''No, you dain't, Mr Crease,' said Clark. 'Yow got on yowr high horse and said yow wanted to know who'd suggested wi talk to yow. Wi dain't say yow were corrupt. So be a good boy and answer me mate's questions.'

'How dare you speak to me like that? And the name is Reece not Crease.'

'Yeah, and me mate's name is Detective Sergeant Collins, not Mr Collins and the next time yow try to insult or intimidate either of us, I'm going to take offence. And yow really don't want to know what I do when I take offence. So cut the fucking bullshit and answer the Sergeant's questions or wi can take this down the station.'

Collins could almost see Reece' mind calculating. He had clearly handled the meeting poorly. These bastards were not going to be cowed by his usual tactics. He decided to change tack. 'It seems we got off on the wrong foot. I apologise. But I've had a very difficult weekend and to be accused of corruption was just the last straw. Ask your questions and I'll answer them as best I can.'

'Good boy,' said Clark. Taking the chair that flanked Reece he moved it to the side of the desk, where he was outside Reece's eye line, and sat down.

'Corruption and Birmingham Council, what do you know about it?' asked Collins.

'I'm not aware that there is any significant corruption. You hear stories of architects and surveyors or purchasing officers getting backhanders but nothing significant. It's all low-grade stuff. I've never heard of any councillor taking a bribe.'

'Not even Councillors Hill and Robbins?'

'That pair. Never.' He paused briefly, before continuing, 'But I can understand why people would be suspicious. Neither of them follows the party whip. They're a pair of mavericks. They've got more in common with each other than their respective parties – who hate the sight of them.'

'So how come them still on the Council?' asked Clark.

'They look after their constituents, that's why. If there's any money going, they make sure that some of it reaches their wards.'

'What about Sir Charles Endbury?'

'Lover boy. Loves the ladies but as straight as a die. He doesn't need the money. He wants power. He's lined up a safe Parliamentary seat at the next election. Give him five years and he'll be in the Cabinet. There's no chance that he'd risk that.'

'And Ronny Charlton, what about him?' asked Collins.

'Now he might be worth looking at. I've got no proof that he's corrupt, but with his background he'd be my number one suspect.'

'Were yow at that do for the Saudi prince a few months back?' asked Clark.

Reece swivelled around in his chair to face Clark, 'I suspect that you already know I was,' he said with a smile that never moved any further than his lips.

Clark leered in return. 'Did yow notice a good-looking woman at the party? About twenty-seven, well built with blonde hair? Spent a lot of the evening chatting to Endbury with her mate.'

Reece paused, clearly pretending to think, before he said, 'No, I can't say that I did. Have you asked Sir Charles about her?'

'Na, not yet,' lied Clark.

'One last question, Mr Reece. Did you ever come across a planner by the name of Simpson?' asked Collins.

Reece spent even longer pondering his answer to this

question than the last. When he did answer he sounded surprisingly regretful, 'No I'm sorry. I've never heard of him.'

'Are yow sure?' asked Clark. 'The poor lad committed suicide.'

'I'm sure.'

Rising, Collins stood up, 'Well, thank you for your time, Mr Reece. We may have further questions for you as the investigation develops.'

Before Collins and Clark had reached the road, Reece was on the phone to Christopher Thorne. 'Chris, I've just had two smart arsed coppers here asking about the Saudi do and a woman with blonde hair. Tell me that you took care of everything?'

'We're covered. No problem. I asked Nugent to deal with it.'

'Well, double-check, will you? And watch out for the smarmy Irish git and the annoying shit of a dwarf that he hangs around with. Keep it tight when you talk to them and whatever you do, don't underestimate them. I think they could be trouble.'

'OK.'

After hanging up, Reece thought about calling Charles Endbury but decided that it would be unwise.

As they walked back to the car Clark asked, 'What do yow think?'

'He's a lying bastard. He wouldn't know the truth if it bit him on the arse.'

'I agree, but what exactly were he lying about?'

'Everything. Everyone he said was clean we treat as dirty and everyone he said was dirty we put on the back burner until we know a bit more.'

'Seems fair to me. Where next? Thorne?'

'Why not?'

Collins had just finished buckling up and was turning the ignition key when his radio burst into life. Picking it up, he said, 'Collins.'

'Mickey, we've been trying to get you for the last thirty minutes.'

'Well, you've got me now. What do you want?'

'Can you get over to Handsworth Cemetery ASAP? Use the Park Lane entrance. They've found a body.'

'It's a cemetery. It has a lot of bodies.'

'Yeah, but not that many who have been murdered and stuck in a hole.'

'Bloody hell. Next, you'll be telling me the victim is female, about twenty seven, well built with long blonde hair.'

'How the bloody hell did you know that, Sarge?'

Collins didn't respond to the question. He put the car in gear and sped away, leaving a track of rubber behind.

## Handsworth Cemetery, 13.08hrs

Heavy rain was falling as Collins reached the top of Camp Lane, turned onto Park Lane and then took a sharp right into Handsworth Cemetery. Just three hundred yards away the red-painted floodlights of the Hawthorns were briefly illuminated by a flash of forked lightening.

Clark nudged Collins and pointed in the direction of a gaggle of police cars off to the right. Collins followed the road around and drew up behind a squad car. Looking at the heavy rain, Collins reached for his wellingtons on the back seat and started to pull them on. Clark looked on with a wry smile as his friend went through various contortions, not helped by the steering wheel sticking in his stomach. 'Yow remind me of a new-born giraffe. All legs and no grace.'

'You know I could easily replace you, Detective Constable. Maybe bring in Marie. She'd show me the respect I deserve.'

'Yeah, and I'd show yow me boot up yowr arse. Ready?'

'Let's go,' said Collins. As they stepped from the car, PC Alex Fletcher detached himself from the tree trunk under which he'd been keeping dry and ran over. 'What we got, Alex?' asked Collins.

'It's a nasty one, Mickey. She's been in the ground about three months. She was buried in the side of a bank. The heavy rain last night flushed her out.'

'Who found her?' asked Clark.

'An old boy walking his dog. Doggie disappeared into the undergrowth and when he dain't respond to being called his master followed him. Poor old sod got a right shock. She's a bit of a mess. Looks like she was smashed up before she was killed.'

'Who says?'

'Mr McEwan. He reckons she was beaten, cut and then hung up.'

'Bloody hell,' said Collins.

'Great. Let's take a butchers,' said Clark and taking a small bottle of Vick from his pocket he opened it and dabbed a spot of the chest rub under each nostril before passing it to Collins who did the same. Both men were used to death. They knew it was seldom the sight of a body that made coppers lose their breakfast, it was the smell which had a way of triggering memories years down the line. Best to kill them at birth.

Fletcher walked up a narrow path that led to a wrought iron pedestrian gate which was never locked. Nearing the top, he turned left and the three men trudged across the sodden turf, between the rose beds, into a dense copse of trees. The holly bushes and spreading rhododendrons formed a canopy over the small glade and provided some shelter from the rain. In sunlight the small dell would have been magical with sunbeams illuminating the secret clearing, constantly shifting and moving as the light breeze moved the tree branches. *Probably a favourite spot for couples,* thought Collins.

'Ah, it's the dynamic duo themselves. Killed anyone this

week?' asked Mr McEwan, City Pathologist and former surgeon. A man universally despised by everyone who know him except, possibly, his mother.

'Nah, but the list of possible candidates just grew by one,' said Clark. Fletcher and the two PCs helping Gerry Dobbs, the SOCO, sniggered.

Ignoring the exchange Collins said, 'Afternoon, Dr McEwan, what do we have?'

'It's *Mr* McEwan. I'm a consultant as you well know.'

'Sorry about that. Anyway, what have you got?'

'A white female, approximately twenty-eight years of age, five feet seven tall with blonde hair. Buried some three or four months ago, I'd say. The cool conditions in the glade and the fact that the soil has a high percentage of peat has kept the body in reasonable condition, so I should be able to confirm the cause of death with some certainty after I get her on the table. What I can say is that she was tortured prior to death and at some stage hung up by the neck. Whether the hanging took place pre- or post-mortem will become clear after the autopsy. Unfortunately for you,' he said smiling, 'she was naked, and has no scars, tattoos, rings or jewellery of any kind that might help you identify her.'

'Ah, sure that would be too easy,' said Collins in the broadest Dublin accent he could manage and winked at the doctor, who sniffed and turned away.

Clark and Collins moved over to the body. The woman had been bent double and buried in a four-foot deep hole in the side of the bank. She'd been well covered up and the body, except for some decomposition, was well preserved. Her head, torso and hands had been exposed when the bank partially collapsed following the heavy rain of the previous two nights. The foxes had wasted no time feasting on the exposed parts of the cadaver and several fingers were missing

Whatever beauty she had possessed in life had been stolen from her by a terrible death and three months in the cold black earth. While Collins examined the body, Clark surveyed the ground. 'Have you checked the ground around here?' he asked, directing his question at the SOCO and his assistants for the day, who were sheltering in the lee of a large rhododendron bush. All three nodded and mumbled in the affirmative. 'OK, then. Have yow got a small fork or trowel I can borrow?'

The SOCO passed him a folk and resumed his place under the rhododendron bush. Slowly Clark started to rake the ground lightly near the body in a series of expanding circles.

Collins stood up from the body, and crossing to his friend, hunkered down. 'What are you doing?'

'Trying to stuff that arrogant bastard. Did you notice, three of her fingers been chewed off by the foxes?'

'Yeah.'

'One of them were her ring finger. It's a long shot but did yow ever hear of a fox eating a ring?'

Collins smiled and standing up said, 'I need a trowel here.'

Over the next ten minutes or so, both men slowly extended the area of their search. It was Clark who found the inch-long stub of a finger still wearing a gold ring with a diamond setting enclosing a large, expensive-looking oblong emerald.

Standing up, Clark looked at Collins and asked, 'Yow or me?'

'It's your honour.'

Drawing himself up to his full five feet five inches and holding the evidence bag containing the finger above his head, Clark bellowed in his best Sergeant-major's voice, 'OK, yow lazy incompetent shits. Stop pissing me about and do yowr job right or yow won't have one. Sergeant Collins and me want every inch of this ground gone over like a mother looking for nits in precious Johnny's hair. And I don't care how fucking long it takes or how wet yow get.'

'I'd like to be associated with DC Clark's comments. If we come back and find any other evidence lying on the ground someone here will be out of a job.'

As Clark passed Mr McEwan, he pressed the evidence bag

into the doctor's chest. 'Yow know Doc. there's always room in this world for a peasant like me who knows how to use a fork.'

Back at the car Clark said, 'We found our mystery lady, Mickey.'

'Just what I was thinking. But it makes no sense why Endbury or Reece would have killed her.'

'Maybe it weren't them. Maybe it's just a coincidence,' said Clark.

'You know that's bollocks, don't you?'

'Yeah it is. Wi need to formally identify her and link her to the do at the Council House.'

'I'll head back to the station and brief Hicks and put her description out. It's too late to call Freeman but I'll see him first thing in the morning. Are you all right handling things here?'

'Yeah. No problem. Hicks will want to see the site anyway. Warn Ridley that we'll need to post a guard here overnight.'

'Will do.'

When Collins returned to the station, he found that Hicks had already left for the cemetery. Checking Clark's desk, he saw the note from the gas board which confirmed that Mitch Williams had done work for the gas board in four of the five houses burgled over the last three months. 'Got you, you little git,' he said under his breath. He had to fight the urge to go around and arrest Mitch immediately but knew that it would be best to do both residences on the same day and for that he needed Clark. Tomorrow would be soon enough. Instead, he spent half an hour writing a full description of the woman and circulating it to all police stations in the Birmingham area, Central CID and adjoining forces. After that he spent an hour thinking about why Reece or Endbury would want to murder a good time girl.

## Wednesday 25th September 1968

### Handsworth, 07.13hrs

There was a new guest in the kitchen when Collins came down for breakfast. Some time in the night he'd been aware of Agnes sliding out of bed to answer the phone, and he rightly assumed that the mature woman in front of him was the cause of her disturbed night.

'Marjorie, I'd like you to meet Detective Sergeant Michael Collins. He's my lodger and offers the extra protection I was talking about, when needed.'

Marjorie held out a limp hand and Collins gripped it lightly. It felt clammy and there was a slight tremble in it.

As Collins warmed his porridge and stirred in a handful of raisins to the mix he examined the woman discreetly. She was only a little shorter than Agnes, at around five foot eight and was probably in her early sixties, making her more than ten years older than Agnes. In her prime Marjorie would have been very attractive but the years had not been kind. Her skin was dry and sickly pale and her eyes lacked any sparkle of life. In contrast to Agnes' shining auburn hair Marjorie's once blonde locks were now a dead mousy grey. But look as he did, Collins could see no bruises on the woman's face or arms. However, her eyes were those of a beaten woman; fearful, sad and hopeless. *The bastard hits her where it doesn't show,* he thought.

Marjorie finished her breakfast and pushed her chair back from the table. She winced as she stood up and Collin knew that his assessment of her injuries had been correct. 'I think I'll have another bath, if you don't mind, Agnes, and then I'll go to bed. I didn't get much sleep last night.'

'That sounds like a good idea,' said Agnes and smiled.

Collins waited until he heard Marjorie open the bathroom door before asking, 'What's her story?'

'One of the Quakers at Bull Street called last night. She's been trying to help Marjorie, but she can't provide accommodation. Marjorie turned up on her doorstep at twenty to two last night.'

'She seems in a bad way. As if she's given up. Is she suicidal?'

'Well she has reason to be. Her husband has turned their adult children against her. For years he's been beating her while acting as Mr Nice Guy to their three children. When she finally told them what he's been doing he denied ever hitting her and demanded that she show them her so called bruises she claimed she had. She couldn't do it. And now he has the children believing she's a fantasist.'

'Why the feck didn't she show them the bruises?'

'Because even if she wore a bikini none of the bruises would be visible. His favourite hobby is kicking and punching her breasts and vagina. He likes to end every session with a cigarette. He's very artistic. The last time he tied her up and branded her with the Olympic Rings on her breasts with a single burn on each nipple to round things off.'

'Bloody hell. What are you going to do?'

'I'm not sure yet. I have to find a way to show her children that she is telling the truth and that their father is a monster.'

'If all else fails, and she's willing, I could get the SOCO to take some pictures.'

Rising Agnes walked round the table and kissed the top of Collins' head. 'Let's hope it doesn't come to that.'

## Birmingham, 09.23hrs

Collins had been sitting in the reception area of Bush House for ten minutes when Henry Freeman came through the front doors. It took Freeman maybe five seconds for his fogged brain to recognise who was blocking his path, and then he remembered the two pints and whiskey chasers. 'Sergeant. I said I'd call you when I had any information.'

'That was before we found a murdered woman matching the description of the woman seen with Sir Charles Endbury on the second of June.'

'Bloody hell, mate. We better take a walk down to the Council House and see my mate Ian Buckley, he does the official photography. I rang him and he said he'd get me the info for Thursday. But if the sheila's dead, you need it now.'

Work started on building the Birmingham Council House in 1874 when the foundation stone was laid by the Lord Mayor, Joseph Chamberlain, father of the future British Prime Minister, Neville Chamberlain. It was completed in 1879 and cost the then princely sum of £163,000. It had been money well spent and was still an imposing building sitting next to the Town Hall, the Museum and Art Gallery and just fifty yards away from the City's magnificent redbrick Library.

The interior of the Council House's was even more impressive than the exterior. An imposing marble staircase greeted all who stepped through the main entrance. Walk up the red carpeted steps and you were on the first floor where two long brightly lit corridors branched off to the Committee Meeting Rooms and the offices of the Clerk of the Council and the City Treasurer. Both corridors had the same fine brass light fittings, which illuminated a long line of dark oak doors, cream coloured walls and expensive red Axminster carpet. Follow the stairs to the second floor and you were in the Council Chamber.

Unfortunately, Ian did not live above ground. He resided in one of the numerous offices, hidden below ground, in a spaghetti of corridors. After following Freeman for no more than thirty seconds Collins felt entirely lost. *This place is like Hampton Court Maze,* he thought. It didn't help that five feet of white tiles covered the walls from the floor to about halfway up the wall and green paint covered the remainder up to the ceiling. The style was utilitarian and uniformly dull. At last Freeman stopped, knocked on a door and walked in without waiting for a response. A small man in his mid-fifties, wearing a light blue suit, white shirt and red bow tie looked up from the pile of photos he was examining.

'Ian, you old queen. This is Detective Sergeant Collins I was telling you about. He needs that info about the Saudi do now, not next week.'

Ian stood up and waved the magnifying glass at Freeman, 'Listen, you Australian lush, stop telling everyone I'm queer or we are going to fall out.'

'Christ, mate, I'm not aware we ever fell in. I must have been really pissed that night. Don't remember a thing.'

'Anyway, why is it suddenly so urgent?'

'As of yesterday, we are trying to identify a murder victim. We think she was the blonde-haired woman who was seen talking to various guests at the reception for the prince,' said Collins.

'Bloody Nora. OK, have a seat. I need to pop down to the storeroom. I won't be more than five minutes.'

Collins sat down in an old green tubular and canvas chair that had been new in 1943 and Freeman took Ian's battered swivel chair. Casually, Freeman started to flip though the photos that Ian had been examining. Halfway down the pile, he let out a loud, 'Bloody hell. Take a look at these,' he said, tossing a handful of photos to Collins.

Collins flicked through them. It was a tasteful portfolio of a young man in his twenties wearing a ridiculously small pair of swimming trunks. He was well muscled with shapely legs, a slim waist and well-developed chest and arms. But the biggest feature in each photo was the huge bulge in his swimming trunks which just about managed to keep its contents under wraps.

'Who'd have believed it? Old Ian is moonlighting for a skin mag.'

'Nothing illegal here. Anyway, they might just be for his own use,' said Collins.

Freeman leered, 'Yeah, I can see how he'd use them.'

Freeman was still grinning when Ian returned looking flustered. 'I'm terribly sorry but all the photos from that night appear to be missing.'

'You mean misfiled?' asked Collins.

'No, missing. I filed them myself. I always do all my own filing. Someone has taken them and not signed them out. I can only assume that they have been stolen.'

'Feck, feck and double feck,' said Collins. 'You've got no pictures of that night.'

'No. None.' Collins felt his heart sink. 'All I've got are the negatives.'

'Bloody hell, why didn't you say so in the first place?' said Freeman.

'You're sure you have the negatives?' asked Collins.

'Oh yes. I keep a second copy of all the negatives in the dark room for six months before I file them with the photos. Just in case anyone wants a copy run off.'

'Can you get them for me, please?'

'My pleasure.'

Ian and Collins spent the next twenty minutes standing under the basement window that was flush with the pavement of Victoria Square going through the 144 negatives that Ian had of the night. Seven negatives appeared to be of interest and Ian disappeared into his dark room to develop them while Collins and Freeman headed for the Copper Kettle Café at the bottom of Christ Church Passage. Two cups of tea each and an interminable lecture on why Australians were superior cricketers to any English team helped pass the time. Freeman's monologue on Australian cricket was even more boring to Collins than listening to Clark explain why the Albion were and always would be a better footballing team than Aston Villa.

Collins took his time walking back to the Council House. Christ Church Passage was his favourite 'street' in Birmingham. Set on a steep hill, it consisted of a series of tiered steps that led up to Waterloo Street. It was enclosed on both sides by a miscellany of Victorian and Edwardian shops, that sold artists' supplies, confectionary, cigarettes and tobacco, stamps, paintings, linen, haberdashery and jewellery. There was even a Ronson lighter repair shop.

Despite two World Wars many of the shops retained much of their original ornate brick, wood- and ironwork. Further up from the Copper Kettle Café Bar sat the smaller Medina Café, and between them they blanketed the entire passage with the smell of freshly made coffee. The Passage was a small time capsule and Collins never lost an opportunity to tread its age-worn steps and for a minute or two to step back in time to Victorian/Edwardian Birmingham. Reaching the top of the steps, Collins and Freeman turned left and headed for the Council House just across Colmore Row.

There were four photos of the blonde-haired woman, two with a female friend and two of her chatting with Sir Endbury. The small dark-haired friend was immediately familiar to Collins. It was Claire Lafferty. But he didn't let it show. 'Ian, do you know either of these women?' asked Collins.

'I've never seen the blonde before. The small one, with the dark hair, is Claire Lafferty. I'm pretty sure she's on the game. High class, but I've seen her at a lot of dos and she always leaves with some bloke.'

'How would they get in?'

'They could be signed in as a guest. Or, if they know the commissionaire, a gratuity might change hands.'

'Can you check who signed them in?'

'I could, but that will take some time. If you give me your phone number, I'll call you as soon as I get it. I've got Claire's address if you want it.'

Collins did not let on that he had Claire's address. Instead he asked, 'How did you get that?'

'I'm a photographer, darling. Loads of girls give me their details just in case I can throw any modelling work their way. Now, if that lump of Australian mutton will get out of my chair, I'll get my contacts book.'

## Handsworth, 12.10hrs

Clark locked his car door and walked over to where Collins was parked. 'What have yow got, Mickey?'

Collins handed Clark the four photos. 'The dark-haired woman is Claire Lafferty, calls herself a model, but according Ian Buckley, the city's official photographer, she's on the game but expensive. I told you about her mother who came to the station on Saturday and reported her missing. Shares the top floor flat, in number 38, with a Christina Murray. That's what the landlord said when I called him. Both were snapped at the Saudi do and Christina looks a lot like our corpse.'

'Yow reckon that Lafferty is at home?'

'Not according to the landlord. Both of them did a runner in June without paying the rent. But there's only one way to be certain.'

Clark knocked on the flat's white panel door twice. There was no response. Taking his lock picks from his pocket he sprang the pre-war lock in less than eight seconds and pushed the door open. The flat was silent, spotless, deserted and had that stale air feel that rooms get when no one has been in them for a while.

Collins drew the curtains and opened the window. Not a cushion out of place. It looked as if no one was living here. A search of the two bedrooms confirmed that every drawer was empty. There wasn't as much as a pair of stockings to indicate that two women had ever lived there. The bathroom was equally bare, with no cosmetics or even a sign of any old make-up.

'It don't look like anyone has lived here in months. How old were the address?'

'Ian said it was only about three months and Lafferty's mother said she wrote her last letter to this address in early May.'

'Well there ain't anyone here now. Let's go. Wi can have a chat with the landlord.'

'Not yet. There's something wrong with this place. Let's have another look around.'

'Yow and yowr bloody hunches. OK. This time, I'll do the front bedroom and yow take the back.'

After a careful check that revealed nothing, Clark sat in the small chair next to the wardrobe and looked at the room. Between the showers, the sun was now streaming through the window into the room illuminating the bed and carpet. It was then that Clark noticed that the off-cream carpet at the foot of the bed looked cleaner than in the rest of the room. Standing, he checked the outline of the clean patch. It was about seven foot by seven. Getting down on his hands and knees, he felt the weave. It was dry but there was no mistaking that it had been recently washed. 'Mickey, get in here. I need yow to help me lift the carpet.'

They moved the bed to the opposite side of the room and laid the two bedside cabinets on it. Clark used his knife to lever up a six-foot run of the carpet from the gripper nailed to the floor. Grabbing hold, they pulled the rest of the carpet away from the wall and rolled it up as they moved toward the lighter patch. The underlay was thick grey felt. As they exposed the washed area it became darker, almost black.

Clark cut a one-foot square of felt from the middle of the dark patch. The floorboards beneath it were also stained black with blood. 'It looks like wi've found where Christina was killed. But where's Lafferty?'

Collins stood up and stretched. He'd spent the entire afternoon at the women's flat. Scenes of Crime had confirmed that the stain that Clark had found was blood. One of the technicians had taken a sample to Mr McEwan to check if it was the same type as the body found the previous day. The landlord had been contacted and he confirmed that the two women in the photo had indeed been the tenants of the flat. When they had failed to pay their rent on the sixth of July, he had called around to find that they had disappeared. 'I assumed they'd done a midnight flit and stuck me for the rent. But I did think it was odd how clean and tidy they'd left the place.'

Scenes of Crime quickly confirmed that the place had been cleaned by professionals. The only fingerprints found belonged to the landlord, Collins and Clark. Other than the blood there wasn't a single sign that the women had ever been there.

'Looks like we have a double murder on our hands,' said Hicks, who was the senior officer responsible for the case.

'Never rains but it pours, boss,' said Clark.

'Why don't you two go back to the station and grab a bite to eat? Write up your statements and then circulate Lafferty's picture to the press saying that her family is concerned for her welfare. You know what's required. Don't link her to Christine at this stage. We'll meet first thing in the morning to sort out our priorities. We need to decide if this murder is in any way connected to the Super's case.'

## Handsworth, 17.30hrs

A file of information from Marie Bolding was waiting for Collins when he returned to the station. He quickly flicked through it before he laid it on the filing cabinet next to the coat stand. He'd read it when he got home. He felt tired and confused. The clean-up at the scene of the murder clearly indicated that they were dealing with professionals. But if that was the case why had they done such a piss poor job of disposing of the body. Sticking it in a hole under a tree was downright amateurish. It was obvious, that eventually it would be found.

He was still thinking of this as he stood in the deserted canteen and stirred his tea waiting for the toaster to pop. 'Put a slice in for me will yow,' said Clark as he headed for the recently brewed pot of tea. 'Did yow get the releases out?'

'Yeah. Sent the details to the newspapers and Lafferty's description to all forces in England, Scotland and Wales. I also sent it to the RUC and the Garda just in case she's back in Ireland.'

'Waste of time if yow ask me. The poor lass is already buried in the ground.'

Collins put his cup down. 'Of course,' he cried. 'How could I have been so bloody stupid?'

'Perhaps because being stupid comes natural to yow.'

Collins ignored the insult. 'You're right. It was a waste of time contacting the other forces. She's already in the ground. In Handsworth Cemetery.'

Clark saw the excitement in his partner's eyes. 'Explain.'

'Don't you see? The killers were professional in how they cleaned the flat. But they just stuck Murray's body in a hole, where eventually it was going to be uncovered. Why didn't they just drop her in an open grave that was ready for a funeral the following day?'

Understanding spread across Clark's face. 'Because them had two bodies but could only find one open grave and if they'd put both bodies in the same grave it would have looked too shallow after they'd shovelled a foot of earth on top.'

'Precisely.'

'But there would have been more than one open grave. They must do well over 30 burials every day up there. Why not just find a second grave?'

Leaning forward, his tea and toast forgotten Collins said, 'The main gates are locked at night. They didn't want to break in as that might have attracted attention. So, they came in by one of the pedestrian gates off Camp Lane. I noticed one just about twenty yards from where the body was found. Now even if there were two of them, they wouldn't want to lug a body far in the pitch dark. They would have wanted to dump the body in the nearest grave they could find…'

'And they found one for Lafferty easily enough but couldn't find a second one for Murray within easy carrying distance,' said Clark.

Collins sat back in his chair grinning. 'I think we'll be at the cemetery first thing in the morning.'

'What wi going to do about Mitch and his mate? Yow don't want to leave them in the wind too long. They might bop another poor sod.'

'True.' Collins looked at his watch. 'The afternoon shift are just coming in for their snap. I'll have a word with Ridley and see if we can borrow four bobbies. We'll pick up Mitch first.'

## Handsworth, 18.25hrs

The two unmarked police cars drew up on Radnor Road. It was raining heavily and the wipers were having problems keeping the windscreen clear. Collins was about to open the door when through the murk he saw Mitch's skinny friend appear at the top of the road. Grabbing his radio, he said, 'Clarkee hold your position. Mr Universe is heading for Mitch's.'

'I see him. Wi'll give it five minutes.'

The six men sat quietly, waiting. They all knew that even a minor raid like this could go wrong and there were a few nerves evident in the slightly pale skin of one of the newer constables and a drumming of fingers by another against the back of Clark's seat. He was about to tell the man to stop or he'd break his fingers when he saw Mickey get out of the car.

Sending PC Moore to cover the back alleyway Collins watched as he trotted quickly up the hill. Another thirty seconds and he'd have the back exit covered. Collins counted to twenty-five then walked up the garden path to the front door and rapped hard on the old wood with his knuckles. Mitch's mother opened the front door. Collins held up his warrant card and said, 'We have a search warrant for these premises. Where is your son Mitch?'

At the top of her voice she shouted, 'Mitch, it's the police.' Then stared sullenly at Collins while blocking the doorway.

Collins heard a window being opened upstairs, pushed the woman aside and took the stairs two at a time. As he neared the top, he could see that Mitch's bedroom door was open and the lad was sitting on the window ledge, Mr Universe standing behind him.

Looking over his shoulder, Mitch saw Collins and the PC. He didn't hesitate, pushed off from the ledge and landed on the coal shed below. The corrugated roof was wet and covered in green slime and Mitch slid off the side to land hard on the garden path.

Grabbing Mr Universe by the arm, Collins flung him towards the PC who was standing in the doorway. As the PC spun the bewildered boy around and cuffed him, Collins dropped onto the shed roof below and half-slid, half-jumped onto the path.

Mitch was already disappearing over the back fence by the time Collins picked himself up and charged at the fence. Scaling the six-foot fence commando style Collins heaved himself into the back alleyway just in time to see Mitch turn left at the bottom and head for Villa Road. *Where's Moore?* he thought, *He's supposed to be watching the back alley.*

Collins exited the alley and followed Mitch. Twice he shouted, 'Police! Stop!' at the top of his voice. Mitch didn't stop. Which was OK as far as Collins was concerned, as it now meant Mitch had resisted arrest. A charge that would keep him on ice while they finalised the burglary charges.

Mitch had youth and muscle on his side, but he was no runner and by the time he reached Villa Road, Collins was less than ten yards behind him and gaining. The wind was blowing the rain into his face and the path underfoot was slick with water and fallen leaves, but Collins knew that he had the lad. Mitch was now visibly slowing. Collins shouted again, 'Police! Stop!'

Oblivious to all around him except Collins, the boy pushed and jostled pedestrians out of his way. Collins was less than a yard behind when he reached for the boy's jumper. Mitch hit Collins' hand away and stepped into the road without looking. Collins barely had time to shout, 'Watch out!' before a bus hit Mitch and sent him sprawling. His body skidded on the wet ground and Collins heard the crack as Mitch's head hit the corner of the pavement.

Collins was first to reach Mitch, quickly followed by the bus driver, who jumped down from his cab. 'It wasn't my fault, sure. He just jumped straight in front of me. Ah, God! Is he all right?'

Collins ignored the man and felt for a pulse in the boy's neck but could find nothing. Pinching the boy's nose closed, he started to give mouth-to-mouth resuscitation and alternated that, after every five breaths, with pumping the boy's chest fifteen times.

The owner of the Milk Bar on the opposite side of the road ran out carrying a sheaf of towels. 'I've rung for an ambulance and the police.'

'I am the fecking police,' hissed Collins as he pressed down on Mitch's chest with the heel of his left hand. By now a crowd was gathering and Collins was relieved to hear a familiar voice, 'Move back now. This is a police scene. Leave the Sergeant to do his job.' Hunkering down beside Collins, Clark asked, 'How's it going?' Collins looked at his friend and shook his head imperceptibly. 'OK,' said, Clark standing up. 'I want everyone back at least fifteen yards.' Looking at the two PCs who'd followed him out of the house he said, 'Organise the traffic. Turn it into a single lane road.'

The ambulance arrived within seven minutes, but they were already too late. Collins had stopped resuscitation three minutes earlier and covered Mitch's face with one of the Milk Bar's towels.

When the Patrick Flynn, the designated traffic officer, arrived at the scene he said, 'Mickey, you get back to the station and write up your statement. I'll sort things out here.'

'OK, but I have to inform his mother first.'

'You ain't going anywhere near the mother, Mickey,' said Clark. 'I'll do that, and I'll bring the skinny kid in when I head back. For now, yow get a cuppa and write yowr report. This weren't yowr fault.'

Collins looked at Clark and tried to smile, but whatever Clarkee might say, this was his fault.

Collins took a circuitous route back to the station, stopping off at St. Francis Church on Wretham Road before returning to the nick. For ten minutes he sat in the silence of the empty church. Trying to pray. Trying to calm the emotions flooding his mind. But peace didn't come. It had been an accident. Collins knew that he had not directly caused the boy's death but he had set in train the events that led to his death. That was enough for him to feel numb with guilt.

Rising, he headed for the station. By the time he had rung Agnes and told her what had happened, Chief Inspector Hicks was standing by his desk. Someone had called him at home. Hicks listened to what had happened and then said exactly what Clark had said, 'It wasn't your fault, Michael.'

Collins spent the next hour writing his statement and had just signed it when Patrick Flynn, the traffic officer, knocked on the CID door. He acknowledged Hicks with a wave and sat down opposite Collins. Collins handed him his statement in silence. There wasn't much to it. Barely three pages, but it contained all the facts and a blow by blow description of the raid and subsequent chase. After reading the statement Flynn slipped it into a manila folder and said, 'I think we can say you're in the clear, Mickey. We've got two witnesses who say they heard you shout "Stop. Police." And several who saw the lad push your arm away and run into the road. None of them say you pushed him.'

'Well, I suppose that's a relief. But what the fuck happened to Moore?'

'He was only half way up Hamstead Road when you went charging up the stairs. He slipped on the leaves and landed hard on his hip. His thigh is covered in bruises. He can hardly walk.'

Collins stood up. 'Thanks, Flynny. If it's OK with you, Boss I'm going to leave the booking in of Mitch's mate to Clark. I think he should write up the report of the raid as well.'

'That's fine. Get off home and try and get some rest.'

## Handsworth, 23.30hrs

Collins had spent the night talking to Agnes about what had happened trying to convince himself that it had not been his fault. But the words of Patrick Flynn about Moore's accident kept coming back to him, "He was only halfway up the road when you went charging up the stairs." *If only I'd waited. If only I'd checked that Moore was in position before I'd gone in*, thought Collins.

That night, in bed, Agnes held Collins in her arms as he

described once more what had happened. She remembered only too well how she had felt when she had shot two Bulgarians in self-defence three years earlier. Nothing she could say would ease his guilt, but her nearness did soothe his troubled mind. She did not let go until he fell asleep and then she said a prayer for him and the boy who had died.

## Thursday 26th September 1968

### Handsworth, 08.56hrs

Collins and Clark sat in silence waiting outside the Cemetery's Registry Office for the Registrar to arrive. Clark knew what was on Collins' mind. It was written in the black hollows under his eyes and the distant faraway look in his eyes. Clark understood the turmoil that was washing through his friend's mind and that the best thing he could do was say nothing until Collins was ready to talk.

Mr Regan, the Registrar, arrived at nine exactly. He was everything you would expect of a man in charge of a large cemetery. He was over six feet tall, stick-thin with a prominent Adam's apple that bobbed up and down every time he swallowed, which was often. He had candlewax skin stretched over sharp cheekbones, a long thin nose and eyes that lay in such deep shadows that it was difficult to say what colour they were. It was a surprise when he greeted the men with a cheerful, 'Good morning. Another beautiful day in the offing, I think.' As he unlocked the office door, he asked, 'What can I do for you gentlemen?'

Stepping into the small, bare office that had a counter running down the middle and a door behind it marked Private, Collins explained the purpose of their visit. Mr Regan disappeared into the back room and retuned moments later with a black ledger marked Burials 1 April – 31 September 1968 embossed on the spine. Flicking over to the June entries, Regan quickly found the burials for Monday the third of June. 'We dig the graves for Monday burials on Saturday morning and we had ...' he quickly counted the relevant entries, 'thirty-three that Monday. Only one grave was dug near where your body was found. The next nearest was down the hill near the Camp Hill and Oxhill Road entrance.'

After taking details of the grave nearest to where the Christine's body had been found Collins said, 'We'd be obliged if you would say nothing about our inquiry to anyone. We'll be back later with an exhumation licence.'

'I understand.'

## Edgbaston, 09.45hrs

John Reece sat at his desk. Spread in front of him was that morning's *Birmingham Post.* Blazoned across the first page was the story of a body found in Handsworth Cemetery. Checking his watch, he picked up the phone and called Thorne. 'Chris, have you seen today's *Post*?'

'No.'

'Well have a look at it, then get over here with Nugent as soon as you can.'

Forty minutes later Thorne and Nugent were in Reece's office. Nugent knew that he'd messed up and the sweat was pouring off him in waves. His blue nylon shirt was sticking to his back and chest and sweat was dripping down his side from his armpits. 'I'm really sorry, Mr Reece. We did as you said,' he lied. 'We dumped the one cow in an open grave, but we couldn't find another one. We must have spent close to an hour looking for one and it was starting to get light.'

'You panicked and stuck her under a bloody tree?'

'We were going to go back but ...'

'But it slipped your mind because you had so many other bodies to think about. Is that it?'

Nugent said nothing.

Leaning forward Reece looked at Nugent and speaking very slowly he said, 'You've fucked up. Big time. Do it once more and I swear that you will be lucky to live long enough to regret it. Do you understand?'

'Yes boss.'

'Now get the fuck out and wait for Chris outside.'

When Nugent had left Thorne asked, 'Do you want me to do anything about his cockup?'

'No, leave him. I've got a job for him but there'll be no bonus in it for him.'

'What do you want him to do?'

'What do you think?'

## Handsworth Cemetery, 14.39hrs

It was normal practice for the police to undertake exhumations after dark, but this was too important to wait. Collins led the SOCO, his assistant and one police car to the site of the grave where he was convinced Claire Lafferty was buried. Two grave diggers and Mr Regan were waiting for him. The Registrar examined the exhumation licence and said, 'That all appears to be in order. You may proceed with the exhumation. I shall be in my office if you need me.'

A seven-foot high canvas screen was quickly erected around the grave and digging began. Collins was amazed at how fast the gravediggers worked. They seemed to dig effortlessly, barely breaking sweat as they dug a trench six feet deep and measuring three feet by seven. He remembered being told that it took a strong man eighteen months to become a navvy who could dig non-stop eight or ten hours a day, six days a week. It required strength, stamina and real skill with a shovel to lift a spade of earth as if it were weightless, and these guys were experts.

The sound of metal hitting wood announced that the heavy digging was finished. Using small shovels, the sides of the coffin were exposed and lifting straps worked under the coffin.

With the coffin lifted clear, the remaining ground was raked lightly until the rake's tines caught on a piece of cloth.

'OK lads, jump out,' said Clark. 'This is where we take over. Thanks for all yowr work.'

It only took a minute to reveal the black hair of Claire Lafferty. She was still wearing the same dress as she had been in the photo. Other than the broken neck there were no obvious marks on her body or face.

'Well, Mickey, seems as if yow were right for a change.'

'Law of averages, Clarkee. Law of averages,' said Collins with a sad smile.

'I think it's time we went to see Sir Charles Endbury again. And this time I ain't going to be on me best behaviour,' said Clark.

'I was thinking just the same. But first I have to deliver the bad news to Mrs Lafferty.'

'OK. I'll wait for you back at the station when I'm finished here.'

## Four Oaks, 19.54hrs

Collins and Clark were exhausted. Clark had spent most of the afternoon at the cemetery and had to put up with the ever-delightful Mr McEwan. Meanwhile Collins had spent a difficult ninety minutes with Mrs Lafferty in Coventry. Then it had been back to the station and report writing. Like twins, two murders did not create twice as much work, they created three times as much aggravation. It was now nearly eight, and they still had to interview Sir Charles Endbury before they could head for home.

'Have yow finished that report?' asked Clark.

'I'm on the last sentence.'

'Good 'cause I'd like to get home before midnight.'

'You're on overtime. What are you complaining about?'

'Having to listen to yow 12 hours a day for a start.'

Collins held up two fingers and said, 'Finished. Let's go and see Endbury.'

'At last.'

Endbury lived in a six-bedroom house in Four Oaks, the most expensive part of Sutton Coldfield. If the rest of the residents in Sutton looked down on Solihull, those who lived in Four Oaks viewed their near neighbours in the ancient town of Sutton Coldfield as very poor relations. Clark drove slowly down the tree-lined avenue. The front gardens were so large that it was difficult to read the house numbers in a street that was without lights, unless they were shown at the front of the lawn or on the gates that protected many of the driveways.

'It's about four doors down on the right,' said Clark. As he spoke a dark coloured Ford pulled out of Endbury's drive, fishtailed and sped away without lights. 'He's in a hurry.'

Collins did not respond and instead turned onto the drive. The house was lit up with lights on in two downstairs rooms plus the hall and landing. The stained-glass window over the front door depicted St George slaying the dragon and saving a woman who appeared to have lost most of her clothes. The sexually confused beast lay dead at the brave knight's feet. Collins used the brass horseshoe-shaped knocker to announce their arrival.

'Do yow reckon that the door will be answered by a butler or just a run of the mill lackey?' asked Clark.

'I think the lackeys just made a dash for freedom in the Ford.'

'Well then, wem fucked. We might as well go home. Sir Charles and his lady wife are unlikely to answer the door to the likes of us.'

Collins smiled and knocked again, only louder. After the third round of unanswered knocking Collins said, 'Let's have a nose around.'

Collins went left and Clark right. Peering through a small window next to the door, Clark saw a woman lying in the hall. 'Mickey, we've got a body on the floor.'

Both men ran to the front door. Fortunately, the deadlocks were not engaged, and the door flew open on the second shoulder charge.

A well-dressed woman lay beside the telephone table in the hall. On the floor beside her was the phone. In her left hand she had two crumpled and bloodstained six-by-four photos. She had been shot twice in the back and blood was still oozing from her wounds onto the royal blue carpet.

Clark knelt and looked for a pulse in the neck. 'Nothing.'

'I'll check the other rooms,' said Collins and moved into the room opposite where the body lay. It was obviously an office-cum-study. Two walls were covered in books. On the third was a display of antiquarian maps in tasteful light oak frames. The fourth was decorated by a range of photos showing Sir Charles meeting famous people including the Queen, and Prime Ministers Winston Churchill, Harold Macmillan, and Alex Douglas Home. Unfortunately, they were now splattered with Sir Endbury's blood, brain matter and skull fragments.

Sir Charles was slumped over his desk, a hole the size of a cricket ball in his skull. A .445 Army revolver lay next to his right hand. Scattered across the desk were several more photos. Collins knew it was a waste of time, but he still checked for signs of life before he looked at the pictures. Some of them showed Sir Charles and Christina engaged in sex. Others were solo shots of Christina and revealed exactly how she had been killed – hung from the chandelier's hook in the ceiling.

Collins stared at the gun and the hand that rested beside it. The right index finger was at an odd angle. He lifted the finger gently and felt the bones of the middle joint grind against each other. *Broken,* he thought.

At the side of the desk lay one of the victim's Italian-made slip-ons. Checking the floor, Collins saw where Endbury's heels had disturbed the nap of the carpet and created two roughly parallel lines.

Clark appeared at the door. 'What yow got?'

'Murder. What about you?'

'Murder. But not by that poor bugger.'

'Five minutes earlier and we would have had the bastards.'

'Ten and wi might have saved them,' said Clark. 'But yow can't think like that. We dain't know that the discovery of Murray's body and our search for Lafferty would panic someone like this.'

'True. I'll call the locals.'

'Bang goes another night's sleep.'

As they waited for the SOCO and the Sutton police to arrive, Collins and Clark continued to search the rooms with their eyes. They touched nothing. It was not their crime scene.

'What do yow think happened?' asked Clark.

'Same as you. Someone, probably Reece, used the photos to blackmail Endbury. When he discovered that we had found Murray's body he was scared that Endbury would reveal all. He had him killed and tried to make it look like a case of murder and suicide.'

'But from what wi know about Reece he's a professional. He, or his boys, cleaned up the flat a treat, so how come he used a pair of amateurs to stage this?'

Collins looked at Endbury's body, then walked into the hall and examined Mrs Endbury. The phone cradle was resting in the middle of a table that measured four foot by three. Even if the table had been knocked, the handset would have remained on the table. Realisation dawned on Collins. 'She had the phone in her hand when she was shot. She was trying to call the police.'

'Yow could be right. She were upstairs, heard what was going on and tried to call for help.'

'Yep. And when they heard or saw her, they couldn't be certain if she had got through to the police or not and panicked. They killed her and hightailed it out of here.'

'Before they had a chance to finish setting the scene or tidying up the giveaway signs like the carpet trails. It makes sense, Mickey lad. It makes sense.'

In the distance, they heard police sirens and went outside to meet Sutton Coldfield's finest.

# Part Two

## Friday 27th September 1968

### Handsworth, 11.58hrs

Collins had finally fallen into bed at five in the morning. As always when he was late in, he had slept in his old room so as not to disturb Agnes. On waking, he took in his old surroundings and smiled. A lot had changed since he had first slept in this room. Stretching, he yawned and shook his head and with consciousness the events of the previous night came flooding back.

Both Collins and Clark had breathed a sigh of relief when they saw that the inspector in charge of the investigation was Dave Archer. Inspector Archer was a thirty-year veteran who had a reputation for honesty, hard work and loyalty to his men. He had turned down more than one chance for promotion because as he said, "I'm a thief-taker and that's what I want to do, not shuffle bloody paper." He was liked and respected by everyone and no one had a bad word to say against him, not even those he had disciplined. After inspecting the crime scene, he told the SOCO what he wanted him to concentrate on. He then spent nearly an hour with Collins and Clark discussing the events that had led them to Endbury's home that night.

'Bloody hell lads, four corpses in two days. That has to be a record even for you pair.'

'Na we've done better than that before now,' said Clark.

Archer smiled and said, 'Write up your statements and get off home. You must be knackered. I'll give you a call tomorrow and we can have a chat on where we go from here.'

Flipping back the bedclothes, Collins checked the time. He had two hours before he needed to be at the station. Stretching, he stood up and moved off to the bathroom.

Agnes heard Collins moving about upstairs and when he finally emerged, dressed and shaved, a bowl of porridge and two slices of brown toast and jam were awaiting him. He kissed Agnes and wrapped his arms around her. 'Thanks, darling. Just what I need.'

'What time did you get in?'

'About five.'

'I thought you just had the exhumation to do. What happened?'

Collins quickly described the events of the previous night and waited for Agnes to comment.

'Someone is trying to contain the situation,' she said.

'And they might have succeeded if the goons who killed Endbury and his wife hadn't messed up.'

'Are you certain that Endbury didn't kill the girl?'

'Ninety-five percent.'

'I've got no meetings this afternoon. Do you mind if I have a look at your file?'

'Mrs Winters, you know that I'm always happy for you to look at my file.'

Agnes smiled, cocked her head to one side and asked, 'When did you say you had to be at the station?'

'Two.'

'Well that gives us plenty of time,' and taking him by the hand Agnes led him back upstairs, his breakfast forgotten.

On arrival Collins found a note from Clark on his desk. A meeting to discuss recent events was in the Superintendent's office at two fifteen and Inspector Archer would be there. *Just time to grab a brew,* he thought. Fifteen minutes later he knocked on the Super's door, cup in hand, and waited to be told to enter.

'Afternoon, Sir,' said Collins as he pulled up a chair to join Acting Superintendent Thatcher, a thirty-five year veteran who had planned to retire the previous summer but had stayed on to fill the gap left by Jock Wallace. He had a reputation for backing his officers and enjoying a good laugh, even if it was at his own expense. Chief Inspector Hicks, and Inspector Archer, along with Clarkee and a young WPC he had never seen before, sat around the Super's small conference table.

'This is WPC Arlington. She's on secondment to my team,' said Archer.

Collins nodded at the WPC and said, 'Glad to meet you,' and sat down.

'You've not missed anything, Collins,' said Hicks and lit up a Gauloise, which prompted Archer to take out his pipe.

*Wonderful*, thought Collins, *I'll be choking within five minutes.*

'It seems blatantly obvious to me that your investigation on behalf of the Super into corruption in Birmingham is linked to the murders of Endbury and his wife. All agreed? asked the Superintendent.'

Everyone murmured, 'Yes.'

'Now I take it that you lads don't want to hand the corruption case over to Central?' Again, Collins and Clark nodded in agreement. 'What the Inspectors and I have agreed is that you pair will continue to investigate the murder of the two girls and see what crawls out of the woodwork as far as the corruption angle goes. And Inspector Archer will conduct a separate murder inquiry into Endbury and his wife on the same basis. But, and this is important, there will be full sharing of information and regular briefing meetings between the two of you. Is that clear?'

'Yes, Sir,' said Collins.

'Good. In that case I want you to give WPC Arlington a copy of all the files you have on the corruption and she'll photocopy them. Likewise, Inspector Archer will copy all his documents to you.'

For the first time Clark sat up straight in his chair and said, 'If wem going to keep what we're doing under wraps from the centre and the press, we need to be careful about who we share information with at our stations. There's always some little sod who wants to pile up brownie points with the top brass or make a few bob from the press. Wi need to keep what we're doing under wraps.'

'I agree,' said Archer, and puffed on his pipe. 'I'll square what we are doing with my Super and brief my team accordingly.'

'Well that's settled, then. Anything else?'

'While Arlington does the photocopying, I'd like a full briefing on the corruption case please,' said Archer.

Ten minutes later, back in the CID room, Collins and Clark outlined everything they had on the corruption investigation to Archer. Much of it had been included in their statement but they all knew that a verbal briefing was invariably better, as it provided opportunities for questions and digressions. Archer listened without interruption, making the odd note in a small unofficial pocketbook.

'OK, let me get this straight. 'You think that Reece, or possibly someone else, was blackmailing Endbury in order to get the land at Birchfield. However, when the girls' bodies were found, Reece was afraid that Endbury wouldn't stand up to prolonged police questioning. So he and his wife were topped and it was meant to look like a murder/suicide. But the boys sent to kill the Endburys ran when they thought she'd called the police and the car you saw hightailing it out of the drive was the killers.'

'That's about it, Sir,' said Collins.

'No other theories?'

'Me and Mickey ain't great ones for theories, Sir. What wi've outlined might be accurate. But it could be a crock of shit. What wi have to do is go and knock a few more heads together before we can say what's really going on.'

'Fair enough. What's your next step?'

Before either Collins or Clark could respond, WPC

Arlington pushed the door open with her foot while she balanced a large wodge of photocopies in her hands. 'Sorry I couldn't knock, Sir,' she said and deposited the papers on Collins' desk. The papers began to slide and both Collins and Arlington made a grab for them, bumping heads as they did so.

'Are you all right?' asked Collins, rubbing his temple.

'Fine, it was only a tap.'

As Arlington split the pile of papers into the originals and copies, Collins became aware for the first time that she was wearing perfume.

'These are yours, Sergeant,' she said handing over the originals wrapped in a new manila cover on which she had written Navarone.

'What's this "Navarone"?' Archer asked.

'Well you said that you wanted to keep the investigation quiet. I didn't think constantly referring to *the corruption case* was a good idea. I thought we could give the case a code name. You can change it if you want.'

'No that's fine,' he said and sat down.

'What are you going to call yowr murder case,' asked Clark.

'I was thinking, "Eagle",' Arlington shot back.

'Well someone likes Alistair MacLean,' said Archer. 'But as I was saying before, what's your next move?'

'We were thinking of interviewing Reece again, and his mate Thorne,' said Collins.

'Why him?'

'Because he runs the muscle for Reece, any killing would be done by him and his mates,' said Clark, 'but I think wi might have to leave it until Monday'

'Why?' asked Collins.

''Cos our mate Mr McEwan called earlier and said he needed to see both of us this afternoon about Mitch Williams. He said it were important.'

Collins' heart missed a beat. If McEwan wanted to see him, it was a pound to a penny that he had found something which would reflect badly on him and he wanted to twist the knife.

## Birmingham, 15.28hrs

Collins had found several reasons not to rush off to see the esteemed pathologist but by half-three he'd run out of 'urgent jobs' to do. As he slipped his jacket on, Clark stood up and did the same.

'It's all right, Clarkee. Whatever McEwan says you don't have to come.'

'But I want to. I want to be there the day yow finally deck the irritating bastard.'

'Well I don't think today is that day.'

'In that case I fancy a drive.'

'Well, we're taking my car.'

'Now there yow go again. Yow always have to spoil it.'

A parking space opened as Collins turned into Whittall Street and he parked just a few yards away from the General Hospital's Accident and Emergency entrance. From there it was less than two minutes' walk to the city mortuary, situated on Newtown Street at the rear of the Coroner's Court. The receptionist recognised Collins and Clark and waved them through. In passing Clark asked, 'How's yowr lord and master today?'

'Same cunt as usual, Clarkee,' replied the retired policeman with a straight face.

There were no bodies on the steel tables in the morgue and everything looked as if it had just been freshly washed down. The door closed behind Collins and Clark and both men looked to the glass cubicle at the end of the room which acted as the doctor's working office in the mortuary as McEwan looked up. He had far more palatial accommodation on the first floor that reflected his position and standing in the community.

'Well, if it isn't Sherlock and his trusty bloodhound,' said McEwan as he crossed the floor to meet Collins and Clark.

Collins ignored the remark and said, 'I had a message you wanted to see me, Mr Mc Ewan.'

'Yes. I left it this morning,' he replied and made it sound like a teacher reprimanding a pupil for their tardiness.

'Sorry, but I only received it an hour ago.'

'Busy catching killers, I suppose. Well I have a spot of good news for you. If that Catholic conscience of yours is bothering you about Mr Williams you can say three Hail Marys and forgive yourself. His death was not your fault. The bus did not kill him and in nine hundred and ninety-nine cases out of a thousand the bang on the head wouldn't have killed any normal man. Unfortunately for young Mitch he was not normal. He had the thinnest skull that I and my colleagues at the Queen Elizabeth Hospital have ever seen. Given his chosen occupation and the fact that he has probably had more than a few fights I'm amazed that he's survived this long. One punch or even the slightest blow on the head could have killed him. You're off the hook, my fine Irish Mick.'

Collins didn't react to Mc Ewan's final insult, and instead thanked him for the information and left.

'How is it that even when he's got good news that bastard has to try and wind yow up?'

'I don't know. I reckon it's a gift he's got.'

'Anyway, how do yow feel about what he said?'

'I didn't kill the lad, but I did set in motion the events that caused his death. If Moore had been where he was supposed to be instead of lying on the floor none of it would have happened. But you know what? I feel really sorry for Mitch and his mother, but I can live with it. '

'That's good. 'Cos I'm telling yow, Mickey, it weren't your fault.'

## Sheldon, 17.35hrs

The rain was lashing down as Martin Cunningham left his office. Ignoring the zebra crossing twenty yards to his left, he trotted to the centre of the road. There he stood with cars passing behind and in front of him for twenty seconds before a break in the traffic allowed him to reach the other pavement. It was a journey he made every day to the newsagent opposite his offices. A man of habit, he always bought the same few items. The *Birmingham Mail* for himself, three different packets of sweets for the kids, and once a week a box of Black Magic chocolates for his wife, although Fiona, the eldest, had announced last week that she was getting too old for sweets. However, Cunningham had noticed that it had not stopped her scoffing whatever he brought home.

Exiting the shop, Cunningham stood in the doorway watching for his chance. He noticed the dark blue Ford Zephyr parked illegally thirty yards away to his right. As he started his run for the middle of the road the Zephyr moved off, accelerating up to thirty miles per hour. Standing on the centre line and watching the oncoming traffic Cunningham saw the Zephyr too late as it pulled over the white line. His reactions were still fast, and he jumped into the air an instant before the car hit him. Landing on the bonnet he slipped off and hit the road hard. His momentum sent him sprawling across the carriageway. The driver of an oncoming bread lorry saw him lying on the road and steered for the pavement while slamming on the brakes. His back wheels caught Cunningham a glancing blow to the head.

As traffic on both sides of the road came to a stop, the

Zephyr swept away and headed for a nearby scrap yard and its appointment with a car crusher.

Cunningham lay unmoving. His left leg was at a very unnatural angle and blood seeped from his forehead and left ear.

## Handsworth, 21.20hrs

News of Martin Cunningham's accident reached Collins later that evening when he received a call at home from Sergeant O'Driscoll. 'Mickey, I'm not entirely sure what you and Clarkee are up to, and I don't want to, but I thought you'd like to know that Martin Cunningham was involved in a hit and run earlier this evening outside his offices. He's been taken to the Queen Elizabeth Hospital.'

Hanging up, Collins immediately called Clark. 'Have you heard the news?,' he asked.

'Yeah, I was just about to ring yow. What wi going to do?'

'Pay a visit to Mrs Cunningham in the morning.'

'I was afraid yow'd say that. I'll pick you up from the station around nine.'

'OK.'

## Saturday 28th September 1968

### Handsworth, 09.13hrs

As Collins walked past the Charge Room, Sergeant Ridley waved him in. 'Glad I caught you, Mickey. I thought you'd like to see this report from Thursday night.'

Collins took the proffered sheets of paper and looked at the heading, "Killing of young dog." 'Not another bloody one?'

'Afraid so. This one took place near St Augustine's Church. I was hoping you could talk to the man who found the dog's body. His details are on the second page.'

'Yeah, I'll go and see him later today. Thanks for this.'

### Solihull, 10.03hrs

The change in Yolande Cunningham since Collins and Clark had last seen her was shocking. She looked drained of all vitality. Her eyes were black from lack of sleep and her skin was as pale as that of a two-day old corpse. In her usually bright eyes there was only bewilderment, while her movements were slow and ponderous.

'Yolande, we're sorry to disturb you, but we heard the news and wanted to wish Martin and you all best for a quick recovery. How's he doing?' Collins asked.

'It's good of you to call. Come in. Come in.' Even on one of the worst days of her life it was impossible for Mrs Cunningham to be unsociable. 'Can I get you a cuppa?'

'Why don't yow point me in the right direction and I'll make us all a cuppa while yow have a chat with Mickey.'

'Ah sure, that's good of you. Just follow your nose through that door,' she said pointing, 'and you'll trip over it. The brack's in the bread bin.'

Collins sat in the same chair he had used only a few days earlier. 'How are the girls?' he asked.

'Sure, they love their Daddy. They're all desperately worried. They feel terrible about it, as he was just buying sweets for them. Did it every day without fail, and now he's in a coma.' Yolande's voice cracked and the tears started to fall again as long, loud sobs shook her body. Collins felt the hairs on the back of his neck rise as a cold chill ran through his body. *He did it every day,* he thought.

Half-recovered, Yolande ground her right fist into the settee cushion. 'The fecking bastard didn't even stop. Ran him over like a dog and kept going.'

Clark appeared in the doorway with a tray of tea and six thick slices of well buttered Irish brack. He laid the tray on the table and handed Yolande her mug of hot sweet tea before taking his and sitting down beside her. 'Where am the girls?' he asked.

'They're out with their Uncle Declan. He caught the last plane out of Dublin last night as soon as he heard the news.'

'It's good to have family around you at times like this,' said Collins.

'Oh, Declan's not family. His name is Boyle. He's Martin's oldest friend. Martin might have left Ireland in 1949 but he's never forgot where he comes from nor the people he loves. I don't think there's a person in the village he hasn't helped over the years.'

'I'm not surprised,' said Collins. 'I only met him the once, but he seemed a decent man to me.'

'That he is.'

Both Collins and Clark knew that there was nothing they could say which would comfort Yolande. She needed her husband to wake up from the coma he was in, so they drank their tea, ate their cake and tried to encourage her to talk about Martin. Occasionally a smile would flit across her mouth as she remembered a specific incident, but it did not last long. The fear she felt obliterated every happy thought as soon as it was born.

After half an hour Collins and Clark made their excuses and left. They were halfway down the path when they saw Yolande's children walking slowly up the road, a tall thin man in his mid-forties beside them. Ignoring the car, the two officers walked towards the sad little group. 'Hello girls,' said Collins. 'We've just been to see your Mammy. We're really sorry to hear about your Daddy.'

The girls mumbled their thanks, all the time looking at the ground.

'Are you the Garda?' asked the thin man. His voice was deep and sounded strange coming from such a slim man. His eyes were set back with black rings under each. He had a large sharp nose and a small mouth. Collins was vaguely aware of having seen the face before but could not place it.

'You must be Declan Boyle,' said Collins, 'Yolande spoke of you. I'm Detective Sergeant Collins and this is Detective Constable Clark,' and held out his hand.

Boyle ignored Collins' hand and asked, 'Are you investigating the hit and run?' His dark eyes never wavered from Collins face. It was if he was committing the younger man's face to memory.

'No.'

'So why are you here, then?'

'We met Martin a few weeks ago on another matter.'

'And what would that be?'

'Best yow ask Mrs Cunningham,' said Clark and touching Collins on the elbow said, 'Wi have to go, girls. Be good to yowr Mom, she needs yow now.'

As Clark drove away Collins looked at him and said, 'You didn't much like Boyle, did you?'

'Bloody right, I dain't. Every instinct I have was telling me that the Karloff lookalike were dangerous.'

Collins smiled as he realised that Boyle certainly did look like Boris Karloff but still, he could not shake the conviction that he'd seen the man before. 'Well, he was certainly unfriendly. But maybe he just doesn't like the police.'

'No, there were more to his attitude than that. He really dain't like yow, Mickey. Now, I know that lots of people who hate the sight of yow, but normally they have to know yow for a few days before they hate yowr guts. He despised yow the minute yow said yow were police. I think it might be worth finding out a bit about him.'

'Do you want me to give Dublin a call?'

'Can't hurt.'

They were on the A45 heading into Birmingham before Collins spoke again. 'I've been thinking.'

'Now yow know what the doctor said about that. It could be dangerous.'

'We'll at least I don't keep me brain in a shoebox at home, like some I could mention.'

'Don't go insulting my box, it's a very nice box. Anyways, whatcha been thinking?'

'Yolande said that Martin always bought his kids sweets, every day without fail.'

'So what?'

'What if he always bought them from the same newsagents, at the same time, most days?'

Clark considered the implications of what Collins had said before replying, 'Yow know, I'm starting to hate this case with all its coincidences.'

'That's what I thought. But at this stage it's only a maybe.'

'And maybe me Auntie was a sergeant major in the war and had her balls shot off.'

'What the feck does that mean?'

'It means that one it's possible, and two if it were a contract killing it would explain why the car hit him when he was standing in the middle of the road and why no one has been able to find it or why it looks like it were using false number plates.'

'Where did you get that info from?'

'I have my sources.'

'And when were you going to tell me?'

'I just have. Where next?

'I think it's about time that we visited Councillor Hill's abode.'

## City Road, 12.35hrs

Councillor Hill's wife answered the door, checked both Collins' and Clark's warrant cards carefully and then shouted up the stairs. 'Bill, there are a couple of policemen here to see you.'

As Mrs Hill led them into a small dining room which had been converted into a very untidy office. Both men heard the sound of bedsprings and Hill's feet hitting the bedroom floor, followed shortly afterwards by the sound of a flushing toilet and running water. When he appeared, Hill looked both tired and hungover. He was a big man, over six foot with a beer belly and a pair of breasts that clearly showed through his grubby shirt. He had the flabby facial features of a town drunk, with thick, slobbery lips, a nose covered in blackheads and pig-like pale eyes that seemed to be examining you like a hungry man looks at a sirloin steak. The stink of last night's drinking seeped from every pore in his skin.

Collapsing into the swivel chair behind the desk, he waved at the two high-backed dining room chairs set against the wall, raised one cheek from the chair and farted. 'Sit down,' he ordered, before delving into the centre drawer of the desk and fishing out a pack of Players cigarettes. 'What do you want?' he asked, lighting up. Every word he spoke seemed to be shouted making even the most inoffensive statements sound belligerent and aggressive. Collins took an immediate dislike to the man.

While Clark prowled the room, Collins sat down, crossed his legs, and picked a piece of lint from the knee of his trousers before asking, 'We're wondering why you signed in a known prostitute to the reception held at the Council House, a Miss Claire Lafferty, for a Saudi prince on the first of June this year.'

Collins watched Hill closely. The distain on his face was easy to read and interpret; he was too hungover to spend time talking to these bastards. Leaning forward, Hill laid both hands on the desk and intertwined his fingers. The fingers of his left hand were stained yellow and his fingernails were long with a rim of dirt beneath each nail. Glowering at Collins, he said, 'Who the fuck do you think you are talking to me like that? I'm not some nigger in the back streets of Birmingham you can intimidate. If you want to talk about Council business, then contact my secretary for an appointment at the Council House and don't bother me at home again.'

'It doesn't work like that,' said Collins amicably. 'We choose the time and place and you answer our questions.'

'Didn't you hear me, you officious cunt?' shouted Hill. 'I'm a respected Councillor and if I don't get an apology out of you in the next two minutes I'll be speaking to the Chief Constable as soon as you've left. You jumped-up Irish prick.'

'Please don't shout, Sir,' said Collins as he watched Clark move behind Hill's chair. 'You see, my colleague doesn't like it when people shout. Next to mentioning the war it's the worst thing you can do.'

'What the fuck are you talking about? What war?'

Clark who had circled behind the councillor, grabbed the back of Hill's head and slammed his face into the desktop.

'I told you not to mention the war, Sir, didn't I?' said Collins.

'Yow see, Mickey. It's like I told yow. No one remembers

the war and all the hardships I had to endure to make the world safe for arseholes like this 'un.'

'You've broke my fucking nose,' cried Hill.

Clark looked at the blood running down Hill's face and grabbed the offending protuberance between his thumb and index finger and waggled it from side to side. Hill squirmed and tried to pull away. 'It ain't broke. Just rearranged.' Hill grabbed at Clark's hand but immediately let go when Clark hit him with a short jab to the side of his face.

A moan of pain escaped the councillor's lips and he said something which sounded like 'Geff thif fuckher offa me.'

'Ah, sure. I can't do that. He's a decorated war hero and I'm just a "jumped up Irish prick". Besides, you've not said the magic word.'

'What fucking magic word?'

'Do yow know something, Mickey? I think Mrs Ashcroft was right all those years ago when she said people are less civil these days.'

'I agree with you. People have no manners these days,' said Collins. 'I blame the war.'

Releasing Hill's nose Clark banged the man's head on the desk for a second time but not so hard this time. 'I told yow Mickey, don't mention the war.'

Flopping back in his seat, Hill took out a soiled handkerchief from his trouser pocket and dabbed gently at his nose before wiping the blood from his mouth and chin. The last few minutes had sobered him up and he was now wide awake. Glaring through hate-filled eyes, he asked. 'What do you want to know?'

'That's better,' said Collins. 'Why did you sign in a known prostitute and her mate to the reception held at the Council House for the Saudi prince on the first of June 1968?'

Hill shook his head and licked his lips. 'I was asked to provide some entertainment for the prince, should he want it. I was told he liked small women.'

'Who asked you?'

'No one. It was just a nod and a wink.'

'And did the prince take what was on offer?'

'No. He left with one of the waiters at the end of the night. No one told me he was a puff.'

'Where did you get the girl from?'

'I'd seen her before at other events. It wasn't hard to see what she was.'

'Answer the question,' said Clark, 'or I'll give yow another slap. Mickey asked where did yow get her from.'

Maybe Hill was confused. Maybe he was thinking about what the least incriminating answer was. Either way, it took him several seconds to reply. 'She's a model. Works out of Pure Gold Modelling Agency.'

'What about her mate? The big blonde?'

'I didn't ask for her. The other girl just brought her along.'

'Did yow see who the girls left with?'

'The blond girl left with Endbury around 10.30. Lafferty left later with some bloke I've never seen before.'

Clark held Hill by the chin and fixed him with an unswerving stare. 'Now that weren't so bad, was it? I'm going to tell yowr misses that yow tripped and banged yowr nose but yow'll be right as rain after a couple of aspirin and a cup of tea. Right?'

Hill lowered his head and mumbled, 'Yes.'

'One last thing,' said Collins, 'don't tell Councillor Robbins or the Agency that we might be calling on them. If you do, Detective Constable Clark here will be back – alone.'

Back on the street Collins said, 'You need to practice your nutter act a bit. I didn't think it had your usual intensity.'

'I was trying to hold the rage back. I dain't want to show everything all at once. I wanted to hint at deeper wells of lunacy.'

'I see. And where the feck did you hear that load of bollocks?'

'One of those BBC arts programmes. Some skinny little shite were talking about his role as Macbeth. He dain't look mean enough to scare Bram.'

'That's it, Get out of the car. Turn around three times and spit each time you complete a turn.'

'Why?

'You just said "Macbeth" in the car. Oh, feck. Now I've used the name. We're cursed for fourteen years.'

'Oh Larry, I hate to tell yow but wi ain't actors. I can say "Macbeth" as often as I like, and it won't bring us bad luck.'

'Ah! but there you are wrong, my good man,' proclaimed Collins loudly in a passable impression of Lawrence Olivier. 'The whole world is a stage and we are but poor actors each with our own entrances and exits.'

'Yow'll have my foot up your exit if yow don't tell me where wem going next?'

'Why my good fellow, let us travel yonder and have a look at the beautiful people.'

'I'm getting really fucking worried about yow. Ever since Agnes started taking yow to the theatre yow ain't been right in the head.'

'No, hang on,' said Collins looking at his watch. 'We've had another report of a young animal being slaughtered. The guy who found the body lives in Greenhill Road. Fancy a slight detour before the Agency?'

'No problem.'

Twenty minutes later Collins drew up outside a small villa. 'You don't have to come,' he said.

'Na, I'm interested. Maybe we can catch the bastard before he moves on to people.'

'You think that's likely?'

'I don't know. But I still think of those three kids regularly and wonder could I have done sommut to stop the bastard.'

Collins' knock on the green door was answered almost immediately. The man in front of them was over six feet tall, with grey hair, soft eyes and the look of a man who was used to manual work. 'Mr Toomey I'm DS Collins and this man is DC Clark. We're here about...'

'The dog. I'm glad someone is taking this seriously. Whoever did this is sick in the head. Let me get me jacket and I'll take you down to the school where he left the poor fella.'

Walking the hundred yards to St Augustine's, Toomey gave a full description of how he had found the animal. 'I'm the school caretaker and I start work at six thirty every morning. On Friday I walked to the school to open it up for the cleaners and found the door open. Someone had used a jemmy to smash the lock. I thought it was a burglary, so I headed straight for Sister Angela's office but that was still locked.' He stopped speaking to show Collins and Clark the damage that had been done to the front door. Then turning left, he beckoned the two men to follow him. 'That's Sister Angela's office, she's the headmistress.' Walking ten yards past the office, he stopped by a statue of Mary holding a baby Jesus. It was a fine piece of work, but the child's swaddling clothes and Mary's white robe were covered by a mucky brown coloured substance. 'The puppy was hung by the neck around the statue's neck. The stomach had been cut open and the guts pulled out. I took the body down and quickly washed the blood off. If you want to see the poor little thing, I have it in the workshop.'

Collins answered for both men. 'No, that's all right, Mr Toomey. You can dispose of the body. This is the second incident of this type in a few days and I can assure you that we will catch whoever is responsible.'

'Fair enough.'

### Birmingham, 16.25hrs

The journey into Birmingham was done in almost complete silence. Both men had been shocked by the level of rage that had been behind the attack on the mongrel puppy.

It reminded Clark of the savagery of the attacks on the animals in the fifties and Collins was angered by how the dead animal had been killed and displayed.

As they climbed out of the car Clark said, 'I want the bastard responsible.'

Collins replied, 'Me too.'

The Pure Gold Modelling Agency occupied the ground floor of a Georgian town house on Calthorpe Road, between St George's Church and Five Ways, Edgbaston. Clark pushed the heavy wooden door open and followed the sign to reception. A tall woman with a short black mini skirt, frilly white blouse and long glistening, black hair down to her waist and beyond, stood up and said, 'Good afternoon gentlemen. Can I help you?' The smile was the full two hundred watt model.

Clark showed his warrant card and said, 'The Sergeant and me would like to see the manager, please.'

The smile faded to forty watts as she replied, 'I'll see if Mr Redford can see you. Won't you please take a seat?'

Collins remained standing by the receptionist's desk. Clark meandered about the room, stopping to look at a range of pictures on the wall and the two catalogues of models that rested on the coffee table. He was flicking through the men's catalogue when the receptionist returned.

'You're in luck. Mr Redford can see you now.'

Turning over the catalogue page, Clark paused before saying. 'Did yow hear that Sergeant? Wem lucky that Mr Redford has the time to see us.' Laying the book down he said to the Receptionist, 'What gave yow the impression that Mr Redford had any choice in the matter, love?'

The receptionist waited until both men had their backs to her and then stuck up two fingers.'

'I heard that,' said Clark.

Mr Paul Redford was average height, average weight and average looking. He had the sort of face that you would forget within thirty seconds after seeing it for the first time. However, what he lacked in looks, he made up for in low cunning and a level of insight unusual in someone from his background. In a business where first impressions were all-important, he recognised that he needed to do something to stand out. The result was an immaculately tailored, blue stripped mohair suit, a pink shirt with white collar and cuffs, electric blue cravat and handmade Italian shoes, worn without socks – very stylish. But his crowning glory was his immaculately coiffured hair, which was dyed dark brown, long and luxuriant.

The accent, when he spoke, was West End of London. 'Morning, gents. What can I do you for? Need a bird to jump out of a birthday cake, do you? I've got a special price for my pals in blue.'

'We're not here about a cake. We understand that you had a girl by the name of Claire Lafferty on your books,' said Collins.

'Name doesn't ring any bells. I'll have to look her up,' he said and went to the low bookcase behind his desk and drew out a black ledger stamped "Register of Models". After a few minutes of seemingly fruitless search he looked up, and with a regretful smile said, 'Sorry, I don't have any record of her.'

Collins looked at Clark and said, 'That's a pity.'

Clark moved quickly and slammed the ledger closed on Redford's hands. Redford gave a high-pitched yelp and pulled his hands clear. As he did so Clark grabbed the manager's left wrist and elbow and in one fluid movement pushed the arm up his back. Holding Redford's left hand with his right, Clark used his left hand to apply pressure to the elbow and push the man's head down onto the blotting paper.

''What the fuck? You can't do this,' he croaked.

'Do what?' asked Collins. 'You're just helping us with our inquiries. But unfortunately, you forgot a few details and we are helping you to remember. The sooner you remember the sooner we'll be out of your lovely hair.'

'What do you want to know?'

'Who ordered Lafferty for the do at the Council House?'

'Which do?'

Clark pushed the trapped arm further up Redford's back. 'Don't piss us about or I'll break yowr arm and then start on the other one.'

'OK. OK. Just loosen your grip.'

Clark relaxed the pressure very slightly.

'The Bosses said to send her.'

*Bosses?* thought Collins, and immediately asked, 'Which one?'

'It was Hill. But Robbins knew about it.'

Again, Collins exchanged looks with Clark, who winked and said to the back of Redford's head, 'Yowr telling me that Councillors Hill and Robbins run this knocking shop?'

'It ain't a knocking shop. We do a lot of legit work, magazines, women's catalogues, posters. But some customers need a friend for the night, and we try to supply their needs.'

'OK. So, the knocking shop part of the enterprise is just charity work, is it?' asked Clark releasing Redford's arm. The manager sat back in his chair massaging first his wrist and then his shoulder.

'Do Reece, Thorne, or anyone else own a part of the business?' asked Collins.

'Na.' said Redford. 'Reece regularly uses our girls to entertain his customers. But he's always charged full whack.'

'What about Thorne? Ever seen him here?'

'I don't know any Thorne.'

'What about Sir Charles Endbury?'

'Never heard of the geezer.'

'Who was it that suggested that Claire should bring a friend to the do?' asked Collins.

'It was Hill who said Claire should bring a friend to the Saudi do. Said it couldn't be one of the regular girls. Needed to be someone totally new to the game in Brum. With big tits and a bum you could get hold of.'

'OK, Mr Redford, you've been most helpful. I don't suggest

that you mention our little visit to Mr Hill or Robbins. If you do, we'll have to tell them just how helpful you were.'

The evening had become blustery. Eddies of paper and leaves chased each other along the gutters and across the open road and gardens. Rain was starting to fall, and the dark clouds overhead suggested that it was here to stay for the night. 'Well that was interesting,' said Collins. 'I didn't think that Hill and Robbins would be running the agency. Maybe we have to rethink their role and position in all that's been going on.'

'Who do yow want to visit next?'

'It's Sunday tomorrow. How do you fancy visiting Mrs Simpson tomorrow afternoon?'

'OK, but any trip to Chasetown is going to take nearly two hours driving plus the interview. So, we best leave about twelve.'

'Fair enough.'

## Solihull, 22.37hrs

Yolande and the kids were in bed when Boyle carried the phone from the hall into the lounge. The lead was just long enough for him to close the door. Sitting on the carpet, he dialled a number in North Dublin from memory. It was answered almost immediately. There was the sound of voices and music in the background.

'Is that Dempsey's Bar?'

There was a slight hesitation at the other end. 'No, you have the wrong number.'

'Ah, sorry to call you. I've been trying for ten minutes to find the right number.'

'Can't help you,' said the man and hung up.

Checking his watch, Boyle went in the kitchen and made

himself a cup of tea and buttered a piece of soda cake. Munching and drinking, he waited exactly nine minutes forty seconds before ringing a green and cream public call box in Grafton Street, Dublin. The phone was picked up immediately.

'Declan?'

'Yes.'

'What's so bloody important that you couldn't leave it until the morning?' I was just about to get the knickers off a lovely girl from Galway.'

'I need help on that family matter I told you about. Would you send me a couple of lads first thing in the morning?'

'If you need them, they'll be there before three o'clock.'

'Thanks.'

'Anything else?'

Boyle remained silent for a few moments then said, 'Yeah see what you can find out about a Detective Sergeant Michael Collins, works for Birmingham police. Late twenties. Judging by his accent, I'd say north side of Dublin.'

'OK.'

'Oh, and one last thing. Give the Galway girl one for me.'

## Sunday 29th September 1968

### Handsworth, 10.00hrs

Collins waited until ten before he picked up the phone and rang his old editor at *The Bray News*. Padraig O'Brian had been well into his sixties when Collins had left for England in 1962 but there was no chance that he had retired. As he himself had often said, "They'll have to carry me out of here in a box."

Collins called *The Bray News* confident that Padraig would be there alone, as he was every Sunday morning. While his wife attended Mass, he used the time to write. He had been writing stories of Ireland ancient and modern since before Collins had been born, but no one had ever seen or read one of them. Instead, they were stored in a large wooden box and only he had the key to open it. The direct line was picked up after four rings.

'Yes,' a voice barked.

'Nice to hear you're still biting people's heads off whenever they ring you direct.'

'That's because only friends and family ever call me direct and I've told them not to call me at work.'

'I'm sure there's some logic in your reasoning, Padraig.'

'There is. It means I'm not usually interrupted at work by some eejit of a junior reporter who gave up a promising career to run off and join the police, in England of all places.' Then relenting, the voice softened and said, 'How are you, Michael?'

'I'm well. Yourself?'

'Grand. Just grand. Joan got your card. It was good of you to remember her birthday. Anyway, what can I do for you?'

'I've come across a guy called Declan Boyle. He's a friend of Martin Cunningham, a big-time builder in England.

Cunningham was badly hurt in a hit and run last Friday. The name sort of rang a bell but there are a lot of Declan Boyles in Ireland.'

'Indeed, there are. Alas, I don't think I can help you. But you said in Joan's card that you would be in Dublin Tuesday next. Why don't we grab lunch at Clerys around two?'

Collins knew immediately what the mention of Clerys meant. Whatever Padraig O'Brian had to say he didn't want to trust it to the busybodies of a local exchange. 'That would be grand. I'll see you then.'

Hanging up, Collins called Chief inspector Hicks at home.

'What do you want, Mickey, that won't wait until Monday?'

'Permission to fly to Dublin on Tuesday, Sir.'

'Why do you need to go to Dublin?'

'When Clarkee and I went to see Mrs Cunningham yesterday to see how she was getting on we met Martin's best mate Declan Boyle. I'm not sure if it was his name or face that rang a bell. Anyway, I've just got off the phone with my old boss at *The Bray News*. He said he knew nothing about the man but suggested that we have lunch at Clerys Tuesday.'

'And I take it this was his way of saying, I can't talk on the phone. Meet me?'

'When I worked for him, a lunch at Clerys always used to signal something serious was up. He's probably got a new word now.'

'You think it might have a bearing on the corruption case?'

'I honestly don't know, Sir.'

'OK. Pay for the ticket yourself and if it's connected you can claim it back on expenses.'

'Thanks, Sir.'

For the rest of the morning Collins went through the information that Marie Bolding had sent and Agnes's analysis of it and every other piece of information they had collected.

For once Agnes had been unable to provide any new insights into the data but she had summarised everything that had been collected. Like an actor learning his lines, Collins read the document seven times. Turning the files over, he took a piece of paper and made a note of the paper's key points. When he compared his list with Agnes,' he'd only missed one point. Collins read the summary three more times and repeated the process of writing out the summary. This time he got them all. With a smile he stored the files in a steel cupboard and locked it before heading for Clark's house.

## New Street Station, 11.07hrs

Declan Boyle drew up outside New Street station in a Ford Zodiac and two young men wearing Levi's and stay-pressed button-down shirts climbed into the car. But that was all they had in common. Shamus, the tall one, was over six foot, with a lanky build and a long narrow face. His hair was dark brown and eyes green and sometime in his life his nose had been broken and reset so badly that it was bent to the right.

His friend Bernie was much shorter, with ginger hair and a mass of freckles that covered his face, arms and chest. What he lacked in height he made up for in bulk, with a large chest, narrow waist and heavily muscled arms.

Boyle smiled at both men, whom he knew well. He'd worked with them before. They could be trusted. Checking in the mirror, Boyle waited for a gap in the traffic before he pulled away and turned left 150 yards down the road.

Boyle drove carefully down Navigation Street onto Suffolk Street and picked up the Bristol Road. From force of habit he constantly checked his mirror to confirm that no one was following him. A mile out of town he turned left and headed for Balsall Heath, home to thousands of single Irishmen working on the roads and buildings of Birmingham. He drew up outside a three-storey house and handed the big man sitting next to him a set of keys. 'Welcome to Brum, lads. The shithole of Europe. Get settled in, you're in flat 2. I'll see you at the Irish Club in Digbeth at nine tonight. The drinks are on me.'

Both men grinned and climbed out of the car. Putting the car in gear, Boyle pulled away, continuing to check regularly in his mirror to see if he was being followed.

## Burntwood, 12.08hrs

Collins pulled up outside Clark's house, trotted up the steps and rang the bell. Even before Clark opened the door, Collins could hear Michael crying and smiled. 'Are you ready?'

'Always, if yow're sure yow can read the map.'

'I can read a map.'

'I dain't know that? Who taught yow?'

'Up yours, you Villa fan.'

'Yow do know, Chasetown is nineteen miles from Brum and it has no train station and a lousy bus service and if yow cheek me again I'm going leave yow stranded there. We'll take my car.'

Instead of going straight across the Chester Road at the end of the Queslett Road and heading into Sutton Coldfield, Clark turned sharp left onto the Chester Road and headed for Brownhills. Parts of the Chester Road had been built nearly 1,800 years earlier by the Romans and while the road was no longer as straight as a yard measure it still contained plenty of straights that allowed Clark to put his foot down.

Chasetown was one of three small mining villages in Staffordshire where a massive house building programme in recent years had changed the character of the area forever. Small two and three-bedroom houses had sprung up all over Chasetown and its near neighbours Burntwood and Chase Terrace. Originally the three had formed a triangle on the map with not very much in the centre except farmland. Now the centre was crammed with houses intended for young married couples working in Birmingham. Thousands had responded to the low prices and the proximity of Cannock Chase with its miles of trees, bridle paths, heathland and 800 strong deer herd, and headed north to start a family.

The Simpsons had lived at 58 Leverson Avenue. Turning off Queen Street. Clark had to drop down to second gear to take the one in eight road. Number 58 was at the top, on a corner. Clark pulled up beside a well-kept lawn. The house was a dormer bungalow with two bedrooms downstairs and the main bedroom and the bathroom upstairs. As Clark locked the car, Collins spotted the lounge curtain twitch.

Collins pressed the bell and waited as he heard someone fumble with the security chain. It was only when the door opened, did he realise that the tired and dispirited young woman in front of him had been putting the chain on the door, not removing it. Her hand was trembling as she asked, 'Yes?'

'Mrs Simpson?' She nodded. 'I'm Detective Sergeant Collins and this is Detective Constable Clark. We'd like to talk to you about your late husband,' he said holding his warrant card up for her to see.

'Why?'

Throughout the brief exchange, Collins had been assessing Mrs Simpson. It was clear she was living on the edge of a breakdown. Her ginger hair looked lifeless and her eyes darted from Collins' warrant card to his face and then his hands. It would only take a single wrong word and she would dissolve into tears or much worse. She didn't need the usual police platitudes. She needed some hope. Collins decided to gamble. 'We don't think your husband John committed suicide.'

The woman searched Collins' face and eyes for any sign of deceit and found none. Tears began to roll silently down her freckle-covered cheeks and she said, 'You'd better come in,' and closing the door, she undid the safety chain.

There was no hall in the house and Collins and Clark immediately found themselves in a neat lounge with a blue settee sporting brightly coloured exotic birds, and matching chairs. 'Can I get you a cup of tea?'

'Maybe later, Mrs Simpson,' said Collins unsure how long the frightened woman in front of him would remain stable enough to answer questions.

'All right, then. What do you want to know?' she asked flopping into one of the armchairs. Picking up a scatter cushion, she held it across her stomach and chest as if it were a shield.

'We're investigating possible corruption in Birmingham City Council and someone suggested that your husband may have been investigating the same matter before he died.'

'What we really want to hear, Mrs Simpson,' said Clark, 'is yowr story about everything that happened leading up to yowr hubby's death and later at the inquest.'

For the first time since they met a thin smile spread across Mrs Simpson's lips. 'It's a long story. Are you sure you want to hear it?'

'Yes,' said Collins.

'In that case we'll all need a cup of tea,' she said rising, 'And please call me Annabel.'

Five minutes later, a mug of tea in her hand, Annabel Simpson started to tell her story. 'John and I were married in 1966, the day England won the World Cup and the same year he qualified as an accountant. We moved out here in early '67 and that coincided with him getting the job of Contracts Auditor at Birmingham Council. Everything was great at first. He loved his job and we loved this house. It's got loads of scope for improvement and we found a wonderful church just up the road at Sankey's Corner. A real evangelical church.

'Then in early 1967 he started to bring home papers from work. Not just the odd memo or report, but boxes of files. He stopped doing any work around the house and spent all of Saturday and even some of Sunday in the back room going through the papers.'

Collins wanted to ask what the papers were about but decided against it. Annabel had that faraway look that people get when they are reliving past events. *All will become clear in time,* he thought.

'This went on for weeks. I was getting worried. Poor John was working himself into the ground. Finally, I asked him what was going on and when would I get my husband back. Well, he just smiled and said, "I've almost finished, just another few days and I'll deliver my report to the Chief Auditor. Then it will be his problem, not ours." I was so happy to hear this that I didn't ask him what the report was about.

'About a week later I got a telephone call from an old friend, Angela Greening. I hadn't seen her since school. She said she was going to be in Brum on business the following week and could we meet up for a meal to catch up on old times. I said yes.

'We arranged to meet at the Belgravia Hotel on New Street for a drink before going on for our meal. Well she was late. Just like she always was, and this chap started to chat me up. I told him I was married, and he said he was just killing time before he met his girlfriend and could he chat to me until my friend arrived. Well he was good-looking, and he was nice, so I saw no harm in it.

'The next thing I can remember is waking up in a hotel room naked. My clothes were all over the floor and my knickers were ripped. I knew I had been raped. I could smell him on me.'

'I spent an hour in the shower and bath that night trying to scrub myself clean. But no matter how many showers I take, I've not felt clean since it happened.' Annabel stopped talking and looked at her hands. Her fingernails had been gnawed down to the quick and a thin line of blood rimmed seven nails. She took a deep breath and shivered, but when she continued her voice was strong. 'When I got home, I told John everything that had happened, and he believed me. But I could tell he was worried. As if he blamed himself.

'The next day I tried to phone Angela, but it was just a hotel number, and no one knew anything about her. Later when the police were checking my story, they traced Angela to Manchester, and she said she'd never called me.'

'About three days after I was raped a package arrived addressed to John and me. I opened it and there were about twenty photos of me and the man I'd met in the bar. Some of them were absolutely disgusting. I was doing things to him that I'd never done with John. With it was a note saying that unless John lost his report on property contracts the photos would be sent to our family and friends and our local church. They said they wanted all the notes, draft reports and the final report by Friday or the photos would go in the post Saturday morning. John was to deliver them to a man he would meet on the fourth floor of the Stirling Street car park.

'We discussed it for two solid days. I wanted John to go to the police. But he didn't want to see me dragged through the press. On Friday night, John kissed me goodbye and the last words he ever said to me were, "After tonight we can get on with our lives." He took everything they asked for, including the photos. Four hours later the police arrived to tell me he'd committed suicide by jumping from the multi-storey car park.

'The inquest was terrible. The police traced the man that I said had raped me and he said that I'd been alone in the bar and that I'd approached him. As for the photos, he said he knew nothing about that. It had just been him and me in the hotel room. Then Mr Hastings, the Chief Auditor, said that he had no knowledge of any report John had been writing.

'It was implied that I'd made the whole story up about the report and being raped because I'd told my husband what I'd done and couldn't face the fact that he'd committed suicide because of me. One paper called me "The Black Angel". John's parents haven't spoken to me since the inquest. Even my own family have disowned me – except me mom who tries to phone when me dad is out. But she always ends up crying.'

'And no copies of this report were ever found?' asked Collins.

'No.'

'How about the files your hubby brought home, are they still here?'

'No. Two men from the Audit office called the week after John's death and took everything that belonged to the Council.'

'And this Chief Auditor still maintains that he knew nothing of your husband's report?'

Annabel nodded.

Collins placed his hand on hers and said, 'I've just got one more question for you. Why did they go after you, rather than try and blackmail your husband? Wouldn't that have been easier?'

'I was pretty wild when I was at school and after. I drank and slept around. I was even arrested once for prostitution, but the case was dismissed. I was so drunk I didn't know what I was doing. It was only after I met John that I cleaned my act up and found Jesus. That's why I loved him so much. He was a decent man who had standards and beliefs and tried to live up to them. It was easier to blackmail a bad girl turned good than a genuinely good man whose reputation would protect him. You do believe me, don't you?' Her voice was beseeching.

'Yes, we believe you.'

Annabel slumped back in her chair and the tears began to

flow freely, but this time there was a smile on her face. After a few moments she wiped her face clean with the back of her hand and said, 'Time for more tea and a sandwich all round. I have no bacon, but I have some Cumberland sausages. How about that?'

Clark exchanged looks with Collins and then answered for both, 'That would be bostin.'

As Mrs Simpson laid the tray of sausage sandwiches and tea on the coffee table the transformation in her appearance was amazing. Collins could see that some colour had returned to her face and life and hope were creeping back into her eyes. After twelve months of being branded a liar, someone finally believed her and there was a chance that her attacker would face justice. As they munched their way through their sandwiches Clark asked, 'Is there anything at all left of yowr hubby's notes and papers?'

'If there is, they'll still be in his room. I've not touched anything in there since he left that Friday night.'

'Mind if I take a butchers?' asked Clark.

'No, feel free.'

While Clark disappeared into the small study off the lounge Collins was playing with an idea. 'Mrs Simpson...'

'Annabel, please.'

'Annabel, you've been cooped up in this house with no one to talk to about what happened. I'm surprised that you've managed so well. My landlady works with women who have been beaten and raped. She knows about these things. I think it would do you good to stay with her for a few nights. What do you say?'

'I'm not sure...'

Collins saw the hesitation and said, 'I tell you what. Just come back with me for tonight and then if you don't like Agnes, I'll drive you home in the morning.'

'Well, I suppose one ...'

'Good. I'll give her a ring while you pack an overnight bag. Then I'd better give Clarkee a hand checking out the study. He's been known to get lost in his own back garden,' he joked and was rewarded with the briefest of smiles from Annabel.

Left alone, Collins called Agnes and without giving any details said that he would be bringing home a woman who needed help. Agnes didn't ask any questions; they would come later. She just said, 'We've got plenty of room.'

Hanging up Collins found Clark in Simpson's small office which was inordinately neat and tidy. Everything you would expect from an accountant, except for the light covering of dust on the furniture, books, files and black plastic floor tiles. 'Found anything?' Collins asked.

'Couple of diaries, a few torn pages in the wastepaper bin. Lots of passages underlined in the Council's Standing Orders and Financial Regulations but nowt of any use.'

Collins wandered over to the desk and ran his hand over the black and gold Remington Rand typewriter on the table. A blank sheet of paper already in the carriage and a quick check showed that the ribbon was brand new. Closing his eyes Collins remembered Padraig O'Brian standing beside him at his interview. "Close your eyes now and type your name and address." The result had been disastrous, but all that Padraig said was, "Sure some of the best reporters I ever worked with couldn't type. You're hired. Start Monday, OK." Still with his eyes shut he typed out his name.

'Whatsha doing?' asked Clark.

'Remembering me past. I used to have the same model when I was at *The Bray News*. Looking down Collins saw his work, but it wasn't what he'd typed. It was gibberish. 'Bloody hell.'

'Whatcha got?'

'I'm not sure but it looks like someone typed a string of characters and then rewound the ribbon to the start.'

'Why would anyone do that?'

'Possibly to check the alignment or to leave a clue.'

'And now yow've just typed all over it. You pillock.'

'I'll take it back to the station and get one of the SOCO lads to have a look at it.' Collins picked up the typewriter and immediately felt something attached to the base. He laid the typewriter on its side and there, stuck to the underside of it by a four-inch piece of Sellotape, was a small key. 'Will you look at this?' he said.

Clark wandered over and bending down, smiled. 'That's either a key for a safe deposit box or left luggage. But I reckon yow've just typed over its bloody address. Like I said, yam a pillock.'

'I found it.'

'Sheer bloody luck.'

## Handsworth, 16.27hrs

Agnes turned down the gas under the pot of soup she'd been stirring when she heard Clark's car pull up on the drive. Opening the front door, she kissed Collins on the cheek and shook Annabel's hand. After the introductions were complete, Agnes said, 'Come in Mrs Simpson – or can I call you Annabel?'

'Annabel, please.'

'I'll show you to your room and you can freshen up before we have a bite to eat. I'm afraid it's just soup and bread. I didn't have time to cook.'

As Agnes led Annabel up the stairs, she nodded at Collins, 'Don't wait for us. Have some soup before you head back to the station.'

Collins immediately knew what that meant. Agnes was going to have a chat with Annabel and depending on how well that went she would be down in either a few minutes or in two hours.

The station was unnaturally quiet when Collins arrived carrying the Remington Rand typewriter. The afternoon shift was out on duty; no one had called in for assistance and both Hicks and O'Driscoll were at home.

Collins ran his finger under the front of his belt. It was tight. *You're getting flabby Michael,* he thought. A waist of barely 28 inches when I landed in this county and now it's tight at 32. No cake for you. Just a cuppa.

Ten minutes later he was sitting at his desk. He rewound the ribbon then removed it from the typewriter. Picking up his diary, he found the home phone number for his mate at Scenes of Crime Office. His call was answered on the third ring, 'Biddeford,' was the one word greeting he received from Sergeant Biddeford, who like Clark had enjoyed a good war.'Joe, it's Mickey. Can you come over to CID on Monday please? I need your help to read a typewriter ribbon.'

'It ain't me you want, Mickey. I know fuck all about typewriters. There's a guy whose number I can give you. Runs his own typewriter business. I've used him in the past. He don't charge us for his services.'

'OK, mate. Give me his number.'

Hanging up, Collins rang Sidney Steptoe's home number, introduced himself, mentioned Biddeford's name and outlined what he was after.

'Well, I can't come immediately but I could make it for five thirty tomorrow, if that's all right?' asked Sidney in what sounded like a woman's voice.

'That would be great. Thank you very much, Mr Steptoe.'

'Think nothing of it. Always pleased to help the police. But please call me Sidney.'

'See you Monday at five thirty, Sidney.'

Picking up his mug of sweet tea, Collins settled back and started to read the crime reports from stations in the city. There wasn't much going on. Give it a few weeks and firework-related accidents and petty crime would increase along with the injuries. For now it was just the usual burglaries, a couple of smash and grabs in the city centre, a fairly big punch-up at a pub in Hockley between two biker gangs and the killing of a pet rabbit in Perry Barr and the nailing of its body to a garden gate. His heart missed a beat as he read the details. The injuries and the display of the body were identical to those of the kitten. Picking up the phone he rang Perry Barr station and asked to be put through to DCI Jameson who had signed the report. After a two-minute conversation, Jameson agreed to circulate a request to all stations in the Birmingham area for any similar incidents of small animals being killed, and promised to send Collins a copy of his findings. Collins hung up and moved on to checking his notes for the inquest into the death of Mitch Williams the following week.

## Monday 30th September 1968

### Handsworth, 11.43hrs

Clark burst into the CID office carrying a large bundle of photocopies. 'Yam never going to guess who oversaw the investigation into Simpson's suicide. I'll give yow a clue. It were handled by Central.'

'Sodding hell. You're not telling me it was...'

'Yowr mate and mine, Chief Inspector West.'

'That's all we need. We better tell Hicks. Flames will be shooting across the bloody sky once West gets wind of us looking at one of his cases.'

'True. But at least wi can be bloody near certain that it weren't a suicide. West has never knowingly arrived at the right conclusion in his life.'

'What else have you got?'

'Newspaper reports and a full transcript of the inquest. Plus, a picture of Adam Strong.'

'Who the feck is Adam Strong?'

'The bastard that screwed Mrs Simpson at the Belgravia. The same man who happens to be on the Golden Model Agency books. From memory his description said, "Adam is six feet one and measures forty-two, thirty-two, thirty-eight." The only thing missing from his profile was the size of his dick and I imagine that information is available on request.'

'Are you sure it was him?'

'Oh yeah. The photocopies I have here are poor, but the originals were good 'uns and they match what I saw in their models' book.'

'Well, he's certainly someone I'd like to speak to. How do you want to play it?'

'I were thinking Marie might give the Golden Model

Agency a ring and say that Adam was recommended to her by a friend.'

'Meeting place the Belgravia Hotel by any chance?'

'How did yow guess? I'll call Marie.'

'OK. We should have a look at what you've found and draw up a plan. I was also thinking we should talk to Robbins and Mr Hastings, the Chief Auditor today.'

'That sounds like a decent day's entertainment.'

'After that I have an appointment with Mr Sidney Steptoe.'

'Who the hell is Sidney Steptoe?'

'I'll tell you on the way to see Robbins.'

'OK, but wem taking my car.'

'Well go and wind the bloody thing up then, while I ring the Council and see where the good Councillor is.'

Collins was informed by a very posh-sounding woman that, "Councillor Robbins was at home and was not expected to be in the Council House until Thursday when he would be attending the Housing Committee meeting." Collins asked if she could give him the councillor's home phone number and address.

Sliding into the passenger seat Collins said, in a fairly good imitation of the woman he'd just been speaking to, 'My good man, you may drive on. The councillor's residence is off the Newton Road, Great Barr.'

'I keep telling ya, no matter how much yow practice yow'll never be as good as Mike Yarwood. If yow want to go on Opportunity Knocks why don't yow try sword swallowing?'

'Bollocks,' replied Collins and settled into his seat for the fifteen-minute drive.

Robbins lived in a large five-bedroom detached house with a three-tier front garden and views of the open countryside from the rear. Clark rang the doorbell, which chimed out two bars of "Jerusalem." Before the tune was repeated for a second time a woman in her late fifties with gray hair, a plump face and dark blue eyes opened the door.

'Yes?' she said. 'Can I help you?'

'We'd like to talk to Councillor Robbins, please.'

'What about?'

Collins found his warrant card and showed it. 'I'm Detective Sergeant Collins, and this is Detective Constable Clark. We think Mr Robbins may be able to assist us in our enquiries.'

'Oh my. Dear me. I do hope that he hasn't done anything.' The worry in her voice was obvious to both men.

'No Ma'am. We just think he may be able to help us with some information.'

The woman stepped aside and allowed the men into the hall. 'If you'll follow me, my husband is in his study on the third floor.'

'Oh, we wouldn't put you to any trouble, Mrs Robbins. We can find our own way.'

'Very well. His office is directly in front of you at the top of the stairs.'

'Thank you, Mrs Robbins, you've been very helpful.'

Collins and Clark walked up the first flight of stairs as normal but crept up the second. Stepping up to the door Clark rapped on it, said, 'Police' and Collins immediately opened the door. Councillor Robbins' head jerked up from the magazine he was looking at and tried to conceal it by pulling a Council report over it.

'Sorry to disturb you, Councillor Robbins. Your wife said you were busy with Council work. My name is Detective Sergeant Collins and my colleague is Detective Constable Clark. We'd like to talk to you about corruption in Birmingham City Council, and your ownership of the Golden Model Agency.'

'Which wi understand is up for an award as Best Knocking Shop in the Midlands, 1968'

'What the hell do you mean by bursting in on a private citizen in his own home.'

'Na don't start that, mate. Yow see Councillor Hill tried that and ended up slipping on the floor and busting his nose on the edge of his desk. Blood everywhere, there were.'

'Are you threatening me?'

'Na, just telling yow about the accident that your mate had, is all.'

'Well I know nothing about corruption in the Council. And as for the Golden Model Agency that is an entirely respectable modelling business.'

'So why is it that Councillor Hill and the manager of the Pure Gold Modelling Agency say it operates a side-line in supplying young ladies to discerning gentlemen,' asked Collins.

'We supply escorts, not prostitutes. What two adults agree to do after they meet is not something we have any control over.'

'Are these escorts anything like the ladies you were looking at when we came in?' asked Collins.

'I was reading a Council report.'

''No yow weren't, mate. Yow were looking at a dirty magazine,' said Clark as he pulled the pile of papers from under Robbins' folded arms and pulled out a Swedish porn magazine entitled *Forced Sex*. 'Now how would yow like me to show this to yowr wife on me way out?'

Robbins didn't answer Clark. Instead he turned towards Collins and said, 'Ask your questions and then get out of my house.'

'Why did you choose Claire Lafferty to attend the reception of the Saudi prince?'

'Men from the Middle East are known to prefer small women.'

'So why did you ask her to bring along a blonde girlfriend?'

'Just in case the prince preferred big blondes.'

'But we've been told that the prince left with one of the waiters.'

'Well, no one told me that he was queer before the reception.'

'Isn't it true that your real target for that night wasn't the prince but Councillor Endbury? You knew he liked the larger women, which is why you asked Lafferty to find a friend who might interest him?'

'And why might I be interested in satisfying Endbury's sexual tastes?'

'So that you could blackmail him into changing his mind on the Birchfield Road planning application.'

'What utter tosh, Sergeant. If you repeat such a calumny in public, I will sue you for slander. Now if you have finished your questioning, I would like you to leave, and next time you want to question me please give me notice of the date, time and place of the interview and I'll be there with my solicitor.'

'Before we go can I ask which evening paper do you read?'

'The *Birmingham Mail*. Why?'

'It's just that the *Mail* has been full of Claire Lafferty's murder since Thursday last. But you didn't mention it once. That seems odd to me.'

Robbins face turned bright red, but he said nothing.

Walking back to the car, Collins said, 'He was a cool customer.'

'Yeah, real annoying, the lying toerag.'

'We'll get him. We've got two people saying that he's the joint owner of a knocking shop and one who says he asked for Claire Lafferty.'

## Birmingham, 15.09hrs

The Audit Office for Birmingham Council was situated at the back of the Council House on the first floor. However, the plush red carpet which covered the floor in the corridor outside the committee rooms was missing here.

Instead, cracked lino covered the wooden floor and the cream walls looked in need of painting. Anything was good enough for the hired help.

The Audit Office was nearly twenty yards long, with fifteen desks arranged in two rows. There were only two people present when Collins and Clark walked in, a middle-aged man, and a young woman busy trying to add up a ledger page of entries. They walked to the far end of the office and asked the man, who was enjoying a cup of tea, where they could find the Chief Auditor. 'Through that door,' he replied and pointed at the door to his left.

Clark knocked on the door and without waiting for an answer pushed it open. The office was large, and the desk was the biggest that Collins had ever seen. Behind it sat a man of medium size, slim, balding and in his fifties. Looking up he asked, 'Who are you?'

'Wem the police, that's who wi am, Mr Hastings. This is Detective Sergeant Collins and I'm Detective Constable Clark. We've come to ask yow a few questions about John Simpson, a one-time member of yowr staff.'

Hastings adjusted the round rimless glasses he was wearing and tried to clear his throat. When he spoke, he sounded terrified, as if he'd been dreading this meeting. 'I thought that was all settled at the inquest. He committed suicide.'

'Why do you think we're interested in how he died?' asked Collins.

'Well I just assumed …'

'I would have thought that an auditor was a bit like a copper. Someone who never assumed anything but always looked for proof,' said Collins.

'I don't know why I thought it was about his death,' said Hastings, his voice rising higher. Imperceptibly at first, Hastings' hands and body started to shake. Opening his desk drawer, he took out a bottle of pills, selected two and swallowed them quickly.

'I think you're lying, Mr Hastings. And I think you want

to tell me what you know about his death and the report he was writing on Trent Tower. The report he gave you, but you denied under oath ever seeing.'

To the surprise of Collins and Clark, Hastings bent his head and started to cry, his shoulders heaving, a low wailing sound coming from his lips. After two or three minutes the crying stopped. Hastings took out a clean white handkerchief and wiped his eyes and blew his nose. His face was mottled with red patches. Finally he said, 'I've been expecting you. I knew you would come some day. I've not slept since I gave my statement to the police about Simson. He was a decent young man and a good auditor. But they had pictures of me and a young woman, and my wife has a bad heart,' and he started to cry again.

Collins exchanged looks with Clark, and the little man said, 'Why don't I make yow a cup of tea, Mr Hastings and yow tell us what happened?'

Hastings was unable to speak but nodded his head and pointed towards a small table near the window. Clark checked the kettle had enough water for three and switched it on. Meanwhile Collins went to the door and turned the key in the lock. They had struck lucky. An honest man blackmailed into lying had found it impossible to live with the lies and now he wanted to unburden himself.

His tea in front of him, Hastings asked, 'Where do I start?'

'At the beginning. When were you approached?' asked Collins.

Taking a drink of tea, Hastings tried to compose himself. Finally, he started, his voice low, 'I received a telephone call, late evening, the night that John died. I recognised the voice. It was Thorne, Reece's attack dog.'

'How did you recognise the voice?'

'He was the one who threatened to send pictures he had of me and Claire to my wife. He told me that John had jumped off the fourth floor of a car park, but before he had died, he'd said that he'd given me a copy of his report. They wanted me to give them the report or else my dalliance with Claire would be revealed to my wife. He told me to watch for a packet of photos in my office post.'

'Would that be Claire Lafferty?' asked Collins.

'Yes,' said Hastings flustered that his train of thought had been interrupted. 'I knew the game was up when you found her body. Poor thing. I loved her; you know.'

After a pause he continued, 'Well, it was Friday night and it would look suspicious if I went into work on Saturday, so I waited until Monday. A photocopy of Simpson's report was in my safe,' he said and nodded towards an old pre-war safe that sat opposite his desk against the wall. 'I'd known from the first time that Simson spoke to me about Trent Tower that Reece would never allow the report to see the light of day. I told Simson that he was not to speak of the report to anyone and that he should report to me directly on all matters connected with it.'

'And he didn't see that as unusual?' asked Collins.

'I told him his report was really important and would bring down senior officers, councillors and contractors. He was far from stupid. He knew the effect that the report would have once it became public, so he stayed quiet. I should have told him to send the report to the Fraud Squad, but I was afraid. I know what Reece and Thorne have done over the years. I told him to save a copy of the report and put it in a bank security box. I don't know if he followed my advice.'

'You mean there might be a copy of his report sitting in some bank?'

'Yes.'

'How could we trace it?'

'It's untraceable. You'd need the bank address and his account number.'

'OK. I can't promise anything, Mr Hastings, but I'll try to keep you out of any court case in exchange for your continued co-operation. I'll speak to the Fraud Squad and suggest that they start their investigation by talking to you. In the meantime, it's essential for your own safety that you don't tell anyone of our visit or the content of our conversation today. Is that clear?'

'Yes, perfectly,' said Hastings. 'I wish to God I'd kept a copy of the report, but I was afraid.'

'But you did read it, right?' asked Collins.

'Yes.'

'OK then I want you to write down as much as you can remember of the report and send it to me at Thornhill Road Police Station ASAP. OK?'

'Yes.'

## Handsworth, 16.53hrs

Clark's phone was ringing as they entered the office and he picked it up. It was Marie. 'Hello, Clarkee. I thought you'd like to know. I just called the Agency and I'll be having an intimate meeting with Adam Strong starting at eight tomorrow, in room 606 of the Belgravia Hotel.'

'Yam a star, Marie. Yow do know, yow don't have to be there if yow don't want to.'

'Are you mad? This may be the closest I ever get to a ringside seat on the Welcome Wagon. I wouldn't miss it for all the tea in China. Room 606 at eight. Bye.'

As Clark hung up, WPC Kennedy knocked on the door and led a small man into the room and introduced him to Collins, 'This is Sidney Steptoe. He says he has an appointment with you Sergeant Collins.'

Sidney was everything his voice had promised. Small and slim, he was about forty-five, with greying blond hair and a suntan. He was dressed like a twenty-five year-old with more money than taste, in bright blue hipsters and jacket, and a white shirt with a blue cravat. When he spoke, his voice was high and very camp. 'Well, two policemen for the price of one. How lucky can a girl get?' he asked.

Collins smiled and held out his hand and was surprised by the strength of the man's grip.

'Well you know who I am, Sidney Steptoe, poof of the parish who has a thing for men in uniforms.'

Collins made the introductions and Clark commented on Sidney's bright blue jacket. 'I like your jacket. Yow should give my mate here the name of yowr tailor. I'm constantly telling him he needs more colour in his wardrobe.'

'Never mind him, Sidney. He's just being daft as usual. Have a seat while I get the typewriter.' Collins went to the bottom drawer of the third filing cabinet and lifted out the Remington and placed it on his desk. 'The ribbon is brand new. I rewound it to the start.'

'What was it you typed over the text?'

'Just my name, Michael Collins. I thought the ribbon had never been used and I tried to type my name with my eyes closed.'

'OK. Let me have the ribbon, please,' said Sidney as he sat down in Collins chair.

Collins took it from his pocket and handed it over. Sidney examined the ribbon from both sides then dived into his bag and extracted a glass perfume dispenser with a rubber tube with a glass ball filled with fine white powder attached. He gently dusted both sides of the ribbon and blew the excess away. He then placed it on the near-pristine green desk blotter and taking a book, he covered it and pressed down hard. Removing the book, he lifted the ribbon clear of the blotter where two separate strings of letters had appeared. It took him less than a minute to write out what had appeared transposed on the blotting paper.

Handing the foolscap pad to Collins he said, 'That's the best I can do. It doesn't look like a code to me. It's just looks like someone checking the alignment of a new ribbon.'

Collins picked up the pad which read *ii;6wq r5 t1x.q5 17954* and looked at the string of meaningless letters and numbers.

Another false lead. 'Well thank you for coming, Sidney but it looks like the user was just testing the alignment.'

'Oh, that's quite all right. You never know when you might need a policeman,' he said with a smile.

Thirty minutes later, Sheba was waiting to greet Collins as soon as he opened the door and he caught her in mid-flight as she leapt into his arms and tried to lick his face. As he crossed the hall with thirty pounds of muscle and bone wriggling in his arms, Collins heard Marjorie and Anabel talking in the kitchen. Agnes emerged from the lounge and beckoned him over, 'Don't go in the kitchen.'

'Why not?'

'That pair haven't stopped talking for the last seventy-five minutes. It's exactly what they both need. So, I suggest we slink off and have a meal in Birmingham.'

'Before we do that, can you have a look at this and tell me if it's a code or not' said Collins handing her the piece of paper Steptoe had given him.

'What do you hope it says?'

'The address of Simpson's safety deposit.'

Agnes examined the slip of paper for maybe thirty seconds and then smiled and asked, 'Can you get me the typewriter from my study please.'

Collins moved quickly. Over the years he'd seen Agnes solve several cyphers and suspected that she knew how this one had been constructed. He returned with an ancient Olivetti and laid it on the table along with a pad of paper and a pen.

'It's the two ii at the start of the cypher that gave it away. If Simpson kept a copy of the report, he'd have taken it to a bank. What's the only bank that starts with two of the same letters?'

Collins thought for a couple of seconds before saying, 'Lloyds.'

'Precisely. Now look at the keys on the typewriter. Where is the letter L on the keyboard?'

Collins immediately saw that the letter L was one key along

from I on the second line of keys. 'So, you're saying that the letters relate to another letter on the line below.'

'Or above it in some cases. Anyway, give me a minute and I'll have it decoded.'

Agnes didn't need a minute; within twenty-five seconds she'd finished and handed the decoded message to Collins. It read *lloyds gt hamp st 17954*.

'Darling, did I ever tell you that you're a genius?'

'Occasionally, but not often enough. I can always do with more flattery. But not in this case I'm afraid. During the war, agents were trained to leave notes as to where they were going. Many of the agents were women who were familiar with typewriters and devised a similar code to the one used by Simpson. Alas, the Germans broke the code quickly and it was not used again, except to mislead the Hun.'

'Well I owe you a dinner out by way of a reward,' said Collins and bending down kissed Agnes on the lips.

## Handsworth, 23.06hrs

When they returned home after eleven, Annabel and Marjorie had adjourned to the lounge with a bottle of Gordon's gin. The bottle was half empty.

Sheba scurried across the polished floor and made a fuss of her master and mistress but soon disappeared back into the kitchen when she realised that they were heading straight to bed and not into the kitchen. There would be no slice of corned beef or lump of cheese for her tonight.

## Tuesday 1st October, 1968

### Dublin, 12.35hrs

Michael had not been to Ireland since he'd left in 1962, but things hadn't changed much. O'Connell Street was still one of the widest boulevards in the British Isles but alas, the iconic Nelson's Pillar was no longer there. The giant granite column and statute of Horatio Nelson had been blown up by the IRA in 1966, depriving Dublin of one of its most recognisable landmarks. But Clerys was still going strong in all its mock Grecian splendour. The famous two-faced clock with its green Roman numerals, white face and gold-coloured hands still hung above the main entrance. "Under Clerys clock" was a favourite meeting place in Dublin where many a first date had started - and a few relationships had ended.

As he walked towards the store Collins remembered holding his mother's hand as they strolled through the front door. *How old was I then,* he thought, *four or five?* But still the memory was clear in his mind. She'd gone to buy a blue polka-dot dress. Collins had been fed-up with the whole rigmarole until his mother went to pay for her purchase. Only then did he see the pneumatic tubes into which the sales bill and money were placed and whisked away to a cashier hidden somewhere else in the huge building. He still remembered vividly the whoosh that the tube made when the sales assistant closed the aperture in the pipe and the ping when the capsule was returned.

Afterwards his mother had taken him to the toy department and bought him a G-Man's gun and plastic badge set. Over the following weeks he'd shot every no-good varmint and gangster in the neighbourhood with that gun. And none of the kids could kill him because he was a G-Man.

Padraig O'Brian was a difficult man to miss. He'd played Gaelic football for Dublin in his younger days and as he was fond of saying, "It was the football that gave me the Roman nose. It roams all over me face." His once dark brown hair was now white and he had let it grow down to his shoulders, which made him look like an Old Testament prophet wearing a green tweed suit and heavy brown shoes.

Standing, he held out a great paw of a hand and smiled. 'I've ordered you corned beef and cabbage. All right?'

'You've got a hell of a memory Padraig. I've not had proper corned beef since I left. They just don't sell it in England. They only seem to sell it in tins.'

'What can I say? They ruled the world but never learnt how to cook.'

While they waited for the food to arrive the men caught up on what each of them had been doing in the previous six years. Padraig had followed Collins' career in the English papers that arrived daily with the mail boat. He seemed to have read everything he could find on the arson case from a few years earlier and the fight at Fradley Airfield earlier in the year.

The catching up only stopped when the food arrived, and the conversation turned to the reason for Collins' visit. 'All right then,' said Collins, 'What's so secret that you couldn't tell me on the phone?'

'It's not a secret who Declan Boyle is. But it's unwise to talk about him in public.'

'OK, who is he?'

'Quartermaster of the IRA.'

'You mean he was quartermaster, don't you?

'No. I mean he still is.'

'Jesus, Mary and Joseph, you're having me on?'

'No. He supplied most of the arms used in the Border Campaign in the fifties and early sixties. But he could never get enough and that's why the campaign fizzled out. Word in

Republican circles is that he's stockpiling weapons for when everything kicks off again in the North.'

'And the British brought that closer by sending troops into the province last August,' said Collins.

'That they did. Put British troops on the streets of any Irish city and it's only a matter of time before the shooting starts.'

'And from what you say, he's all ready for it.'

'Not quite. He is still short of money but that will flow in from the Yanks once the first Catholic is shot. But he's a good strategist. He knows that if any future campaign is to be successful, they will have to strike on the mainland. For months now there are rumours that he's looking to build an operation in England. Sort of sleepers, you know.' Padraig fell silent and waited as Collins laid his knife and folk down and with elbows on the table made a steeple with his fingers.

'If he wants sleepers, they'll need jobs if they're to blend in,' said Collins, 'and no one would notice a few extra lads working for a big building company.'

'That's what I thought the moment I heard that Martin Cunningham had been injured and his friend had rushed to console his distraught spouse.'

'Do you think he organised the hit and run?'

'He's ruthless enough. But I'm not sure. Is there anyone else who'd want Cunningham dead?'

'Maybe. I'm looking into corruption in the Council. Some of the people I'm looking at would benefit from Cunningham's death.'

'Well I'd look at them first. But if you find nothing take a good long look at Boyle.'

'OK. Anything else?'

'Boyle is a smart cookie. A good strategist and a right cunning bastard. Don't underestimate him. Also, he's well known for despising any Irishman who joins the British armed services or police force. He considers them traitors to Ireland.'

'I need to watch me back, is that what you're saying?'

'Front and sides as well. Here,' said Padraig, 'I put this file together yesterday,' and reaching down, he lifted an untitled, quarter-full lever arch file onto the table. 'It has most of what I know about Boyle in it. Don't read it on the plane.'

Collins took the file and laid it by his feet. 'Thanks, Padraig. I owe you.'

'I know you bloody do. When it's over, all I ask is that you remember where you got the file from.'

'Will do.'

On his way back to the airport Collins ran over the likely suspects in the attack on Martin Cunningham. The most likely scenario was still that Martin had been injured by a hit and run driver. Second on his list was either Reece or his mate Thorne had arranged the accident. In third place was Charlton but he could see no reason why he would have done it and in last place the IRA. He knew that the boyos were vicious enough to carry out such an attack, but they seldom attacked other Irishmen who were civilians. However, now that Martin was in hospital, Collins was certain Boyle would exploit the situation to the IRA's advantage. He knew he had to try and stop the IRA getting a foothold in Birmingham, because if they did Birmingham would become an extremely dangerous place in which to live and work. Especially if the North did explode into flames in the New Year.

Only once on the taxi ride from O'Connell Street to the airport was his reverie broken as he passed the Comet Pub, named after the first passenger jet aircraft. His father was probably in there now, drinking in the small lounge at the rear. There he'd sit with his cronies until they were thrown out at 11pm. Collins realised that he had no wish whatsoever to stop and speak to his father, and he dismissed the man he'd hated for most of his life from his mind.

## Belvedere Hotel, Birmingham, 18.26hrs

The Aer Lingus flight was on time and landed at 18.26. Collins grabbed a sandwich in the airport café and then drove to Birmingham and his meeting with Mr Adam Strong at the Belvedere Hotel.

He met Clark in the foyer and both men took the stairs to the sixth floor. Collins knocked on the door of room 606. Seconds later, Marie eased the door open and said, 'Come on in.' Standing aside she let both men into the mid-size hotel room. Turning to Collins she asked, 'How do you want to play this?'

'Hard from the start,' said Collins and outlined what he and Clark had in mind.

Adam Strong knocked on the door at two minutes to eight. Marie went to the door and slipped the security chain on before opening it. 'Yes?' she asked.

'I'm Adam.'

'Oh, yes, you are, aren't you,' she said and supressed an excited giggle. 'Let me get the chain off.' Closing the door, she undid the chain and opened the door. Adam brushed past her and didn't give the bathroom on his left a second glance.

Standing with his back to the door, Adam took his overcoat off and dropped it on the bed.

Turning to face Marie he said, 'Nice room but not as nice as you. You look fabulous in that dress. Red really suits you and the high heels make your legs look great. I really think we're going to have a fabulous night.'

'Thanks,' said Marie and pushed the bathroom door open.

Collins stepped past Marie and into the room. 'Evening, Adam. You don't mind if I call you Adam, do you?' asked Collins.

'What the fuck? This ain't an orgy, love. It was meant to be just you and me.'

'A man of principle. I like that, Marie,' said Collins. 'Sit down, Adam. I have a few questions for you, and you will answer them.'

'Who the fuck are you?'

'Detective Sergeant Collins.'

Strong marched towards Collins. Only when he was a couple of feet away did he see Clark standing against the door jamb of the bathroom and thought better of starting anything. His eyes still on Strong, Collins said, 'Oh I see you've spotted my friend. He's going to handle most of the questioning. I suggest you don't try and lie to him. He gets really angry when people lie to him.'

'Really angry,' said Marie, who smiling, sat down on the side of the bed and crossed her legs.

Strong sat on the only chair in the room. Clark made a show of locking the door and slipping the chain on. Strong did not match his photo or description. He looked five years older and was under six foot and the well-chiselled physique so obvious in his modelling pictures had lost a lot of its ripped perfection.

Clark walked slowly towards Strong and stopped three feet away. 'So, Adam, me mate here tells me that yow were very friendly with Mrs Annabel Simpson. Wi'd like to know who asked yow to drug, rape, and take dirty pictures of her?'

Strong's face reddened. 'What the fuck are you on about? I don't know any Annabel Simpson. Now I've done nothing illegal by coming to this room tonight and now I'm going to leave. If you try and stop me, I will report you for kidnapping and false imprisonment.' Standing, he pushed the chair back, but before he could take a step a knee hit him flush in the groin and he bent double. His face turned red, then puce; his mouth opened wide as he tried to breathe. A short left to the side of the face sent him sprawling on the floor.

'Don't try to be tough, Mr Strong or I'll do so much damage to yowr face that yow'll never fuck another woman again without paying.'

Strong lay on the ground still clutching his testicles. As always, Collins was impressed at how quickly Clark had taken down the bigger man.

'I don't ... fucking know ...what you're talking about,' gasped Strong.

'Wrong answer again,' said Clark and kicked Strong in the side. Collins heard a rib snap.

'Fucking bastard,' groaned Strong.

'When I want yowr opinion I'll ask for it,' said Clark, and kicked Strong again in the ribs. A second rib broke. 'Now answer me question. Who ordered yow to drug, rape and photograph Annabel Simpson?'

Strong groaned and tried to sit up. Clark placed his foot across his throat and said, 'Stay there and start talking.'

Strong sank back onto the floor, desperate to take a deep breath, but unable to do so because of the pain in his ribs. He lay quietly taking short breaths trying to work out some sort of plan of action. After maybe thirty seconds he said, 'OK. Help me up. I'll talk.'

Clark bent down, grabbed him by the lapels and started to drag him upright. Strong was almost perpendicular when he pushed Clark and pulled a flick knife from his back pocket. Clark backed off at the sight of the slim and deadly five-inch blade. 'Not so fucking hot now, are you, copper?'

There was no change in Clark's expression. Strong stepped forward, the knife slashing through the air. Clark blocked the hand holding it with his forearm and punched Strong in the face. The man's knees crumpled, and he sank to the floor. Grabbing the hand that held the knife Clark stepped over the arm and twisted it hard to the right. There was a loud crack as Strong's wrist broke and the knife dropped to the floor. Clark kicked the knife towards Collins who picked it up, snapped it shut and slipped it in his pocket.

'You cocksucking bastard. You've broke my arm.'

'Just the wrist,' said Clark. 'Mickey, open the window. This bastard don't think I'm serious.'

Collins crossed quickly to the window and levered it up to its maximum open position. Clark grabbed Strong by his broken wrist and hauled him to his feet. Strong started to scream with pain and fear but was unable to resist. Clark slapped him across the face and shouted, 'Shut up or I'll break the other wrist and then yow won't be able to enjoy yowr own company. Now, put yowr head out the window.' As he did so Clark kicked the back of his knees and he slumped onto the windowsill.

'Now yow piece of shit, tell me what happened,' as he said this Clark let go of the wrist and grabbed the back of Strong's trousers with his right hand and with his left pushed him a further 12 inches into the abyss.

Strong's scream of fear was loud and long but he was six floors up and all the hotel windows were double-glazed. Only Clark heard the sheer fear in the man's voice. *He don't like* heights, thought Clark and pushed him another foot out the window. A dark stain started to develop on the legs of Strong's trousers.

'OK, OK. I'll talk,' he shouted.

'If yow don't yow're going to find out what it's like to hit a concrete pavement from six floors up. So, don't fuck me about.'

'I'll talk. I'll talk. Honest.'

Clark reeled the terrified man back into the room and he slumped to the floor. The stain on the front of his trousers was enough to convince Collins that he was going to be very cooperative from now on.

Strong seemed to know he was beaten. He couldn't take the guy standing above him with both arms. With just one good arm, he had no chance. He didn't wait to be asked a question before he started to pour out everything he knew.

'OK. I don't know who paid for it. I just got an order from Hill. He gave me a picture of the woman and where I was supposed to meet her. He gave me the Mickey Finn as well. It was easy. I slipped the Mickey in her drink and then walked her to the lifts. When I got to room 555 Gus was already there.'

'Gus?' asked Collins.

'The photographer. We stripped her and Gus got started on the pinups. Job done, he gave me the roll of film and went on his way and I hung around until she woke up.'

'Why wait?' asked Collins.

'Make sure she was all right. I didn't want her passing out cold and choking on her own vomit. I made out we'd had a great time and left about eleven.'

'And that was it?'

'Yeah until the hubby topped himself and I got called in as a bloody witness.'

'Who did you give the roll of film to?' asked Collins.

'Thorne. I need to go to a hospital.'

Collins ignored Strong's pleading and asked, 'How did the coppers track you down?'

'Barman downstairs knows me. Saw me that night and put two and two together. Now for fuck's sake can I go to the hospital. Please?'

Collins nodded and said, 'Stay in Brum. We may want to speak to you again.'

Outside the hotel, Clark turned to Marie and Collins, 'How about a Chinese on me?'

'I'd love to, but I'm knackered. I need me bed,' said Collins.

'Typical of the younger generation, no stamina.'

'Well I'm up for it,' said Marie and linked arms with Clark.

As he drove home Collins realised that he'd not briefed Clark on what he had learned in Dublin, but it could wait until tomorrow.

# Wednesday 2nd October 1968

## Handsworth/Sheldon, 09.13hrs

'So what wem doing today, O great and wise Sergeant?' asked Clark from behind his desk as Collins hung up his coat.

'I'm grand, thanks for asking,' Collins said with a smile.

Clark knew that smile. Collins was on to something. 'OK. Out with it. What have you got?'

'Agnes broke Simpson's code.'

'Well what is it?'

'It's a safe deposit box.'

'And where's this box located or do wi have to go through every bank in Brum?'

'It's in Lloyds Bank on Great Hampton Street.'

'Bloody hell! Are yow sure?'

'Absolutely.'

Clark smiled broadly. Both men knew that if the report was still in the deposit box it would blow the corruption case wide open.

'When are wi going to the bank?'

'I thought I'd wait until a certain Black Country yob was able to attend.'

'I'll ignore yowr poor attempt at an insult and just say, let's go, now.'

'OK. But for God's sake remember that we need the co-operation of the bank manager if he's to let me open the box without a warrant. So be nice to him.'

'I'm always nice to me social betters. Mind yow, I ain't met anyone better than me since 1943.'

As they drove to the bank Collins reported what he had learnt in Ireland and discussed their meeting with Adam Strong. On balance both men agreed that what Strong had said was probably the truth or as near to the truth as they would ever get.

The Lloyds Bank branch on Great Hampton Street had been built in the late 1880's, but it had an elegance that was unusual in so many Victorian buildings. It consisted of two tall storeys consisting of painted stone and terracotta, with Gothic, Renaissance and Dutch gable motifs. It certainly stood out from most of the other business premises on the street, such as the huge Lucas's office block which was squat, large and box like without any decorative touches.

It was ten past ten when Collins and Clark walked into the bank and asked one of the cashiers if they could speak to the manager. At first the cashier said that they would need to make an appointment. When they showed him their warrant cards, he disappeared quicker than the lodger when he heard the landlady's hubby arrive home early.

Three minutes later the manager appeared. For a moment Collins almost laughed. He looked exactly like Arthur Lowe who had been Leonard Swindley in Coronation Street and was currently playing Captain Mainwaring in *Dad's Army*. The only difference was that when the manager spoke, he had a Yorkshire accent. 'Good morning, officers. My name's Stokes. I am the manager. I understand that you wish to speak to me?'

'Thank you for taking the time to see us, Mr Stokes. I'm Detective Sergeant Collins and my colleague is Detective Constable Clark. Is this key one of yours?' Collins asked and handed the small balding man the key.

Mr Stokes turned the key over and said, 'Yes, it is.'

'We need to open the box as a matter of urgency.'

'Do you have a warrant to open the deposit box?'

'No, we don't.'

'Then I am unable to permit you to access the box,' he said his eyes flicking to the side as the front door opened and a young woman entered the bank.

'Mr Stokes, you are aware that the box was rented by Mr

Simpson prior to his death last year. We believe that it contains evidence pertaining to those responsible for his death.'

'I'm sorry. I really would like to help but my hands are tied.' He said as his eyes watched the mini-skirted young woman cross to the counter. 'As you surely know, you must provide me with a warrant before I can give you access to the box.'

Collins found it irritating that the man avoided eye contact. But before he could say anything Clark moved closer to Stokes and leaning forward whispered in his ear. The manager's face turned from florid red to deathly pale as he listened. After twenty seconds Clark stepped back and said, 'Now, Mr Stokes, given this new information yow've just received, are yow willing to cooperate.'

Mr Stokes took a handkerchief from his jacket pocket dabbed at the sweat that had sprung up on his forehead and said in a strangulated voice, 'Yes.'

Twenty minutes later Collins and Clark left the bank with the report securely wrapped in a cloth money bag. 'What did you say to him that changed his mind?'

'I said that I would lodge a complaint with Lloyds about his behaviour towards women. How he can't concentrate on anything except the next woman to walk into the bank. Then, I'd find out which toms he visits, arrest him and make sure his case gets reported in the *Mail*.'

'Well it certainly worked.'

'Anyways, what are wi going to do with the report?'

'Find someplace safe to copy it and then we'll pop over and see our favourite copper in the Fraud Squad, Superintendent Patterson.'

'That sounds reasonable to me.' There's a place on Newhall Street wi can use.'

Forty minutes later Collins and Clark knocked on Superintendent's Patterson's door and were told to enter.' The man behind the desk had not changed very much since the first time Collins had met him. He was wearing a dark grey check suit, black brogues and a white shirt and was puffing away on his pipe. As he stood up, a smile spread across his face. 'What brings you pair of rascals to my humble lodgings?' he asked.

'We have a present for you, Sir.'

'The last present you gave me occupied my team and me for nearly six months.'

'But it were worth it? asked Clark.

'That it was. What have you got for me this time?'

Collins placed the brown paper bag that Quick Printers had given him on the desk and said, 'This might just be the case of your career, Sir.'

Sitting down, Patterson pulled the report out and started to skim-read the pages. As he read the headings his skimming slowed down as he stopped to read entire paragraphs and odd whole pages. After ten minutes he looked up and grinned at the two men. 'Who gave you this?'

'We sort of acquired it from a safe deposit box. But the man who asked us to look into it was Superintendent Wallace.'

'I was sorry to hear of his health problems. How is he?

'Dying, Sir. He's been investigating corruption in Brum for two years but had only managed to get a few names and facts together. He asked us to look into it and try to break the case before he died.'

'And this John Simpson, the writer of the report, is he available to interview?'

'No, Sir we believe he was murdered about twelve months ago. We're investigating his death along with those of Claire Lafferty, Christina Murray, Sir Charles Endbury and his wife. We're also looking into a hit and run on one of the builders named in the report, Martin Cunningham, and trying to stop the IRA from establishing a bridgehead in Brum.'

'OK. I take it MI5 are sniffing around.'

'They ain't yet, Sir,' said Clark.

'Does anyone know that you've given me this report?'

'No, Sir.'

'Good, keep it that way. I'll read the report tonight and I'll call you tomorrow afternoon when I've had a chance to consider it fully.'

'OK. Thank you, Sir. There was also a letter written by Simpson attached to the report.' Collins dug in his pocket and pulled out an envelope and handed it to Patterson. It was a statement written by Simpson the day before he died outlining his meeting with Reece the following day. 'As you can see, Sir, he thought he might not survive the meeting.'

'A brave man,' said Patterson. 'Leave it with me.'

Outside, the skies had opened and it was raining heavily. Pulling their macs over their heads they made a run for the car. They only just made it to the shelter of the Capri before a ragged fork of lightning lit up the darkening sky and the rain became torrential.

As he pulled on his safety belt Collins said 'I was thinking it's time we had a chat with Mr Thorne.'

'Steady now. Don't overwork the two brain cells yow have.'

'At least my two brain cells are still working, unlike yours.'

'Bollocks,' said Clark and to prove it continued, 'I've been thinking about what yow said about me being too soft with some of the wankers we meet. I've reached an age when I need to practice being an unreasonable, slightly mad bastard with violent tendencies.'

'Well don't bring them out too strongly or we'll have a dead interviewee on our hands.'

'No chance. I only kill people who are trying to kill me. Just one thing, park well away from Thorne's office. I have a reputation to uphold as a tough bastard and tough bastards don't drive around in poncy Capris painted yellow.'

'You still on that record?'

'Yep and I will be till yow get rid of this load of yellow crap.'

Neither Collins nor Clark noticed the black Humber Hawk start its engine and follow them down the road towards the Cathedral. The driver of the Hawk knew his job and stayed at least two cars back all the way from town to Thorne's office in Sheldon.

Thorne's business premises were off the main A45 on Wagoner's Road and consisted of a two-story building that boasted workshops and a factory shop on the ground floor and offices on the first. Collins pulled into one of the three bays reserved for customers. If he'd checked in his rear-view mirror, he would have seen the Humber Hawk drive past and park on the opposite side of the road outside a greengrocer's.

Both men flashed their warrant cards at the receptionist, and Collins said, 'We'd like to speak to Mr Thorne, please.'

'Is he expecting you?'

'I think yow could say that,' said Clark and smiled.

Without waiting for the receptionist to provide them with directions both men headed for the stairs. The name plate on the third door on the left said "Mr C. Thorne, Managing Director". They walked into the small office occupied by Thorne's secretary without knocking. Before she had finished standing up, Clark knocked on the connecting door and without waiting for a reply walked into Thorne's office.

'Morning, Mr Thorne,' said Clark. 'I'm Detective Constable Clark and this is Detective Sergeant Collins. Wem here to ask yow what yow know about the deaths of Christina Murray and Claire Lafferty.'

Thorne stood up and glared at Clark, a vein in his temple pulsing. Taking a deep breath, he sat down again. By the time he spoke he was calm and friendly sounding. 'I've been expecting you.'

'Oh, why so?' asked Collins.

'Well, you visited John Reece. It was inevitable that you'd get around to me sometime.'

'Why inevitable?' asked Collins. 'You're not joined at the hip with him, are you?'

Thorne smiled and shook his head. 'No, we're not, but I do a lot of business with John.'

'Yeah, we heard about that. Yow supply the muscle in the partnership. Did yow bring someone in to do the two girls found in the cemetery, or do yow have a stone-cold killer on your books already?'

'Don't be ridiculous. I don't employ killers. I run a legitimate company selling fire and burglary alarms and security services.'

Thorne's responses were irritatingly calm and reasonable. Collins was annoyed with himself. He'd thought that a full-frontal attack might have angered Thorne. It hadn't and now he had nowhere to go other then let Clarkee try some rough stuff and Thorne was too cute to give him an excuse.

'So how come two ladies, one of who entertained Sir Endbury shortly before he changed his mind on the Birchfield deal ended up murdered?' asked Clark.

'I've no idea what you're talking about. Charles Endbury was a well-known womaniser. But he had a reputation of being honest. I doubt that he would have his views changed by a shag. No matter how good it was.'

'Wi was thinking more along the lines of blackmail than a roll in the hay,' said Clark.

'So you're now accusing me of being a blackmailer?'

'Lots of people seem to change their minds after receiving a visit from you. And nearly always the change benefits Mr Reece,' said Collins.

'What can I say? I have a gift for negotiation. Besides, where's the evidence to back up your wild claims and accusations?'

'Wem in what's called "the process of collecting it".'

'Well until you've actually got some evidence, would you mind leaving please? I have a very full day ahead of me.'

'Not at all Mr Thorne,' said Collins 'But you can be sure of one thing, we'll be back.'

It had started raining again and both men ran to the car. Wiping his face with a handkerchief, Collins asked, 'What do you think?'

'Hard to say. Reece warned him wi was coming. He were prepared for us. The only thing I'm sure of is that he's a bloody good liar. When he said he had nowt to do with the killing of the two girls I almost believed him.'

'Well, me Lud, I have to admit that I am in accord with my learned friend's opinion.'

'Bastard, ain't it, when a plan don't work out? Anyway, where to now, Tonto?'

'Hang on a minute. I thought we'd agreed. I'm the Lone Ranger. You're Tonto.'

'Bollocks to that. It's me that has the widest knowledge and experience of police work, not yow.'

'But the stripes are on my arm.'

'Yeah, and they'll be up your arse if you don't stop arguing with me.'

'OK, Kemosabe. But you do know what Kemosabe means in English, don't you?'

'No. What?'

'I can't say. It's one of our tribal secrets. I can never reveal the name we have for small, annoying, white men with a penchant for violence.'

'Sod me. Where did yow pick up a word like penchant? I dain't think the Green Reading Book Two covered it.'

'That's because you never got passed Orange Book 1.'

'Bollocks,' said Clark. 'Anyways where to now, Tonto?'

'We need to head back to the station, and report to Hicks. The investigation is heating up and we need to keep him onside.'

'OK.'

## Handsworth, 15.12hrs

Collins picked up the phone on the third ring. It was Superintendent Patterson. 'Well, Michael, you were right. You've given me the biggest case of my career. Simpson was one hell of an auditor. He would have had a stellar career in the Fraud Squad if he was a copper. He's named Reece, Thorne, Charlton, Hill, Robbins and at least five other bigwigs in the Council who were involved in corrupt practices. I'm seeing the ACC this afternoon to get more manpower. For everyone named in the report there will be five, ten or twenty others with their hand in the till. I'm going to be busy. I'll call you and we can meet up when I've got a good picture of who's involved.'

'That's great, Sir.'

Hanging up, Collins checked his watch. It was still early but he felt knackered. He needed an early night. Leaving a note on the office noticeboard, he headed home to give Annabel the good news.

An unknown car was parked outside the front door when Collins arrived home. Only when he turned his engine off did he hear raised voices from inside the house. Collins ran to the front door and opened it quietly. A large man was shouting and pulling Marjorie across the hall towards the front door. 'Come on, you fucking bitch. You think you can humiliate me in front of our friends and neighbours. Just wait until I get you home.' Annabel was pulling at the man's free arm and screaming at him. There was no sign of Agnes or Sheba.

Collins closed the three yards between himself and Marjorie's husband, grabbed him by the hair and pulled him backward over his outstretched leg. The man let go of Marjorie at the same moment that Collins let go of her husband's hair. He landed hard on the parquet floor and banged his head with a loud crack. Before he could move

Collins dropped on the man's stomach with both knees. He felt the air from the man's lungs brush past his face. Turning, he smashed a right hook into the side of the man's face just under the eye.

Collins stood up. Not a sound could be heard except the man's attempt to suck some air into his lungs. 'OK, ladies. I think you should pop out and do a bit of shopping while I speak to Mr Burns.'

Both women nodded silently and crossed to the cloakroom for their overcoats and bags. On their way-out Marjorie stood over the prone figure of her husband. 'Not so fucking big now, are you?' she said and spat in his face.

Collins grabbed Burns by the lapels and dragged him upright. 'Now that we're alone, we can talk without any interruptions. Now you can either walk or I can drag you but we're going in the kitchen.'

'I'll walk.' Stumbling, Burns headed for the kitchen. Just before he reached the door he swung around and tried to punch Collins. He was off balance, and Collins easily blocked the punch with his left forearm and smashed a straight right into Burns' face, breaking his nose. Blood spurted and flowed over his chin and dripped onto his expensive white shirt and the floor.

Collins pushed him into the kitchen, closed the door and told him to sit down. He looked groggy and disorientated. Collins filled a half-pint glass with water and laid it on the table. Burns picked it up and drained the glass in one go. Exchanging the glass, for a small hand towel Collins said, 'First, you are finished beating your wife and burning her with cigarettes. Second, you will write a letter to your children telling them the truth, in detail, about what you have been doing to your wife. Third, you will go home, pick up your clothes and move out of your house tonight, and you will never return. Fourth, you will visit your solicitor tomorrow and transfer the house to your wife, and finally you will never attempt to see or speak to your wife again.'

'What makes you think you can tell me what to do? I'm heading straight to the police once I leave here and tell them how you attacked me.'

'Not a good plan. For two reasons. Firstly, I've got two terrified women who will testify to what happened and secondly, I *am* the police, Detective Sergeant Collins and to prove it, here's my warrant card.'

'Bastard.'

'Yes, I am, but I'm not a cowardly bastard like you. Now while I go and get you a pen and paper, I'm going to handcuff you to the cooker.'

After two poor attempts to write the letter Collins dictated Burn's confession cum apology to his family, and watched with satisfaction as he signed it. 'Now if you ever go near your wife again, I promise I will put you in hospital for three months. Now, piss off and pick up your belongings from your wife's house.'

Burns rose from the table and dropped the towel on the chair. The blood had congealed and there was now a clear bend in his nose.

'You can keep the towel. I suggest you visit the hospital on your way home.'

Collins walked Burns to the door and watched as he climbed into his car. As he drove off, Agnes and Sheba came into view.

'Who was that driving away?' Agnes asked as she slipped out of her overcoat and Sheba, nose to the floor, followed the drips of blood into the kitchen.

'Marjorie's husband,' said Collins and gave his fiancée a hug.

When Marjorie and Annabel returned, they told Agnes the full story and Collins handed Marjorie the letter Burns had written. The two women both embraced Collins with tears in their eyes.

When Collins told Annabel what Superintendent Patterson

had said about John's audit report the tears began to flow. It was Agnes who broke into the sniffles and laughter, 'I think we should go out and celebrate. All those in favour say "aye".' Collins was the last one to agree as he waved goodbye to an early night.

## Thursday 3rd October 1968

### Sheldon, 02.03hrs

The police telephone call woke Thorne at exactly three minutes past two. His latest squeeze was snoring gently beside him. Picking up the phone, he confirmed his name and then listened as an Irish copper told him that a regular patrol had found the front door of his premises on Wagoner's Road open. As the registered keyholder, he was asked if he would attend the premises and accompany the waiting officer into the building.

It wasn't the first time this had happened, and it wouldn't be the last, but it was annoying. *I'll have to change the name of the keyholder,* he thought, as he pulled on his trousers and an old jumper. He quickly went through possible candidates for the job. No one struck him as trustworthy enough. Either they would be out shagging the night away or would be so pissed when they got the call that they'd listen, hang up, turn over and fall asleep immediately. No, there was no one he could trust, and he preferred it that way.

There were no lights on in the building when he drove onto the forecourt and parked in his reserved parking spot. Stepping from his car he saw a figure in the familiar uniform of a policeman standing beside a powder-blue Ford Anglia panda car, with the broad white stripe running across the top and over the front doors.

'Mr Thorne?' asked the policeman walking towards him.

'Yes.'

'Thank you for coming out so quickly. If you could accompany me into the building?'

The door had been kicked in and was open four inches. 'Bloody amateurs,' he said, turning towards the policeman. That was when he saw the blackjack being swung at his head by the copper who had just greeted him. As he ducked, the cosh missed its target and smashed against the door. Rising, Thorne swung an uppercut into the midriff of his attacker and followed it up with a right cross that sent the smaller man crashing to the floor. But the man was up almost immediately, reaching inside his jacket. In the moonlight, Thorne saw the handle of an old army revolver. Springing forward, he hit the gunman in the neck with his shoulder and fell on top of him as they both hit the ground. The man tried to break Thorne's grip on the hand that held the gun. Suddenly, there was a loud report and the man screamed in agony as the bullet ripped into the top of his thigh and embedded itself in the bone. Struggling free of the man, Thorne stood up and kicked him in the face, breaking his cheekbone. Grabbing the unconscious man under the arms, he dragged him back to the panda and was just about to bundle him into it, when he heard someone running down the stairs. Dropping the man on the ground, Thorne ran to his car and started the engine just as a small man with ginger hair appeared at the door and fired two shots at the accelerating Aston Martin.

The ginger-haired man knew that he would never catch Thorne in an Anglia, even if it had been repainted to pass as a panda car in the dark. Lifting his friend into the passenger seat, he reversed away from the building and headed towards Birmingham in the opposite direction to that taken by Thorne.

## Handsworth, 07.50hrs

Annabel and Marjorie were chatting in the kitchen, and Agnes was stirring a large pot of porridge when Collins returned from his early morning walk with Sheba. Hearing voices in the kitchen, Sheba made a beeline for her favourite room in the house. Long ago she had worked out that if there were humans in the kitchen there was always a good chance that they'd give her something to eat.

Collins was about to join Agnes when the phone rang. A call this early in the morning had to mean it was the station, but when he lifted the receiver, he didn't recognise the voice at the other end. 'Sergeant Collins?'

'Yes.'

'Can you hold, please? I've got Inspector York for you.'

Collins waited as he was put through to his old sergeant.

'Morning, Mickey, how are you?'

'Grand, Sir. And yourself and the family?'

'All well, thanks. Which I suspect is more than I can say for Mr Christopher Thorne.'

'Thorne? What's happened to him?'

'I'm not sure. He may have been kidnapped or murdered or just done a runner. Someone phoned him early morning and lured him to his office where they jumped him. Judging by the amount of blood spilled, I'd say he put up quite a fight.'

'Bloody hell.' Collins paused trying to think who would want Thorne dead. The only name that came to mind was Declan Boyle. 'You're calling because Clarkee and me paid him a visit yesterday.'

'Yep.'

'OK. I'll pick Clark up and be with you within an hour. Where are you, the station or Thorne's offices?'

'His offices.'

Agnes emerged from the kitchen and asked, 'Who was that?'

'Inspector York. I have to go over to Sheldon. One of our suspects has gone missing. Look, I don't think I'll have the time to take Annabel home today to pick up some more clothes.'

'Don't worry about that. I'll take her and Marjorie. We'll make it a girl's day out.'

Collins kissed her on the lips and set off to Clark's.

## Sheldon, 09.23hrs

Once through Birmingham, the traffic was light with most of it heading towards the city. Collins and Clark made good time in the lemon monstrosity. When they arrived, there were two police cars, the SOCO's van and a couple of spectators outside Thorne's office and workshop to greet them. They drove onto the car park and ducking under the police cordon, waved their warrant cards at the young constable standing guard by the broken front door, asking where they could find Inspector York. Following the constable's directions, they made their way to the workshop at the back of the building on the ground floor.

Inspector York saw the two men and waved them into the workshop. A heavy wooden chair had been placed near a basinful of water and an old set of jump leads on the floor. On a bench nearby a variety of tools had been laid out. All of them had innocent uses in the workshop. But the way they were displayed reminded Collins of numerous films where the hero was tied up and the villain took delight in displaying his toys and explaining what he was going to do with each one.

'Can I have a butchers?' asked Clark, nodding in the direction of the chair.

'By all means. You know more about this sort of thing then I do,' said York.

There was no sign of any blood or vomit on the chair or floor. Nor was there any blood on the tools on the bench. Straightening up, Clark said, 'He was called here early morning you say?'

'Yes,' said York.

'Why would he come out in the middle of the night?' asked Collins and then answered his own question, 'Because the call he got was from the police, or so he thought.' 'That's what I think,' said York, 'and whoever called him jumped him outside.'

'So, either he duffed them up and did a runner. or they did him,' said Clark. 'But there's no sign of blood on any of the tools laid out, or on the ropes, chair or floor. Which means they dain't get him inside.'

'Precisely,' said York.

'Which means either he's dead or he got away,' said Collins.

'Any ideas who might have done it?' asked York.

'Let's grab a cuppa across the road and wi'll fill you in,' said Clark.

The small café catered for workmen from the local workshops and warehouses. There was no heavy industry or engineering around here. Most of the firms were like Thorne's, small businesses turning out electrical components for a range of industries including car and aircraft.

York insisted on paying and Collins carried the tray of three teas and two bacon butties and a sausage sarnie over to the corner window seat. 'OK, lads. Tell me what you're up to this time. And please don't tell me it involves MI5 again.'

As the three men munched their way through their doorstep size sandwiches Collins outlined everything that had happened since they had visited Superintendent Wallace, right up to the interview they had held with Mrs Simpson. The only interruption was when a small ginger-haired man from the nearest table asked to borrow their brown sauce.

'Bloody hell, lads. This sounds worse than last time.'

'It's not as bad as it sounds. We've got no evidence that the IRA is involved. Sure, every family in Ireland has a Declan Boyle of sorts. And on Easter Sunday every family in the twenty-six counties claims that their father or grandfather was in the Post Office with Padraic Pearse and James Connolly.'

'I agree with Mickey, wi have no hard evidence, but what I've seen and heard this morning, I think Thorne had a run-in with the IRA.'

'But why would they go after Thorne? If it is the IRA and they are making a play to run building in Birmingham wouldn't they go after Reece?' said York

'Maybe they wanted to remove any chance of reprisals from Thorne before they took out Reece,' suggested Collins.

For the next fifteen minutes the conversation continued without coming to any firm conclusion as to why the IRA might have attacked Thorne. As the three police officers finished their teas the conversation changed to how well Sheldon Flight were doing in the Birmingham Police Football League this year. As the conversation ended, it was agreed that Collins and Clark would pay a visit to Mr Reece to break the news and that York would follow their visit up later that afternoon. They would compare notes on Reece tomorrow.

## Five Ways, Edgbaston, 11.57hrs

Reece was on the telephone when Collins and Clark burst into his office, followed by his secretary. 'I'm so sorry, Mr Reece, but I couldn't stop them.'

'That's all right, Janet. Please call my solicitor and tell him to get around here immediately. Tell him I'm being harassed by two police officers.'

'Yow might want to hold off on that Mr Reece. Wi've come bearing news of yowr mate, Mr Christopher Thorne,' said Clark.

'What news?'

'He's either dead or done a runner,' said Clark.

The colour drained from Reece's face and he fell into his chair. 'How? Who? What do you mean, "dead"?' he demanded.

'You can leave us now, Miss,' said Collins and led the shaking secretary to the door and closed it.

'He was called to his office in the early hours and a fight ensued. Someone, either Thorne or one of his attackers, lost a lot of blood,' said Collins. Do you know anyone who would want to kill Mr Thorne?' asked Collins.

Reece staggered to his feet, and going to the drinks cabinet behind his desk, opened the doors and took out one glass and a bottle of whiskey. Sitting down, he poured himself nearly a full glassful and drank half of it in one gulp. Some colour returned to his cheeks. 'Do you have any suspects?' he asked.

'No,' lied Collins.

'Chris has been a friend of mine for twenty years. Find out what happened and there will be a hefty drink in it for both of you.'

'We'll find out what happened, but we won't be accepting any reward from you, Mr Reece. Now if Mr Thorne does contact you, please let us know immediately.'

'I will.'

## Handsworth, 14.15hrs

Despite the slurring of his words Clark recognised the Australian tones of Harry Freeman immediately. 'Is your mate about, Shorty?'

'Na, he's out of the office. Can I help yow?'

'No one can help me, mate. But that's another story and my God is it one boring crock of shit. Just tell the Irish bloke that it was Councillor Robbins who signed in Claire Lafferty and Hill signed in Christina Murray to the Saudi do. Got that?

'Yep.'

'Good man. Now I'm gonna have a shit and go home. I'm pissed.'

Clark smiled to himself as he heard the Aussie hang up. As a rule, Clark didn't like drunks. They were usually selfish arseholes who caused all sorts of pain to their wives, families and themselves. But for some, it was the only way that they could deal with memories that no person should have to endure, and Freeman was definitely one of those.

Slipping his jacket on Clark went in search of Collins and found him in the Charge Room talking to Sergeant Ridley.

'Whatcha doing hiding in here?' asked Clark.

'Talking about a report that DCI Jameson from Perry Barr just sent us. It seems there have been seven reports of small animals being killed and their bodies put on display in the last few weeks.'

'Anything else?'

'Yes, all of them have taken place within a three-mile circle of the first one and that was in Handsworth.'

'So, yow reckon that whoever is doing it lives locally?'

'Seems a reasonable assumption,' said Ridley. 'I'll ask the lads to keep an eye out for anything suspicious.'

## Handsworth, 20.07hrs

The transformation in Annabel that had started when Collins said he believed her and had accelerated by whatever Agnes had said had continued. For the first time since he had met her, she appeared animated as she moved around the kitchen helping Agnes to tidy up and feed Sheba.

Thirty minutes later Annabel and Marjorie said they were going for a walk and left Collins and Agnes alone. Neither Collins nor Agnes said anything until they heard the front door close.

Collins and Agnes were watching TV when the phone ringing. Collins recognised Clark's voice immediately, 'What's up?' he asked.

'Just had a call from Freeman. He confirms it were Robbins who signed in Claire and Hill signed in Christina.'

'Now that's interesting. I think we need to visit them again.'

'Tomorrow?'

'No, it will have to be Monday. It's the inquest tomorrow and I need to check the file.'

'Fair enough. I'll stay out of your hair. But you've got nowt to reproach yourself over. Remember that.'

## Friday 4th October 1968

### Handsworth, 10.20hrs

Ever since Collins had mentioned Declan Boyle and the possible IRA involvement in the corruption case, Agnes had been fighting the temptation to call Sir Aubrey Nichols, Deputy Head of MI5. She knew how much Collins disliked the man and how he would never forgive him for putting Agnes in harm's way during Petrov's defection. But every fibre of her security service training was telling her that Boyle was a potential threat to the country and MI5 needed to be alerted.

At twenty past ten Agnes finally gave in, picked up the phone and called Sir Aubrey on his direct line. On the fourth ring the phone was answered. 'Aubrey speaking.'

'Hello Aubrey, it's Agnes.'

'Agnes, what a lovely surprise. I wasn't sure if we were still on speaking terms.'

'We'll always be on speaking terms. It's Michael you have to watch out for.'

'Quiet,' said Aubrey. 'How can I help you?'

*He must be busy,* thought Agnes, *he has no time for the usual small talk.* 'Do you know a man called Declan Boyle?'

'Now there's a name I've not heard for a few years. Big in the Border Campaign for the IRA, but nothing to worry about these days.'

'Are you sure about that?'

'Yes, the IRA is finished. It no longer speaks for the Catholics of Northern Ireland. The Civil Rights Movement has succeeded them. The IRA have no money, precious few weapons and an organisation that leaks like a colander. Besides which they threw Declan Boyle out of the organisation over five years ago. No, he is yesterday's man. I'm more worried about what the Protestants will do if the Civil Rights Movement wins substantial concessions. Why the sudden interest?'

'A well-known builder in Birmingham, Martin Cunningham, was involved in a hit and run. Within hours Declan Boyle turned up to console his wife, Yolande. Now one of the possible suspects in the case has disappeared.'

'There's no chance that the IRA are on the rise. I'd stake my job on it.'

'Michael's contacts in Ireland say otherwise. They say Boyle is preparing for another campaign. If Martin Cunningham dies, Declan Boyle may effectively be running one of the biggest independent building companies in the UK. An organisation that will provide the IRA with money and a bridgehead in Britain for agents.'

'I really don't think that there is anything to worry about, but I'll ask someone to look into it and get back to you. Now I really must go, I have an appointment with Prince Philip in ten minutes.'

'Still misbehaving, is he?'

'I will pretend I didn't hear that.'

After he hung up, Sir Aubrey pressed the button on the intercom for his secretary. She responded immediately, 'Jenny I'm just leaving. Please ask Mr Rhodes to see me on my return.'

'Yes, Sir.'

## Handsworth, 12.10hrs

Clark looked across at Collins' empty chair. If he believed in God, now would be the time he said a quick prayer for his mate. It was the inquest into Mitch Williams' death and both Hicks and Mickey were there. It was an open and shut case and no blame could be attached to Collins. However, Clark knew that with his over-developed conscience, Mickey would find a way to blame himself. Looking to the heavens Clark muttered under his breath, 'How the fuck was he supposed to stop the bleeding rain?'

Clark was in the canteen doing his pools when Collins and Hicks returned from the inquest. Clark bowed to no man when it came to the finer points of football. He even understood the offside rule and what the semi-circle at the edge of the penalty area was used for. But he knew that it was impossible to predict football results based on form, league position or past performance. So he quickly placed an x against the sixteen numbers he habitually used, wrote his name and address on the back of the coupon, and slipped it into his jacket. After collecting their fish and chips plus an extra mug of tea for Clark, both men slid into the seats opposite Clarkee, 'How did it go?' he asked

'Pretty good,' said Hicks. For once McEwan was a real help. He made it clear that Mitch was an accident waiting to happen. He even praised the efforts of Mickey here to keep him alive.'

'Bloody hell. Will miracles never cease?'

'What about you? What have you been up to?' asked Hicks.

'Been checking the inquest transcripts and newspaper stories about the Simpsons' case.'

'Well, if you fancy a trip out, I was thinking of paying Charlton a visit. Want to come?' asked Collins.

Clark took a penny from his pocket and tossed it in the air. Catching it, he said, 'Heads Charlton, tails court papers.' Turning his hand over he slapped the coin down on the table.

'Heads it is,' said Collins.

As he stood up and slipped his jacket on, Clark said, 'Yow know what I find disconcerting about Scousers?'

'You can't understand a word they say?'

'Besides that. Them's all live in Liverpool, right by the seaside. But them's so full of bullshit. I mean where do they get all the shite from?'

'That's a question for the great thinkers of our age. You should write to Malcolm Muggeridge,' said Collins.

## Great Barr, 13.51hrs

'We'd like to see Mr Charlton,' said Clark showing his warrant card to the red-headed woman behind a sliding glass partition.

'Sorry love,' she said. 'He's out on site, but he should be back any minute now. Why don't you take a chair and I'll get you a tea?'

'Ta, that would be bosting.'

Collins and Clark eyed the plastic-covered waiting room chairs and settled on the corner unit, which was green, cheap and nasty, but surprisingly comfortable. Two mugs of hot sweet tea arrived within a couple of minutes, along with a plateful of ginger nuts and the men tucked in. Ten minutes later Ronny Charlton bustled through the swing doors clocked Collins and Clark and asked, 'Who are you?'

Collins stood up and held out his warrant card. Charlton took it and examined it closely. 'You looking for me?'

'Just a few questions.'

'OK, you better come in. Maggie, can I have a brew please?' Looking at the empty cups on the table he added, 'And refills for the coppers.'

There was nothing grand or spacious about Charlton's office. The desk was cheap plywood, covered with a teak veneer. The chairs were foam filled and covered in blue plastic. The remaining furniture consisted of three filing cabinets that seemed to have been bought prior to the Boer War and a scarred set of shelving, buckling under the weight of lever arch files and papers. Not a single item of furniture matched any other, and there was no discernible colour scheme.

'Have a seat. Just chuck the papers on the floor.'

Collins was surprised by Charlton. He had been expecting

a Scouser with an accent as broad as the Mersey and an attitude that saw police as the enemy. Instead he found a middle-aged man who had no discernible accent and a seeming willingness to speak to the police without demanding that his brief be present. He also seemed to possess something approaching charm, then he remembered what Freeman had said about him, "A man who would steal the pennies off a dead man's eyes, screw the widow and throw the kids out of their home." *Don't be fooled*, he thought.

Maggie arrived with three teas and an open packet of chocolate biscuits. Leaving the tray on Charlton's desk, she smiled and said, 'Get stuck in.'

'What's this about? Cunningham?'

'Why should it be about him?' asked Collins.

''Cos I knew him and he was run over in a hit and run. Which is a crime, ain't it?'

'You think you're a suspect, is that it?'

'You wouldn't be doing your job if you didn't think I was.'

'OK, did you have any part in Cunningham's hit and run?' asked Collins.

'No.'

'Do you benefit from it?' asked Collins.

'Yeah, I did benefit a bit from Cunningham's accident.'

'How so?' asked Collins.

'Cunningham is number two builder in Brum when it comes to Council work. With him out of the picture for a while I stand a chance of taking some of his business.'

'And Thorne?' asked Clark.

Charlton looked confused by the question and took a couple of seconds to reply. 'Has something happened to him?'

'He's missing,' said Collins.

'Bloody hell. They must have been big bastards to take him down.'

'Why so?' asked Clark.

Charlton hesitated before replying then said, 'Off the

record. Thorne likes to scrap. He does four or five bare-knuckle bouts a year. I ain't never seen him beat yet.'

'What's his relationship to Reece?' asked Collins.

'People think he's Reece's number one. But what you might not realise is just how much Reece relies on him. It's him that manages much of Reece's organisation. If he's out of action, it will weaken Reece. So again, that's good for me.'

'Were yow at the Saudi prince's do back in June?' asked Clark.

'I had an invite but didn't go.'

'Why not?'

'Family do, in Liverpool. Me Dad's in his seventies now. Even so he would have skinned me alive if I'd missed his and me Mam's golden wedding anniversary.'

'Did you know a young woman called Christina Murray?'

'No. But I'd known Claire Lafferty, the other woman you lot found dead, Of course I didn't know her name was Lafferty or that she was on the game the night she shagged me.'

'Anything happen after that memorable encounter?' asked Clark.

'Such as?'

'Photos in the post.'

'Na. It never got that far.'

'How do you mean?'

'I'm forty-seven, a bit overweight, going bald and I'm starting to have to take three pisses a night. I'm not what you'd call every woman's dreamboat, unless their idea of a dream boat is a broken-down old bugger with plenty of money. I saw Lafferty coming a mile off. She wanted to go back to her place, but I insisted on mine. Even before we started, I clocked she left the curtains open a few inches. Then I heard the photographer outside the window start clicking away as soon as she peeled me pants off. But I did what every Englishman should do in such situation. I fucked her to a finish.'

'What then?'

'I shot at the bastard outside my window with my legally registered shot gun. Don't worry, I aimed to miss. But it did the job. He shit himself, fell over, smashed his camera and almost broke the hundred yards record running away.'

'What did yow do to Lafferty?'

'What could I do? She was so busy laughing at the little ponce running down the drive, she nearly peed herself. We went upstairs to bed and continued shagging uninterrupted. She didn't charge me, but I gave her a small gratuity. I thought the entertainment value had been worth it. Especially when she told me that it was Reece and his mates Robbins and Hill who were behind the blackmail attempt. After that she provided me with some useful info which I paid her for and received a free shag as a by-product of my generosity.'

'What sort of information?'

'Nothing to do with the building trade or Reece's business. More to do with who Reece had in his pocket. Which girls were screwing which councillors or businessmen? Then it all stopped, and you discovered the reason for that when you dug her up. She was all right, was Claire. She didn't deserve to die like that.'

'And I don't suppose yow had anything to do with that?'

'Not a thing. In fact, I'm willing to offer a five grand reward, anonymously of course, for any information leading to the arrest of Claire's killer.'

Collins looked at his watch and stood up, 'Well thanks for your time, Mr Charlton. We'll probably be back.'

'Not what I expected,' said Collins as he walked back to the car.

'No, he weren't but did yow notice what he said about Christina Murray.'

'Yeah the newspapers don't know that the two deaths are related. So how did he know that Lafferty was Murray's friend?'

As Collins was opening the car door Clark said, 'You know I reckon you've got a flat tyre.'

'Where?'

'At the bottom.'

'Pillock. Which wheel?'

'Not sure. Give me the tyre gauge.'

Collins fished the tyre gauge out of the door pocket where he kept it with a set of point gauges, a couple of new spark plugs, a fan belt and hose clamps of various sizes.

Collins stood by the driver's door as Clark examined each tyre in turn. Clarkee had taken the pressure of two tyres before Collins realised that he was not concerned with tyre pressures. He was interested in the black Humber Hawk on the opposite corner with the ginger-haired driver.

Kicking the last tyre for effect, Clark slid into the passenger seat and asked, 'Yow clock him?'

'Yeah, same kid who asked to borrow the brown sauce in the café in Sheldon.'

'Maybe more than that. I got a feeling I've seen the car before that.'

'Where?'

'Maybe outside the station. I can't be certain.'

'What do you want to do?'

'What do yow think? Grab him. Yow block him in and leave the rest to me.'

'OK.' Collins put the car in gear, waited for a break in the traffic and then executed a three-point turn.

The lad realised he had been spotted when Collins was twenty yards away and tried to jump out of the driver's door. Collins accelerated and stopped inches from the driver's side. Collins looked at the lad and smiled as the realisation that he was trapped spread across his face.

Clark was already moving, the passenger door open, when the driver's window exploded in a cascade of glass followed immediately by the passenger's window. Looking across Collins saw the lad level the .45 again, threw himself across the passenger seat and started to scramble towards the open door. He knew he would never make it before the next shot was fired. Then he felt Clark's hands grab his shoulders and pull him clear as the second shot was fired. A third and fourth shot went off in rapid succession.

Huddled behind the Capri's front wheel arch Collins' noticed a rapidly expanding patch of blood on Clark's waist and his eyes looked small and unfocused. Collins heard the passenger door of the Hawk open and slam shut as footsteps approached. *He's still got two bullets,* thought Collins. With no truncheon and no gun Collins realised that his only chance was to rush the man as soon as he appeared. But which end of the car would he come from? Collins decided he would approach from the front and clambered over Clark to protect him from the first shot.

When he did appear, it was from the rear of the car. Collins heard his footsteps and turned just in time to see the gun go off. He expected to feel the hammer punch of the bullet as it ripped his chest apart but there was nothing. Just a surprised look on the young man's face as he saw the throwing knife sticking out of the centre of his chest. His gun pointing skyward and his eyes closing for the last time. Looking down Collins saw Clark grinning at him. 'Thank fuck for the overconfidence of youth,' he said before he closed his eyes and his head dropped onto his chest.

By now shopkeepers and shoppers were rushing to see what was going on. Charlton pushed his way through the crowd. One look at Collins cradling Clark's head while applying pressure to his wound was enough for him to immediately take charge. Turning to Maggie, he said, 'Call the General Hospital tell 'em a copper with a gunshot wound to his stomach is on his way in. Then call the coppers and tell 'em that two of their own have been involved in a shooting.'

Looking around Charlton spotted a man in his fifties sporting a blue blazer and the badge of the Parachute Regiment.

'Mate, you're in charge until the coppers come. Keep 'em back and don't move the kid's body.'

'Come on, Sergeant, we have to get your mate to hospital. You go with him in the back. I'll drive.' With the help of a couple of bystanders Clark was lifted gently into the back of the Capri. Collins slid in beside his friend. Not once did he let up on applying pressure to the wound which was still bleeding profusely.

Wheels spinning, the two litre Capri fishtailed away and was doing fifty before it reached the end of the street. The mid-afternoon traffic was light on the A34 and ignoring the speed limit, Charlton put his foot down. Blowing his horn as he approached traffic lights and zebra crossings, his speed seldom dipped below sixty. As he approached Perry Barr a police motorcyclist roared up beside him, lights flashing, and tried to wave him down.

Collins saw what was happening and wound the rear window down. 'Officer shot,' he shouted twice and held up his warrant card, his hand covered in blood. 'Get us to the General Hospital.' That was enough for the motorcyclist. He accelerated in front of the Capri and waved Charlton to follow him. With the motorcycle's sirens blaring and lights blazing, cars, vans and buses pulled over to the side of the road and let the small procession pass. At some stage, the police rider called Central Control and told them what he was doing. By then Control had heard of a shooting involving a police officer and every car and motorbike in the city was tasked with clearing the roads to the Accident Hospital for Collins and his yellow Capri.

At the hospital, a trolley was already waiting for Clark. A young nurse gently removed Collins' hand from Clark's stomach and quickly applied a clean compress to the wound. The nurse was still pressing hard down when seconds later Clark was wheeled into the operating theatre. It was only as the doors swung shut that Collins realised that Charlton and the police motorcyclist were still with him. 'Can I buy you lads a coffee?' asked Collins.

'Na. We'll buy you a cup of tea,' said Charlton. 'Looks like you could use one.'

'Ain't that the truth?' said the motor cyclist, and holding out his hand said, 'The name's Ward, Richie Ward.'

For fifteen minutes Collins, Charlton and Ward sat and chatted in the small waiting area outside the operating theatre and drank some hot, sweet tea provided by a friendly nurse. As if by some unspoken agreement none of them spoke about what had just happened. Formal statements would come later, and it was best not to indulge in any activity that might imply collusion between witnesses and participants. It was only when Ruth appeared with Bram, Agnes and Hicks that the gathering broke up.

It was twenty past six when the surgeon, Mr Conway, came out of theatre and spoke to Ruth. Although he was nearly ten years her junior, his tone was condescending. 'It's my opinion, Mrs Clark, that your husband was incredibly lucky. The bullet went straight through his side and shaved his liver which was the cause of so much bleeding. We have been able to stich the liver and stop the bleeding. He will have some pain for a week or so but should make a full recovery. One thing is certain. He owes whoever maintained pressure on the wound his life.'

'Will he make a full recovery?' asked Ruth.

'There's no reason why he shouldn't.'

'How long will he be off work?' asked Hicks.

'If you confine him to desk duties, I think he could return after a week or so. Provided all goes well, that is. Personally, I would be more concerned about his mental health than his physical if I were you, Mrs Clark.' The young doctor spoke as if he was delivering a message inscribed on stone tablets from the slopes of Mount Sinai. 'I've been reading recently about the impact that violent incidents can have on individuals who haven't been specially trained. Now your husband has been trained to deal with violent thugs, but to be shot in his line of work is extremely rare. It's highly likely that he will suffer what we call traumatic memories concerning the incident which may cause him to have panic attacks or suffer problems coming to terms with the fact that he killed a young man.'

Ruth started to smile, and Collins found it difficult to stop himself from laughing. Taken aback by the reaction, Mr Conway was clearly irritated by the reaction to his words of professional wisdom. 'I'm sorry but I don't see what's funny about a man's mental health.'

'We're not laughing at your advice, Doctor,' said Collins. 'It's just that Detective Constable Clark had a highly eventful war. I doubt that this incident will even count as a blip on what he's seen and endured.'

Once Clark was wheeled into a single room and everyone had satisfied themselves that he was breathing, Ruth was left alone to await Clark regaining consciousness. Agnes took a sleeping Bram home and Collins and Hicks headed back to the station for what would be a frantic night's work.

# Part Three

## Handsworth, 18.34hrs

Handsworth nick on a Friday night was usually deserted until after closing time. The on-duty coppers were out on the streets getting ready for the usual fights and scuffles that occur around the time the pubs empty. The off-duty men and women were at home, enjoying a break from dealing with drunks. Not so tonight. Every officer who could walk or crawl had come in as soon as they heard about Clark and none of them were leaving until they knew how he was.

The atmosphere was one of anger, and it would not take much to set the coppers off. All they knew for sure was that a red headed kid had shot Clark, but it didn't take long before stories of IRA involvement started to spread. Collins immediately realised that it would only take a rumour of Clark's death to start reprisals with anyone Irish in the eye of the storm.

Assailed on all sides for answers, Collins shouted, 'In the canteen, lads and I'll give you the latest.'

The men assembled in a large semi-circle around Collins and Hicks. Collins looked at Hicks, who leaning forward said, 'Best if it's from you, Mickey.'

'OK, quiet, lads. Quiet!' shouted Collins and waited for the noise to abate. Then said, 'Clarkee is out of danger.' A huge cheer of relief went up from everyone present. Again, Collins waited until the noise died down. 'Ruth's with him now. The Doc says he will be off work for a week. Less if I know Clarkee. No lasting damage has been done. A single bullet grazed his liver. So now in a message direct from Clarkee, "Fuck off home and get some sleep, yow'll all be on duty in a few hours."

A second, even louder, cheer went up and for perhaps the

first time Collins fully understood the importance of Clark to the station. It was not just that everyone could see beyond his gruff sergeant-major's exterior to the man beneath, who would do anything for a mate. Or that they all recognised him as the best man in Brum to have beside you in a scrap. It went deeper than that. Clark was the station's mascot, flag carrier and one true leader. The man behind which the coppers marched. As long as Clarkee was there, they really believed that nothing truly bad would befall them.As the men filed away, Ridley approached Hicks and Collins. 'Nice speech, Mickey. Well done.' Turning to the Inspector he said, 'The ACC and Acting Super are in the Superintendent's Office. They have also got some guy called Sir Aubrey Nichols in there with some young buck who looks like he can handle himself. I'd say they're either MI5 or the Security Service. They want to see the pair of you as soon as. Which leaves me with just one question. Who the fuck was the kid that Clarkee did for?'

'I'll tell you as soon as I find out,' said Hicks.

Chief Inspector Hicks knocked on the Super's door and waited to be called in. Four men were already in the room seated around the conference table. ACC Knowles, who'd been such a support following the investigation into Norman Yates, sat in pride of place at the top of the table. On his right was Acting Superintendent Thatcher. To the left of the ACC was Sir Aubrey Nichols, a man whom Collins heartily despised, and beside him the young man Ridley had referred to.

Collins guessed that the young man was about two inches taller than him and had that loose-limbed elegance that many natural athletes possess. Fair-haired, he was lightly tanned with high cheekbones and a wide mouth. It would be easy to mistake him for a leading man in a Noel Coward play until you saw his eyes. They were pale green, cold as a freshly frozen icicle and watchful. He was a man used to assessing people and situations according to the level of threat they posed him. He reminded Collins of Peter O'Toole's portrayal of Lawrence of Arabia. *I wonder what Clark will make of him,* thought Collins. The man was introduced to Collins as Stephen St Clair Rhodes and they shook hands.

'How's Constable Clark?' asked ACC Knowles.

'He's out of surgery and the doctors say he'll make a full recovery,' replied Hicks.

'Good, and how about you, Sergeant Collins? Still bearing up?'

'I'm fine, Sir. If I'm honest I was shaken up a bit when I saw how bad the bleeding was. I thought Clarkee was a goner. But now that he's OK ... I'm fine.'

'Good. Well, while you were at the hospital, we've been working our nuts off. It seems that Sir Aubrey here got a tip-off that the IRA might be in Brum and had already started looking into that when news of the shooting came in this afternoon. His vigilance gave us a bit of a head start once we heard of the shooting. His team were able to identify the young killer as Bernie Meehan, aged twenty-one. He's been associated with the IRA for nearly eight years.'

'Eight years?' said Hick.

'Yes,' said Sir Aubrey. 'Started running messages and more for Declan Boyle just as the Border Campaign ended when he was thirteen.' Aubrey paused as if he expected Collins to say something about Boyle, but he remained stubbornly silent.

'The gun found near Meehan was a Webley .455, standard British Army issue. So Chief Inspector Hicks, would you like to explain how your current investigation involves the IRA?' asked ACC Knowles.

'The simple answer is that I didn't know of any connection until just now. All that Sergeant Collins and Constable Clark had was that Declan Boyle was a family friend of Martin Cunningham.'

'And who's Martin Cunningham?'

'Chairman and founder of Tricolour Construction, one of the biggest independent house builders in the country,' said Collins.

'Right, we need to speak to the pair of them,' said Sir Aubrey.

'That will be difficult, Cunningham was run over last Friday and is in a coma.'

Rhodes shifted in his seat, and speaking for the first time asked, 'Is Boyle a suspect in the hit and run?'

'Yes,' said Collins, 'but only one of four suspects.'

'I think you had better brief us on your investigation, Sergeant,' said ACC Knowles.

For the next twenty minutes Collins proceeded to outline what he and Clark had discovered following Superintendent Wallace's request that they investigate possible corruption in Birmingham.

'Very well,' said the ACC, 'Before you arrived, we had been discussing how this investigation should proceed. You will appreciate that what was a delicate enquiry has now become one with national security implications. There is also the matter of you losing your trusted right-hand man, Sergeant Collins. We have agreed that Stephen here will be seconded to you until such time as the case is concluded. On all police matters he will defer to Chief Inspector Hicks and you, Sergeant Collins, but on matters pertaining to national security he will have seniority. Is that clear?' The ACC looked at Hicks, Collins and Rhodes in turn. All three men nodded. 'Good. Then bugger off and sort this mess out before it escalates any further.'

It was past midnight when the trio of officers left the CID office and headed for the now deserted canteen. Collins picked up the small kettle, filled it half full and placed it on the cooker before switching the gas on and checking that it had ignited. 'Have you got any place to stay while you're here?' he asked.

'No, not yet, 'said Rhodes. 'I'll sleep here overnight and find a hotel room tomorrow.' Rhodes voice was smooth and deep, and pure Received Pronunciation English, but he didn't sound like the product of a public school.

'No need for that. Agnes and I have plenty of room. You can come home with me tonight. Provided you don't wet the bed or upset the other tenants.'

'How can I turn down such an offer?' said Rhodes and smiled.

All three men were dog-tired and didn't have the energy to discuss the events of the day. Twenty minutes later Hicks drove out the station entrance, followed by Collins sharing a ride in Rhodes' Ford Cortina. For the first time since the shooting Collins wondered, *Where in God's name did they take me car?*

## Saturday 5th October 1968

### Handsworth, 08.25hrs

Rhodes was sitting at the kitchen table trying to enjoy his freshly cooked bacon and eggs, but it was difficult. Every time he raised a forkful of food from his plate to mouth Sheba watched the ascent. With her head on one side, her slightly opened mouth watering, the occasional drop of saliva dripped into her basket. Twice, Agnes had told him to ignore the dog, but it was no use, and in the end, he threw the black beast a full rasher of bacon while Agnes wasn't looking. The evidence disappeared in one gulp and Rhodes wondered if it had even touched the animal's mouth or tongue on the way to its stomach.

When Collins entered a few minutes later, Rhodes was smoking a Dunhill cigarette and finishing his tea.

Kissing Agnes on the cheek, he said, 'Where's Bram?'

'He woke up at three thirty and finally feel asleep again at five this morning,' said Agnes. 'I assume it was because of the strange bed.'

'Bram?' asked Rhodes.

'He's Clark's son. Michael Abraham Clark,' said Agnes. 'Ruth stayed at the hospital last night, so I brought him home. Which reminds me I should really call her, but I don't want to wake her if she's gone to bed.'

'She's not going to go to bed until she's spoken to you about Bram. Call her,' said Collins.

Agnes nodded and went to call Ruth.

'Thanks again for putting me up. It really is much appreciated. I'll find something later today and be out of your hair.'

'You're more than welcome. Just one little hint, Agnes hates smoking in the house, especially at mealtimes.'

'Oh Lord,' said Rhodes, and immediately opened the

kitchen door, dropped the offending article on the concrete and stamped on it, before he picked it up and dropped it in the kitchen bin.

*Good manners,* though Collins, *perhaps a little too good for the upper class.* For the second time since he met him Collins found himself wondering about Rhodes and his background.

'So where do you want to start, Michael? Is it all right if I call you Michael?'

'Michael, Collins, Mickey. They're all OK. Just don't call me Paddy. While we are at it, what do I call you?'

'Steve or Stephen is fine.'

'I thought we'd start with a quick visit to Clarkee. Then we can pay a visit to Mr Declan Boyle. Before that, I want you to call your boss and check out the latest information MI5 has on Meehan and Boyle. At the moment, we have very little to connect him to Meehan.'

Rhodes' 1966 Ford Cortina Mk1 GT sat on the drive with the early morning sunshine glinting on its red bodywork and chrome. 'Your own car?'

'Yes, we don't all earn enough to run a Bentley or a DB5.'

'I know how you feel.'

'You'll have to direct me.'

'Just turn left and head for town and I'll tell you when to turn again.'

Pulling away Rhodes asked, 'How do you want to handle Boyle?'

'I've no idea. Clarkee and me always played it by ear. If the person was reasonable, we were reasonable. But if they put on the big, I am, start lying to us or became aggressive we'd slap them down. Or I should say Clarkee would slap them down.'

'Is he as good as they say he is?'

'Well, he saved my life yesterday, so I'm prejudiced, but I'd say he's better.'

'It's hard to believe that he's better than his reputation. A lot of the guys in MI5 know about him. Some say they served with him. But how does he do it? I mean, he's getting old.'

'Don't let him hear you say that, he may feel the need to show you he isn't past it.'

'So, how does he do it?'

'It's difficult to explain. He doesn't have to psyche himself up. He just moves from peace to all-out war in the time between breaths. It's not that he's lost it or is angry, he's not. He's always totally calm. It's just like a switch has been flicked. He told me once that in a fight he sees everything in slow motion and doesn't have to think about what his next move will be. It just happens. That makes him quick and unpredictable. Because if he doesn't know what he's going to do until he does it, how can an opponent counter it?'

'I'm looking forward to meeting him.'

'He's an acquired taste, and he's not keen on toffs.'

'I see,' said Rhodes and said nothing else until Collins told him to turn left after St. Chad's Cathedral.

## General Hospital, 09.48hrs

The PC outside Clark's room didn't recognise Collins and asked to see his warrant card before he would allow him in. The bulge in the man's tunic indicated that he was either armed or else he had brought his own sandwiches. Collins' money was on a gun.

Clark was propped up in bed, his eyes closed, dozing. There was an IV drip attached to his left arm, the strapping around his wrist clearly visible beneath his pyjamas. Tidied up and wrapped in pristine bandages, the wound looked nothing like the bloody mess that Collins had nursed in his arms just twenty hours earlier. Clark looked tired and hungover, but with the sound of footsteps on the lino covered floor his eyes snapped open. Seeing Collins, he said, 'I hope yow brought me a bacon butty. Sister Hitler and her strapping Bavarian staff nurses say I'm on fluids today. I mean how's a man supposed to get better on bloody liquids?'

'Good to see you're back to your old self.'

'Yow dain't bring me a sarnie?'

'No.'

'Yow ungrateful sod. I took one for yow.'

'No, you didn't. You were just too slow to duck.'

'Bollocks. Even on me slowest day I'm twice as quick as yow. Anyways, what you doing hanging around with someone who's just been shoplifting in Austin Reed?' asked Clark while checking out Rhodes.

'Clarkee, I'd like you to meet Stephen Rhodes. He's with MI5.'

'Pleased to meet you, Constable Clark. How do you feel?'

'Bloody hell, another sodding public schoolboy. That's just what the security service needs, another public school boy,' said Clark as he shook hands. Clark held the handshake for a second or two longer than was necessary. His eyes searching Rhodes face. When he let go he said, 'In answer to your question I feel as if Muhammed Ali has been thumping me for two days non-stop. But give it twenty-four hours and I'll be fine.'

'I'm glad to hear it,' said Rhodes.

'Now, I have a question for you. When the shit hits the fan yow ain't going to let me mate down, are yow.' It was a statement, not a question.

Rhodes said, 'No.'

One of the "Bavarian" staff nurses, a small woman with a soft Devon accent, entered and laid a cup of tea on Clark's locker, fluffed his pillows, took his pulse, entered it on his chart and left. Collins did not spot any Nazi insignia on her uniform.

For ten minutes the men chatted about the events of yesterday and what it meant for the investigation into the deaths of Lafferty, Murray, the Endburys, Thorne's disappearance, and corruption in the City Council. As the meeting started to wind down Rhodes looked at his watch and said, 'If you'll excuse me, I need to check in with London. I'll see you outside, Mickey.'

Clark waited until the door closed before he said, 'Mickey, I know that you don't like being overruled, but you should avoid any and all battles yow can't win on this one. National security will always trump any civilian enquiry, and if that means letting murdering scumbags off the hook to catch or take out a senior member of the IRA, so be it.'

Collins started to speak but was cut off by Clark, 'How much do you know about Rhodes?'

'Nothing. I only met him yesterday. Why?'

'He's not an ordinary operative.'

'What do you mean?'

'MI5 employ all sorts of people. Common or garden spies, investigators, analysts, linguists, filing clerks. They also have a small team of killers who get rid of problems for the government. Permanently. Rhodes is one of them.'

'How do you know?'

'It takes one to know one. My bet is his orders are to find and kill Boyle and any other members of the IRA he comes across. That is why he's been teamed up with yow. Yow are the one most likely to find Boyle.'

'But it was the ACC who teamed him with me, not Nichols.'

'Yow don't know what he agreed with Nichols in their chat before the meeting, Mickey.'

Collins thought for a moment before saying, 'I'm in the bloody crossfire again, aren't I?'

'Yep. But that's what yow're paid for. Now how's Bram?'

'Aren't you going to give me any advice on how to survive?'

'Na. Yow should have brought me a bacon butty. How's Bram?

When Collins left five minutes later, he looked back at his

friend from the doorway. Clark's eyes were closed, and he was sleeping.

## Solihull, 12.45hrs

It started to rain as Rhodes pulled up outside Yolande Cunningham's house. It seemed to add to the worry that had enveloped the house and which Collins felt as he walked up the path. Several windows had the curtains drawn and there was a stillness that Collins usually took as a sign that the house was empty.

Yolande answered the door. She was dressed to go out.

'I'm sorry Michael, I'm just off to the hospital. They've just called me. Martin has woken up, thank God.'

'Sure, that's great news. We won't keep you,' said Collins. 'We were wondering, is Boyle in?'

'No. He's not here. He's gone back to Ireland to arrange a few things.'

'Do you know when he'll be back?'

'He said he'd be back tomorrow night.'

'Did he give a time? We really do need to speak to him. It's important.'

'Ah Michael, he's not in the IRA any more. He left them in the early sixties. He knows nothing about the shooting of your friend yesterday – if that's what this is about. How's the little fella anyway?'

'He's going to be all right, but I still need to speak to Boyle.'

'Thank God. I liked the wee fella. Boyle's coming in on the last flight from Dublin tomorrow. I think it gets in about six thirty. I'll have a houseful of Martin's people here by then, so Declan is going to stay at the Henley Hotel on Stratford Road.'

"Thanks. Can we give you a lift?'

'No, I'll be grand. I have the car, but thanks anyway.'

As Collins and Rhodes returned to the Cortina, Rhodes stared to ask, 'Where to, now?' but was cut short by Collins upraised hand. He was thinking. Slipping into the passenger seat Collins pulled out his notebook and flicked back through the pages. Finding what he was looking for, he tapped the book with his index finger.

'What is it, Michael?'

'It might be something or nothing. When you spoke to Sir Aubrey, he didn't know that Boyle had left England did he?'

'No. But I'm not sure if we had anyone watching him. That sort of operation can take up to twenty-four hours to arrange.'

'Take me back to the station. I have a few calls to make.'

## Handsworth, 13.50hrs

Back in the office, Collins sat down and looked out the window at the rain. He was thinking. He knew what he wanted to do but had not yet settled on the order to do it in. Finally, he said, 'Steve, find another office with a phone and call your mates at MI5 and MI6 and Special Branch. I want to know the whereabouts of Declan Boyle on every day for the last nine months. That means an address and proof that he was there. Both here and in Ireland.'

Rhodes had been trained by the British Army and knew that now was not the right time to ask questions. Picking up a notepad, he went in search of an empty room.

Collins' first call was to Aer Lingus Information. Their responses to his enquiries were swift and clear. 'Yes, our last flight from Dublin to Birmingham is at five-fifty, arriving in Birmingham at twenty-six minutes past six, and, "Yes, the time of the last flight was the same, seven days a week." Collins declined their kind offer to book him on a flight but thanked the young man with the Kerry accent.

Next, he put a call into *The Bray News* and Padraig O'Brian.

As soon as his old editor identified himself Collins said, 'Padraig, don't speak. Just listen. This is important. I need to know exactly where our friend has been every day for the last nine months. That includes any trips he made abroad, especially to Ireland. You can reach me anytime on the station's number. Just say you're my uncle calling about my sick aunt and I'll phone you back. Don't call from your office or home. Got it?'

'Indeed, I have Mr Brennan. I'll look into it for you and get back to you. It will probably be Monday.'

'That's fine,' Collins paused, considering if he was being overly melodramatic, then decided that safety was more important than sounding like an actor in a cheap B film. 'Be careful. If this is what I think it is, you could end up dead if you approach the wrong person.'

Without any delay Padraig replied. 'Sure, that's exactly what I was thinking meself. Good day now, Mr Brennan.'

Finally, Collins called Agnes. The phone was picked up by Annabel, whose cheerful greeting indicated that between the information contained in her husband's report and the influence of Marjorie and Agnes, she was starting to come out of her cocoon of pain and sorrow. After a brief exchange of pleasantries, she put Agnes on the phone.

'Michael, is everything all right? Nothing has happened to Clive?'

'No, all's well. I need you to contact Sybil Harker for me. I want to know if her contacts in the Irish community have picked up any whispers about IRA activity in Birmingham, London, or any other cities with a big Irish community. Also have there been any sightings of Declan Boyle in London since the start of the year? If possible, I'd prefer that MI5 and Special Branch didn't know about her enquiries.'

'This is to do with the current case, I take it?'

'Yes.'

'Be careful, Michael. Your countrymen have been fighting their war with us for eight hundred years. They're a dangerous enemy, and you don't have Clive to watch your back.'

'I have someone better than that.'

'Who?'

'You.'

Hanging up, Collins headed for the station garage and borrowed a squad car. He needed to speak to Clarkee.

## General Hospital, 15.10hrs

'You've brought me a bacon sarnie?' asked Clark even before Collins was fully in the room.

'Sorry, mate. No bacon. But I do have a tub of jelly.'

'I'm bloody starving in here and yow bring me a bloody jelly.'

'Well if you don't want it, I'll eat it meself.'

'Not a chance. Give it here.'

Collins passed over the small bowl of jelly Agnes had made earlier in the week and fished a dessert spoon out of his jacket pocket. He sat back saying nothing as Clark took his time to devour his raspberry jelly.

Finished, Clark lay back, a look of contentment on his face. 'Anyways, what do you want? Twice in one day, people will start to talk about yow.'

'I think I've got something, but I want you to tell me if I'm completely off me trolley.'

'We already know yam mad. What's it yow got?'

'Yolande said that Boyle took the last flight out of Dublin after hearing of Cunningham's accident.'

'Yeah, so?'

'When was Martin run over?'

'About twenty to six.'

'When do you think the police informed her of the death?'

'He were known in the area and had his ID on him. It would have been quick. Say between six fifteen and six forty-five.'

'The last Air Lingus flight from Dublin to Birmingham leaves at five fifty and arrives at six twenty-six.'

It didn't take Clark long to recognise the significance of what Collins was saying. 'Boyle's lying about being on that plane. He were already in Brum, or England at least. The lying toerag. There's nowt mad about that as a theory. Which I admit is a bit unusual for yow. What else is going on in that tiny mind of yowrs?'

'What if we've been played all along? What if everything that has happened since the Saudi do has been orchestrated by Boyle? Reece did intend to blackmail Endbury. But Boyle wanted Reece out of the picture, so he killed the girls. He gambled that Endbury wouldn't want to be a part of murder and would go to the police, but Reece cleaned the scene up and buried the bodies.'

'There's a lot of bleedings ifs in there, ain't there?'

'I know. It's the weakest bit of me idea. But stick with me. It wasn't Reece's men who we saw driving hell for leather away from Endbury's. It was Boyle's boys. He wanted the Endburys dead because he knew it would throw more pressure on Reece. That's why the murder/suicide hadn't been set up properly. He wanted it to look like a double murder.'

'Why attack Thorne?'

'To put even more pressure on Reece. Remember what Charlton said about Reece relying on Thorne for more than just muscle. The bastard was building pressure on Reece waiting for him to crack or us to pick him up. What do you think?'

'Yow can't take it to anyone as it stands. Yow'd be laughed out of court. Yow need to fill in the gaps in yowr story and get some evidence. What yow got planned?'

Collins told him of his request for information from Padraig and Sybil, and Rhodes calling MI5.

'OK, well that's a good start. Yow should also check out with Marie if there have been any rumblings among the Irish in Brum. Even if yow prove that Boyle was in Brum every day since New Year's Day, all yow've got is circumstantial. Yow need hard evidence, a witness.'

'I know. But do you think it's worth pursuing?'

'Of course, I do. I trained yow and there's nowt wrong with yowr instincts, it's just yowr brain that I worry about.'

Collins smiled, held up two fingers and walked out. As the door closed Collins said, 'See you tomorrow, Clive,' he was out of the door before the jelly spoon hit the door.

## Handsworth, 16.30hrs

Collins found a note on his desk from Rhodes when he returned to the CID office. "My colleagues are looking into what we discussed. I'll see you later." It was signed "Steve".

Collins took a match from the box on Hicks' desk, opened the window and burned the message. *Now, I really am becoming paranoid,* he thought. As he pulled the window down, Hicks bustled into the office. 'Afternoon, Mickey. How are things going? How's Clarkee?'

'He's on a liquid only diet today and is threatening not to talk to me if I don't bring him a bacon butty.'

'Sounds like he's on the mend. Take him a small jelly. Nothing in it. That will shut him up. He just wants the feel of food in his mouth. What about the case? Any developments?'

Collins remained silent and said nothing about the jelly he had given Clark that afternoon. He was also trying to decide if he wanted to reveal his theory about Boyle. He surprised himself when he said, 'I'm looking at the possibility that Boyle may have been behind all the deaths and Cunningham's accident. But I must do some more digging before I can provide any evidence. Give me a couple of days to firm it up, Sir?'

'OK. But given how close Clark was to getting killed, you need to write down your ideas – just in case.'

'Will do, Sir.'

Collins spent half an hour writing up an outline of his theory then headed home.

## Handsworth, 23.07hrs

Agnes stood up, crossed to the TV and turned it off before the final credits had finished rolling. 'Well, I think you've had more than enough excitement for one day. It's time for bed.'

'What a good idea,' said Collins.

'My idea is sleep, what's yours?'

'The same for me, darling, the same.'

'Why don't I believe you?'

They had reached the landing when the phone rang. Agnes was about to go and answer it when Collins said, 'I'll get it.' Picking the phone up, he was in the process of giving his number, when Hicks' familiar voice interrupted him. 'Mickey, I need you back at the station ASAP. MI5 have something.'

## Handsworth, 23.44hrs

When Collins arrived at the station, the meeting between Hicks, the Superintendent, ACC Knowles, Sir Aubrey and Rhodes had already started. To his surprise, Inspector Archer was also there. 'Grab a seat Sergeant,' said the ACC. 'We're just starting. Sir Aubrey has some information that has changed the nature of the investigation. Sir Aubrey, if you would...'

'Thank you. I received a report earlier this evening from a source in London which has been confirmed by the FBI. Declan Boyle had a meeting with Dwight McCloud, an arms dealer in Mississippi, eight weeks ago and arranged for a major shipment of arms from America to GB. We have no information on when or where the shipment will arrive, or if the guns are destined for Northern Ireland or will be stockpiled in Britain for safe keeping.'

Collins was the first to speak, 'So his supposed break with the IRA was a sham?'

'Yes. I am afraid that the IRA have hoodwinked us. And of course, we don't know what other shipments have been made in the last five years.'

'What's our next move, then?' asked Archer.

'We need to find Boyle and watch him until such time as he makes a move to collect the weapons,' said Aubrey.

'Finding him won't be hard,' said Collins. He will be at the Henley Hotel tomorrow night. He's returning from Dublin on an Aer Lingus flight which arrives at six thirty. The difficult bit will be tracking him.'

'Any ideas? Suggestions?' asked the ACC.

Rhodes raised his head and said, 'Mickey and I should pay him a visit. Let him know that we have suspicions. I'm sure he's already looking for tails, so we provide him with someone to avoid but have a backup team that he won't be looking for.'

'Sounds like a plan. Can we resource it?' asked the ACC.

'Leave that with me,' said Sir Aubrey. 'What we need now is to flesh out the plan.'

The meeting continued for nearly three hours as each possibility was considered, changed, rejected or accepted. They had just run through their plan for the second time when Sir Aubrey looked at his watch and said, 'I think we have a plan, gentleman. What we all need now is a good night's sleep. I suggest we reconvene later today at 16.00 hours.'

## Sunday 6th October.

### Birmingham, 12.13hrs

Collins set out on his walk to St Francis for the quarter to one mass. As he walked the near two and half miles his mind drifted back to last night's meeting. Most of the time had been taken up planning for the surveillance of Boyle and any contacts he made. Unfortunately, without knowing how many men he already had on the mainland it was impossible to plan accurately the resources required. This had made Collins uneasy. He was still worried, and kept thinking of his boyhood hero, General George Custer. Custer had charged after a small war party of Indians at Little Big Horn, only to find himself surrounded by two thousand Indian braves. Collins did not want to follow a handful of IRA volunteers into a trap and total annihilation.

In the end it had been agreed that MI5 would send as many agents to Birmingham as they could, while also covering London, Liverpool and Glasgow. Their agents would be dispersed around Birmingham but work out of Thornhill Road.

Aubrey had also revealed the details of the order made by Boyle, worth near three million pounds. Most of the money had been spent on Armalite rifles, hand grenades, revolvers and a large consignment of an explosive called Semtex that Collins knew little about.

Collins went over the plan again. It was a good plan. The only part he did not like was the possibility of walking into a hundred plus IRA men on the warpath.

As he entered St Francis he dipped his hand in the small font of holy water, made the sign of the cross and asked God to protect all involved with the operation.

## Handsworth, 14.52hrs

With the dinner dishes and cutlery washed up, Collins kissed Agnes and said, 'I don't know what time I'll be back darling. Rhodes and I will be paying a visit to Declan Boyle this evening. With a bit of luck, we might catch him with his guard down.'

Agnes knew that something was going on. An all-night meeting at the station was unusual, but she and Collins had not had the opportunity to discuss it. She held him tightly and said 'I doubt that Mr Boyle ever lets his guard down. Please be careful Michael – for me.'

'Will do.'

## Hall Green, 18.24hrs

The afternoon had been taken up with meetings which Collins believed had been a complete waste of time. The information discussed the previous night had been re-examined, and how Boyle was going to be watched discussed again. The only new piece of information was that thirty-two agents had been moved into Birmingham and would stay until either Boyle was captured or killed. Collins was relieved when at five thirty he and Rhodes drove out of the station yard and headed for Hall Green.

An hour after they had arrived, Collins and Rhodes were still sitting in the car park of the Henley Hotel, a two storey, two-star hotel that had been built in the 1950s and tried to look like an American motel. Across the road two other MI5 agents, a man and a woman, were parked in a Ford Zephyr also watching the hotel. Just before eight o'clock a Ford Escort pulled onto the forecourt and found a place to park. Collins and Rhodes watched as Boyle and two other men got out of the car. The driver, a medium sized, black-haired man with quick movements, went to the boot and lifted out two suitcases. The biggest man of the trio picked them up and followed Boyle into the hotel. Rhodes picked up the camera and took several pictures of the three men until they disappeared into the hotel.

'Give them five minutes, then we'll go in,' said Collins.

After Collins had shown his warrant card to the blonde receptionist, she was only too pleased to answer his questions. The two men sharing were in room eighteen, but Mr Boyle was alone in room twenty.

Rhodes knocked on number twenty and waited. A moment later the door opened a few inches and Boyles's face appeared, 'Yes?' he asked.

Rhodes stepped aside and Collins said, 'I have a few more questions for you, Mr Boyle. May we come in?'

Boyle's eyes remained unreadable. 'Sergeant Collins. I didn't expect to see you… tonight. But come on in.' Stepping back, he opened the door.

The room was modern, functional, clean and tidy. Boyle's case lay unopened on the bed. A cup of freshly made tea sat on the bedside cabinet. Taking out a packet of Senior Service, Boyle selected one and lit it with a silver Ronson lighter. He didn't offer the pack to either Collins or Rhodes.

Collins went to the window and opened it.

'You don't smoke, Sergeant. That's unusual in the police?'

'That it is, but I never took to it.'

'Wise man. Costs a fortune. Now what can I do for you?'

'Yolande said that you flew in on the last flight from Dublin. Is that right?'

'Yes. It was three minutes early. The British still can't believe that we're able to operate a successful national airline.'

'Is that the same flight you caught the day Martin was run over?'

'Ah, no, sure. I was in Manchester when I heard about that. I came straight down.'

'Yolande thought that you flew over on the last flight. Why would she say that?'

'I've no idea. All I can say is that when I arrived, she was in a terrible way. Your lot had told her what had happened and took her to the hospital. Sure, she didn't get home until gone midnight. Mind you, there was no police car to take her home. They'd all pissed off, quicker than the day's favourite at Leopardstown. No, she had to catch a taxi.'

'What about the two lads who came in with you?'

'You saw those did you?' Boyle's eyes were alive. He was enjoying himself. 'Friends of Martin's. They wanted to see Martin and came back with me from Dublin.'

'What are you planning to do after Martin's recovered? Stay here or return to Ireland?'

'Oh, I'll stay on a bit. Give Yolande a hand. She needs a bit of help now.'

'What sort of help?'

'The usual. Don't get me wrong, Yolande is a powerful woman, worth two of most men, but she's not at her best just now. I'll help manage the business and the men until she's feeling a bit better and Martin is back on his feet.'

'And then?'

'I'll head home, job done.'

'You wouldn't be tempted to keep it for the IRA?' asked Collins and held Boyle's eyes.

'You've checked me out, have you? Well you can't be any good if you didn't know that I left the IRA nearly six years ago.'

'Kicked out for incompetence and poor performance as quartermaster, I heard.'

Boyle's lips grew thin and some colour left his face. 'Ah sure, you don't want to believe everything you hear, Mr Collins.'

'Which part shouldn't I believe? The part which says you were kicked out for doing a piss-poor job or the part that says you left the IRA?'

'Ah, it's interesting you should say that. You know why I

hate the bastards that leave Ireland and join the Crown's forces? They become the lackeys and lickspittles of their country's oppressors. But one day they'll be judged as the traitors they are.'

'And I assume they will all be found guilty?'

'That they will,' said Boyle with a smile.

'And what then?'

But Boyle was not going to be drawn further. With a broad smile he said, 'You'll have to excuse me I'm very tired and that bed has me name on it.'

Sitting in Rhodes' Cortina, Collins asked, 'What did you think?'

'He knew you were going to ask the question about the time of the flight.'

'And...'

'He was playing with us.'

'That's what I thought too. But why?'

'Maybe he doesn't expect to see you again.'

Collins understood the unspoken warning contained in Rhodes' response. After a few seconds' thought, he said, 'Check out who the boys with him are and radio the watchers to keep a good eye on all three of them overnight.'

'OK,' said Rhodes.

On returning home Collins kissed Agnes and ran his hand down her back, coming to rest on her backside. Agnes removed it and smiled, 'You don't look capable of doing anything. Go on and sit down and I'll make you a pot of tea and some toast.' Eight minutes later Agnes carried the tray into the lounge, but she was too late. Collins had slipped off his shoes and jacket and was curled up on the settee, asleep. Crossing to the table, she laid the tray down and returning to the settee she bent down and lightly kissed his forehead and whispered,

"We are such stuff As dreams are made on, And our little life Is rounded with a sleep."

Turning the light off, Agnes closed the door and returned to the kitchen and the BBC Radio Four news.

## Monday 7th October 1968

### Birmingham, 09.33hrs

Rhodes parked outside the General Hospital and he and Collins walked to Steelhouse Lane. The overnight rain had washed the skies clean and added to the number of leaves that were starting to accumulate in the gutters. *Another week or so and the trees will be bare,* thought Collins. He had not spent any time thinking about how he'd handle West, but he had promised himself not to lose his temper with the overweight, pompous, arsehole. Now, he was about to find out if he could keep that simple promise.

Passing the Charge Room, the two men headed for the second floor and Inspector West's office. Knocking on the door Collins walked in, followed by Rhodes. West's two Sergeants and three Detective Constables looked up. Collins could feel their animosity roll over him. They were never going to forgive him and Clark for how they had been humiliated in the Yates multiple killings case five months earlier. Collins didn't think it was worth telling them that their own boss had been the cause of their embarrassment. A quick look at the glass corner office confirmed that West was out

'We're looking for Inspector West,' said Collins.

After an awkward silence, the youngest person in the room, said, 'He's with the Superintendent. If you want to hang around you can.'

'Thanks,' said Collins. 'You'll find us in the canteen when he's free. Give us a shout, would you please.' Leaving the office Collins turned left, rather than head for the stairs, turning the corner he pushed open Marie Bolding's door. Marie looked up from the file she was making notes on and smiled when she saw him and Rhodes. 'I suppose you're here to see West.'

'Got it in one,' said Collins. 'This gentleman is Stephen Rhodes. He is helping me out until Clarkee is back on duty. Did you manage to get any additional information on the names I gave you?'

'Yep,' said Marie and going to the filing cabinet nearest her desk, opened it and withdrew a black lever arch file in a brown paper bag.

Collins picked it up and flicked through the papers. There were over twenty pages of information. 'Anything that you want to tell me?'

'Yeah. Boyle's been in England most of this year. He's spent some time in London but mostly in Manchester. He was in Manchester when Cunningham was run over. Flew back to Dublin last Friday and returned last night. The word among Irish narks in Brum is that he was thrown out of the IRA in 1963 and now works for himself.'

'Doing what?' asked Rhodes.

'That's difficult to say. Putting people in touch with other people is the best description I can give you. He's travelled to Europe, the Middle East and America this year and talked to people.'

'What sort of people?' asked Collins.

'Manufacturers, builders, bankers and the odd politician here and there. He's registered a small private company in Ireland called Eire's Voice. He's making money but not a huge amount. He seems to spend most of what he earns on travel.'

'Has he got any employees?' asked Collins.'

'He's got three full-time employees in Ireland and a part-timer who works from a one room office in London. Her name's Fiona McGuinness. There's a picture of her in the file. She's quite a looker.'

'His woman?' asked Rhodes.

'So, rumour says.'

'OK. I'll take the file and give you a call when I've read it. In the meantime, can I buy you a cuppa?'

'No, sorry. I need to finish a report for the ACC by tonight. Otherwise I won't be going out and I have a red-hot date. Another time?' Marie stood up and kissed Collins on the cheek and shook hands with Rhodes.

As they headed down to the staff canteen Rhodes asked, 'What happened to her arm?'

'A bullet broke her left elbow about six months ago. But she saved my life and Clarkee's. We owe her.'

'Will she ever get full movement back?'

'I don't know. They are still operating on her. I hope so. We need coppers like her.'

It was a few minutes after eleven and the early shift were piling out of the canteen after their second breakfast of the day. Both men were tempted by the smell of bacon and sausages but neither wanted to leave an entire plateful of uneaten food if West deigned to call them. They settled down in the corner with a slice of toast and a tea each. 'What made you join the Service?' asked Collins.

The question did not surprise Rhodes. Most people were curious, but few ever asked it in such bald terms. Rhodes took a few seconds to frame any sort of answer. Collins had treated him well since they had been thrown together and he deserved at least a partially true account of how he had been recruited. 'You don't beat about the bush, do you, Mickey?' Collins shook his head and waited.

'As you've probably guessed my name is not St Clair Rhodes. It used to be plain old Stephen Rhodes. I'd never thought about joining any service, but I got in a spot of bother when I was twenty-two and thought it would be better if I could tell the judge that I'd applied to join the Guards. It probably kept me out of jail. Anyway, I joined up as a regular soldier. I thought I'd do my five years and leave but I found I enjoyed it and they seemed to like me. I worked hard and the harder I worked the more I enjoyed it. I came out of basic training as top recruit. After a tour in Aden in 1962 I was promoted to Corporal and my Sergeant suggested I try out for the SAS. They're a specialist ...'

'Yeah, I know about them,' said Collins.

'Well that went very well, and I joined the regiment. After some work I did in Africa, MI5 contacted me and the rest is, as they say, history.'

'What does your family think of your success?'

'I have no idea. I've never met my father and my mother died when I was six. I spent the next ten years in a children's home. Then two years on the streets of London before I got a job that put a roof over my head.'

Collins didn't inquire how he had survived. He had a fairly good idea. Instead he asked, 'What was the job?'

'Bellboy at the Savoy. Someone I met on the streets coached me for the interview. They taught me how to speak, how to eat and how to remain invisible. All vital skills if you want to succeed at the Savoy – or MI5. I was one of four front desk managers when some money went missing. The suspects were me and a French nobleman. Guess who they blamed. Thus, my court case.'

'I'm surprised you were able to trade a career in the army for a place in jail.'

'My friend from the street was, what shall we say, influential.'

Collins wanted to ask if he had kept in touch with his friend but decided it was none of his business.

They had just finished their second cup of tea when West barrelled into the canteen with one of his sergeants. Spotting Collins, he bent down and said something to his sergeant, who then headed towards the corner. It was now ten past eleven and the room was nearly empty. Pulling back a chair the fat detective dropped into the seat. His thighs slopped over the sides of the chair. Sitting down he looked like an adult who had just joined a couple of children at their play. *He's put on at least another stone since spring,* though Collins. *Fat git.*

'You were after me, Collins?'

'Yes Sir. I've been looking into corruption in the Council, and it appears that a Mr John Simpson who it was thought had committed suicide was probably murdered. It was your case and I thought you should know that it's now being actively re-investigated.'

'And what proof have you got that it wasn't suicide?'

'The man who slept with Mrs Simpson has admitted that he drugged her and arranged for the pictures to be taken.'

'Fair enough. But that don't change the fact that her husband jumped off the fourth floor of a multi-storey car park.'

'No, it doesn't. But it does support her story about her husband writing a report on corruption and being killed when he refused to be blackmailed.'

'Who are you reporting to on this case?'

'Acting Superintendent Thatcher and ACC Knowles.'

West sat quiet for a few moments. Standing up he said, 'Well it sounds like you've stitched me up, again you little shite. Just don't expect any help from me, my team or your lezzie friend Marie Bolding.'

Rhodes waited until they were outside before he said, 'Bloody hell, that fat slob really does need taking down a peg or two.'

'True, but he didn't learn anything about you. Nor has he learned that we have a copy of Simpson's report.'

'Why didn't you tell him about the report?'

'He'll build up his defence based on the info I did give him and when he raises it in a meeting with the ACC, I'll be able to stuff the bastard.'

'Bloody hell, you really don't like him, do you?'

'That's a fair assumption.' said Collins.

## Handsworth, 14.00hrs

When Collins arrived back at Thornhill Road, Rhodes said, 'I have a little job to take care of. I'll be back tomorrow early. I've left an envelope with the info from the centre which you asked for in your pigeon-hole.'

'OK. See you tomorrow.'

Collins stopped off at the Charge Room to pick up the post and then headed for the empty CID room. Hicks had taken a day's holiday and was somewhere in Cardiff with his wife.

As he walked, he started to flick through the envelopes he'd picked up and took out an A5 brown envelope with HMSO printed on the front and addressed to him by hand. It contained a three-page summary from Steve of the data he'd received from Sir Aubrey.

Over the next four hours the phone rang several times, Collins studiously ignored it each time and continued to read and take notes from Simson's audit report. By 6.20 he'd finished his second run through of the document and the paperwork from Marie. Much of the information appeared in both files but there were a couple of pieces that seemed to contradict each other, usually concerning dates and times. Picking up his notes, the file and Rhodes' summary he headed for home. He wanted Agnes' opinion.

As he opened the front door Sheba came bounding across the wooden floor to welcome him and he heard Agnes shout 'Hello,' from the lounge. He laid the files on the phone table and took Sheba into the kitchen where he found the bone from yesterday's shoulder of lamb and broke it at the joint. Bending down, he gave the smaller bone to Sheba, who didn't bother to say "thank you," but instead disappeared at speed out of the dog flap and into the garden. After putting the kettle on, he went to see Agnes.

Agnes was sitting at the dinner table, a large collection of Metropolitan Police papers spread across its surface. Most had "Confidential Met Police" stamped across them. 'Sybil has been busy,' he said. 'Found anything of interest?'

Agnes looked up, her mind clearly somewhere else. 'I've nearly finished. Go and make some tea and I'll tell you what I've found.'

When he returned five minutes later with a tray of tea and a couple of slices of sponge cake Agnes was leaning back and stretching. He set the tray down, went behind her and kissed the back of her neck. Within seconds she was giggling and telling him to stop.

'We have work to do.' she told him. After a final nibble of her ear lobe he let her go. 'I'm starting to think that you are a big bully Mr Collins.'

'And here's me thinking I'm Don Juan.'

'You have the passion, my love, but not the language.'

'There you go again. It's always languages with you.'

'Not always,' said Agnes and standing, she crossed to Mickey and sat on his lap. 'Sometimes,' she paused, 'it's work. What did you find in your files?'

Collins picked up his summary notes. 'If you'll just sit on one of the other five chairs in the room, I'll tell you.' Agnes kissed him hard on the lips before moving. 'Marie tells me that Boyle has been living in England for most of 1968 He arrived on the fourth of January and has flats in both London and Manchester. He returns to Dublin at least once a month to see his mother.

'He's well-known in the Irish circles in both cities and gets on well with the local Irish lads. Always willing to buy a round. He does not attend any political meetings and based upon what the IRA has said about him and his actions in England it doesn't look as if he has anything to do with the Cause.

'He's not been seen very much in London. His girlfriend, Fiona McGuinness, runs the London Office of his *Eire's Voice* and spends most weekends with him.

'Last February he had a two-week trip to the USA and

again in July. Visited New York, Chicago and Washington. On his return he went to Manchester and had a lot of meetings in and around the city. But none in Liverpool.'

Collins stopped for breath and picked up his tea and took a sip.

Before he'd had a chance to bite into his cake, Agnes said, 'So either his meetings in the US are entirely innocent, or he doesn't want anyone to know that he's speaking to people in Liverpool who could help him import guns and ammunition from the States.'

'That's exactly what I thought.'

'Do you know who he met over there?'

'Marie didn't, but Sir Aubrey did. All of the men he met are known supporters of the IRA. Several of them are suspected of supplying arms to the IRA during the Border Campaign.

'On top of his visits to the States he's been to the Middle East twice. Neither file tells me who he met. But both visits were to Lebanon, and on both occasions, there was a delegation of Palestinians in Beirut at the same time, but there is no proof he met with them.'

'The Palestinians don't have enough weapons to arm themselves adequately. Of what possible use would they be to the IRA? Unless it was their paymasters he was interested in,' said Agnes.

'Of course, the Russians. They'd welcome an uprising in Northern Ireland. Anything to embarrass Britain and the West would be good for them. What about you? What have you found?' asked Collins.

'Well Sybil's information is mainly from narks, and is dubious at best. But she's identified a couple of characters that Boyle has met in London. An American called Dwight McCloud and one Mohammed Ali. He met them separately. Both are known to be active in the field of illegal weapons. Anything from a revolver to an RPG launcher, with munitions. She has also provided us with a list of people Boyle has met or spoken to in the last nine months. Obviously, it has gaps.'

Before Collins could reply, the front door was opened and Marjorie and Annabel half fell into the hall chatting. They weren't drunk but they had been drinking and the world was a much better place for both of them. Seeing Agnes and Collins, they waved, and Annabel said, 'We've bought some fish and chips. There's plenty for the four of us.'

'How could we turn down such an offer?' said Agnes, 'Put the kettle on.'

It was nearly eleven thirty by the time Marjorie and Annabel had described every scene in *Bullitt* to Agnes and Collins, and the fish and chips party broke up. Both Agnes and Collins were tired, and neither were keen to reopen their earlier conversation. As Agnes turned her bedside light off, she said, 'If you leave your files. I'll go through them tomorrow and summarise all our notes.'

'That would be great, love,' he said and fell asleep.

## Tuesday 8th October, 1968

### Handsworth, 09.05hrs

Hicks was reading the reports from the weekend when Collins arrived. 'Sorry I'm late, Sir. I called in on Clark. The hospital released him yesterday.'

'How is he?' asked Hicks.

'Better. He'll be back tomorrow or Thursday.'

'Strange things, shots in the gut. They can lay you out for months or a few days. No telling with them. How did yowr meeting with Boyle go?'

'He's a cool one, that's for sure. Admitted nothing but implied a lot. I'd like to get him in an interview room.'

'With Clarkee, no doubt. What have you planned for this morning?'

'Not a lot.'

The conversation was cut short when Collins' phone rang. Picking it up, he heard Ridley's familiar voice. ''You'll like this, Mickey. DCI Jameson has just called. One of their lads saw a young guy and girl acting strangely near the Villa ground last night. As he moved towards them, they did a runner. When he reached where they'd been standing, he found a cat hanging by its neck with one paw nailed to the fence of a two up two down. Poor thing was still alive. The copper reckons he could identify the pair.'

The hair on Collins' neck stood up as he remembered the meeting with a young man and woman as he was checking out a dead kitten nailed to Mrs McCann's rear gate. 'I think I know where they can be found,' said Collins. 'I'll call Jameson.'

## Handsworth, 12.10hrs

Collins was enjoying his hake, chips and peas when Stephen Rhodes dropped into the seat opposite him. The young man looked tired and Collins wondered what job he'd had to finish the previous evening. 'You look terrible,' he said, 'Grab yourself a cuppa and a bite to eat.'

'No, I'm fine. I had something on the motorway. What's happening?'

'Not too much at the moment. If you want to join me later tonight, I'll be picking up a couple of vicious little sods who enjoy nailing animals to fences and back gates.'

'Well I've no appointments tonight, so I'd love to join you. But what are we going to do until then?'

'Well, Thorne is still missing. I was thinking it might be useful to visit Reece's offices and see if he's heard anything.'

Forty minutes later, Collins and Rhodes parked behind Reece's office and took the elevator to the sixth floor. As the door opened it was obvious that not all was well. A heavy-set man wearing a gray pinstripe suit was holding a meeting in Reece's office, the largest room available. The room was packed, and the overspill extended into the reception area.

The man seemed to be coming to the end of his speech. 'As I've said, Mr Reece will be away from work for a period of four weeks. I'll be in temporary charge until his return.'

A rumble of surprise and doubt ran through the gathering and a middle-aged woman in the centre of the crowd started to ask a question.

Collins decided he did not have the time to wait for the meeting to end. Raising his voice, he said, 'My name is Detective Sergeant Collins. I need to speak to the gentleman talking, so I must ask you to return to your offices.' There was a murmur of discontent which Collins quickly silenced with a firm command of, 'Now, please. My business is urgent.'

The office emptied within forty seconds. Collins closed the door and asked the middle-aged man for his name.

Wiping the sweat from his brow he said, 'I'm Nelson Thurston, the Chief Accountant.'

'You must know everything that goes on here?' said Collins.

'If only. I've been here less than three months and I'm already looking for a new job, but when you're the wrong side of forty-five, it's not easy. Now the bastard has gone on holiday and left me in deep shit.'

'You're not a fan of Mr Reece?'

'God, no. I had no idea what I was getting myself into when I joined.'

'What do you mean?'

'That's it. I don't know. I just know that all he wanted me to do was pay the bills, advance him large amounts of cash whenever he demanded them, and draw up a set of accounts for the Inland Revenue and Companies House that would satisfy them.'

'Didn't you ever ask him what he used the money for?' asked Rhodes.

'Once. He told me he spent it on three things. Entertaining clients, promoting the business, and paying experts for their services.'

'Did he ever give you receipts or invoices for these services?' asked Collins.

'He did occasionally. Mostly it was just a memo signed by him. I'd be amazed if the Inland Revenue accepted them as genuine receipts. I've spent the last day and a half going through his files and I still have no idea or any record of what deals he's done or the conditions under which they were made.'

Collins looked at Nelson Thurston. He did not look like a career criminal. He was an overweight, middle-aged man who had been used by Reece to make his accounts look legitimate. As for any tax audit of his affairs, Collins was fairly certain that there had been audits and Mr Reece had managed to entertain, pay off or frighten Her Majesty's Inspectors of Taxes enough to ensure a clean bill of health every time.

Taking Thurston by the elbow, Collins said, 'It's Tuesday today. Tomorrow, you will talk to the firm's solicitors, bankers and accountants, after which you will call Superintendent Patterson, at the Fraud Squad, Steelhouse Lane. Tell him you have spoken to me and that you think Reece's entire business was built on a fraud and ask him to investigate. He's a decent man. He'll look after you. Any problems, ask him to give me a ring.' Collins took a sheet of paper from Reece's desk and wrote both his and Patterson's name and telephone numbers on it.

Thurston took the page, his hands and lower lip shaking in unison,' 'Thanks,' he said.

Outside, Rhodes asked, 'Are you sure we can trust him?'

'I don't know,' said Collins. 'But I do know that I can trust the Superintendent. I worked with him a few years ago. A great copper. I gave him a copy of John Simpson's audit report on Friday. With Thurston's help, Patterson will find every piece of shit that Reece was ever involved with and prosecute every politician, builder and lowlife who got anything from Reece.'

'Aren't you worried that you're making it easier for Boyle to take over the building industry in Birmingham?'

'Not really.'

'Why not?'

'Because you, me and Clarkee are going to take him down.'

Rhodes smiled and said nothing.

Thirty minutes later, Collins and Rhodes pulled onto the car park in front of Thorne's offices. A hand-painted sign on the front door read "Closed until further notice".

Next to it was a letter from Thorne's solicitor stating the same in formal terms.

The reception area was empty, and after ringing the bell three times Collins resorted to banging on the desk. In place of the attractive young woman who had been present on his first visit a man over six feet tall with dark Italian looks appeared from the workshop area. Looking at the two men, he said, 'What the fuck do you want? Can't you read? We're closed,' and started to walk away.

Collins nodded at Rhodes, who grabbed the man's shoulder and spun him round. The man was a pro and he had started his punch the moment Rhodes hand had touched him. But he was not quick enough. Rhodes left elbow blocked the punch and his right fist plunged deep into the man's solar plexus. He bent double as every drop of air in his lungs was expelled from his body. A much less ferocious punch hit him on the side of the face, and he collapsed onto the floor and curled up.

Neither Collins nor Rhodes moved to help him. After thirty seconds he sat up and leaned against the reception desk, still trying to fill his lungs with air. Another fifteen seconds passed before he asked, 'Who the fuck are you?'

'That's better,' said Collins and showed the man his warrant card. 'And what's your name?'

'Morgan. Richie Morgan.'

'And what do you do here?'

'I'm the foreman.'

'I see. And what are you doing today?'

'Thorne's solicitor came in this morning and said he had been told to sell the business.'

'Who told him to sell it?'

'He dain't say.'

'And what about the receptionist and other office staff, where are they?'

'The solicitor paid them two months' salary and told them they'd no longer be needed.'

'What about the books, who's got them?'

'Books?'

'Accounting books.'

'The solicitor.'

'OK. Do you have Thorne's address book?'

'Na. If it's still here, it will be in his desk.'

'One last question what's the name and address of Thorne's solicitor?'

'Carrington and Ridgeway, somewhere on Great Charles Street.'

'Well thank you for your co-operation, Mr Morgan. We'll just have a quick look for Mr Thorne's address book.'

Morgan didn't reply. He was too busy watching Rhodes and planning what he'd do to the ponce next time he saw him.

It was a disappointed Collins and Rhodes who returned to the lobby ten minutes later. Every piece of paper and record had been removed from Thorne's office. The safe's door was open, and a quick glance was all that was required to confirm that, it too, was empty.

At the front door Collins copied the solicitor's address into his notebook and walked slowly back to Rhodes' car.

'Where to now?' asked Rhodes, 'The solicitor's?'

'Not yet. I need to check them out. I've not heard of them before. I need to go back to the station and give Marie a call.'

'Why not call in and see her on the way back?'

'Because that sack of potatoes Chief Inspector West will be monitoring every person she sees.'

'What I don't understand is why Reece has gone on the run.'

'I don't think Reece is running. He's trying to find out who's coming after him and Thorne and kill them before they can attack again.'

## Handsworth, 18.24hrs

The afternoon had been spent digging up information on Thorne's solicitors, and Collins was only too glad when his wristwatch showed twenty-five past six and he went in search of those who would accompany him on the arrest of June Gregg and Andy Dewar.

Collins, Rhodes, Jameson and PC Brown, the young constable who had seen the boy and girl the previous night, pulled up two hundred yards from the house June Gregg lived in. Rhodes and Jameson got out, walked to the back of the building and waited.

Five minutes later Collins knocked on June's front door which was opened by a middle-aged woman.

'Mrs Gregg?'

'Yes.'

Holding his warrant card up, Collins said, 'I'm DS Collins, I'd like to speak to your daughter June, please.'

'What about?' she asked her voice unsteady.

'I just need to speak to her.'

'Well you'd better come in.' Both men stepped into a short hallway and were directed to the front parlour. Collins heard a back door slamming shut, followed by the sound of high heels on the hall's tiled floor. As soon as June entered, PC Brown lent over and whispered, 'That's her, Sergeant.'

'You sure?'

'Positive.'

'Miss June Gregg, I am arresting you under Section (1) (a) of the Protection of Animals Act 1911 for cruelty to animals, namely four kittens, two puppies and one rabbit and for their killing. You do not have to say anything ...'

'What! You can't? I ain't done anything.'

'I can and I am,' said Collins, and spinning the young women around, he took her by the arm and led her past her crying mother in the hall and out to the car. Tears had formed in June's eyes, but she fought hard to stop them falling.

The door that had slammed shut five minutes earlier had been the Greggs' kitchen door as Andy made a run for it. He pulled the back gate open and immediately ran into a fist in the face from DCI Jameson. His eyes went blank and he stumbled two steps backwards before he collapsed onto the floor. Rhodes and Jameson lifted him up, pushed his arms up his back and led him down the alley and back to the waiting police car.

At the station Gregg was locked in the cells while Dewar was put in Interview Room 1 and the police doctor was called. Collins thanked DCI Jameson and PC Brown for their help and asked them to write up their arrest reports and send him a copy within the next twenty-four hours. Rhodes and Collins then headed for the canteen and an appointment with a late dinner.

It was nearly eight before Collins had Gregg taken from the cells by WPC Coates and brought to Interview Room 2, where her mother and father were sitting. When Collins saw her, he was surprised. She didn't seem afraid or scared. She looked sullen and angry. She sat sideways in the chair and refused to look directly at Collins. 'Do you know why you are here?' Collins asked.

'No. I ain't done anything illegal.'

'Cruelty to animals is illegal.'

'I've never hurt any animals, and you can't prove that I have.'

'We have an eyewitness who saw you and your boyfriend nailing a small puppy to a back garden gate.'

'You mean some old biddy who's half-blind.'

'No. I mean a young Constable who has excellent eyesight.'

'Well he's lying if he said that I were nailing the puppy to the gate. 'Cos I wasn't.'

'You may not have, but what about your boyfriend? Did he hurt them and let you watch?'

'No. Andy's not like that.'

'So, what is he like?'

'He's kind and gentle. He wouldn't hurt a fly.'

'Well he's been telling me that it's you who always suggests going out and finding some defenceless little animal to torture and kill,' lied Collins.

'Now I know you're lying. Andy would never say that. He's told me all about how the coppers frame people for things they haven't done.'

'And you believe him?'

'Course I do. He knows what he's talking about.'

'OK,' said Collins, 'you will spend the night here and tomorrow morning be taken to a Special Magistrates Court. Where you will face charges of cruelty to animals, along with your boyfriend.'

Twenty-five minutes later Dewar was brought into the interview room by a constable who Collins didn't know. Andy Dewar smiled when he saw Collins, and flicking his head, cleared his fringe from his eyes. A middle-aged women accompanied him into the room. Collins correctly guessed that she was Dewar's mother.

Collins was confident that Dewar would be found guilty. He'd seen his likes before. Overconfident, arrogant young men who thought they knew it all. Court appearances seldom went well for such people.

'You will be held in custody overnight and appear in a special magistrates' court tomorrow, for the torture and killing of various small animals. If found guilty you will probably be sent to an approved school where you can be kept for training until you reach the age of twenty-one.

'That's a load of bollocks. I love animals, I do. I'd never hurt any animal.'

'That's not what your girlfriend told me. She said you had a thing about torturing and killing young animals. It turned you on.'

'No, she dain't.'

'And why are you so sure she didn't?'

Looking at Collins straight in the eye he said, 'A, because she loves me and even if I had done what you say she would never shop me, and B, I dain't do it. You've got the wrong man, so you have.'

'Well I'm certain we've got the right man, and so is the eye-witness who will identify you in court in the morning.'

## Wednesday 9th October 1968

### Liverpool, 07.02hrs

James Charlton and his two eldest sons, Mark and Peter, climbed into the grey 3.5 Rover and started out on their eighty-mile journey to north Birmingham. They took the A-roads, ignored the recently built sections of the M6 and kept within every speed limit. Peter, the younger of the two sons, sat in the back and looked out of the rear window. After half an hour he said, 'There's no one following us, Dad.'

'OK, keep looking.'

Four hundred yards behind the car, a Vauxhall Viva driven by a middle-aged man continued to follow the Rover. Beside him his younger companion stared at a small screen which showed the Rover as a black dot. 'Where do you think they are going?' asked the younger man.

'My guess is Birmingham. I'll give them another hour and then call in their position to Central.'

### Warwick, 07.50hrs

Reece put the phone down and walked into the kitchen where Thorne was standing by the cooker, flipping an egg over. Looking over his shoulder, Thorne asked, 'Well did your snout manage to find out who tried to take me out.'

'The fucking IRA, that's who.'

'I thought those bleeders had disbanded or were dead.'

'Not yet. It seems that it was Cunningham's best mate Declan Boyle who set him up for the kill. The same Declan Boyle is a bigwig in the IRA. It seems Boyle turned up the night of the accident to offer the distraught wife all the help and support she needed in her hour of need,' said Reece, and flopped into one of six chairs around the large kitchen table.

'What's he after?'

'They think he's after Cunningham's business,' said Reece.

'Why would the IRA want his business and why come after me?'

'Bloody hell Chris, don't you ever listen to the news? Northern Ireland is primed to explode. Once that happens, the IRA will want some place to hide its men who are wanted by the police. What better place than among all the Paddies working on the roads and building sites of Brum?'

'What do you want to do?' asked Thorne.

'Simple, kill the bastards, especially Declan Boyle. Call the boys to a meeting. We'll use the house in Erdington. No Irish cunt is going to try and kill you and threaten me without paying a heavy price.'

## Hall Green, 08.03hrs

Declan Boyle sat on the bed and pulled on a pair of clean socks, slipped on his shoes, and looked at the door. He was feeling impatient, but he looked calm and composed. Within a couple of minutes he heard a woman's heels in the corridor. They stopped, and a small white envelope was pushed under the door. Then he heard the woman walk away.

Rising, he went to the door and picked up the envelope. Ripping it open, he read the short message. He pushed the note and envelope into his coat pocket, left the room and headed for his car.

As he pulled away Boyle immediately noticed the tail. 'So, you're playing games are yea?' he muttered under his breath and started to look for the real tail. He was almost in Birmingham when he spotted the red Ford Escort a hundred yards back. He slowed down and let the Ford come closer. A quick look in the rear-view mirror was all he needed to confirm that the two men in the car were MI5 agents. Pulling a small notebook from his pocket, he scribbled down the registration and headed for St Chad's Cathedral.

He parked outside the Gunmaker's Arms on Bath Street. There was no sign of the red Ford, but he knew they were nearby. The Queensway was busy as usual, and he could smell the stench of petrol as he walked to the Cathedral. Looking to his right as he entered the church, he saw the two agents nearly ninety yards behind him. A smile tugged at his lips.

Stepping into the empty church, he trotted silently down the side aisle. At the communion rail he turned left and exited the building through a side door marked "Fire Exit". Closing the door, he ran down the steps and jumped into a black Jaguar E-Type, pushed the seat as far back as it would go and hunkered down. The car accelerated away and two minutes later the familiar voice of Ronny Charlton said, 'You're all right Declan, we're clear. No one is following us.'

'Thank God for that. Where's the meeting?'

'At the farm. Dad and me brothers will be there.'

## Handsworth, 09.17hrs

Clark slid into the canteen seat opposite Collins and added one large spoonful of sugar to his dark coloured tea before asking, 'Anything happen last night?'

'What are you doing here?'

'Office duties. Answer me question.'

'We picked up June Gregg and lover boy. The RSPCA will be prosecuting the case today.'

'Good, let's hope they get what's coming to them. Yow've not had any info on the whereabouts of Reece?'

'Not so much as a passing rumour.'

'What are wi going to do?'

'See what Ridley has for us and wait. I hate waiting.'

'Yow should know by now that policing is 98% waiting and the other 2% are periods of bum puckering bloody terror. Something will drop in our lap.'

'I'll bow to your vast experience, O Ancient One.'

'Not so much of the Ancient One.'

Back in the office, Collins' phone started to ring just as he opened the door. Picking it up he heard Rhodes' familiar tones, 'Mickey?'

'Yes.'

'I've got some bad news, Boyle has disappeared. He left the hotel this morning. Drove to St Chad's Cathedral and before our men had got inside, he'd vanished.'

'Sod it. Do you think he made the second team?'

'I think we should assume that he did. He just disappeared into thin air.'

'OK. Thanks for letting me know.' Checking his watch, Collins realised that he was cutting it close if he was to make the court in time to give evidence. 'Make yourself useful Clarkee and give me a lift to the Magistrate's Court, will you?'

'OK but only because yow asked so nicely. That, and it will be a pleasure to see Romeo and Juliet sent down. Well, stop dawdling then. Grab yowr coat. I want to see the bastards responsible.'

## Elm Farm, 10.07hrs

Ronny Charlton turned off the A38 just after the sign for Minworth. Changing down through the gears, he drove slowly up the twisting farm track. The grass on both verges was over two-foot-high and the fields hadn't been planted with any crop for three years. After five minutes the road opened out into a concrete area on which had been built a four-bedroom farmhouse, a barn, a milking shed and a couple of smaller buildings. As with the fields, the yard looked in need of maintenance, with weeds growing freely outside the house and other buildings.

Charlton drove towards the barn and the doors swung open. Rolling the windows down, he shouted a welcome to his father and brothers. Climbing out of the Jaguar, Ronny was enveloped in a powerful bear hug from his father, and handshakes from his brothers.

Boyle hung back, waiting for the family reunion to end. When the welcome abated, he held out his hand to Jimmy who took it and pulled the younger man into a warm embrace. 'My God, Declan you're looking fine. How are you?'

'I'm fine, Jimmy. But I'd kill for a drink.'

'Get the man a drink. You'll find the whiskey in the boot.'

John Charlton followed his father's order and took five glasses from the Rover's boot before returning with a full bottle of Powers Gold Label. With glasses full Jimmy Charlton raised his glass and said, 'To Ireland and a free North.'

After five minutes of catching up on family affairs, Boyle finally asked, 'You've got the goods?'

'That we have, Declan. The stuff is already loaded on the truck. All I need is a time and place to deliver it to.'

A broad smile spread across Boyle's face. 'No problems then?'

'None.'

'I was worried about that Yank. But by God, he came through for us.'

'That he did.'

'OK. We stick to the original plan. Bring the stuff to the farm tonight and then if everything is still OK, you can deliver it to Martin's yard tomorrow night at ten.'

'Will do. How is Martin? I heard he's in a coma?'

'He's going to be fine. He woke up last Saturday. He's still in hospital so he's got a perfect alibi if things turn tits up.'

'Grand.'

## Handsworth, 14.07hrs

Collins was feeling good as he sat down to his lunch in the canteen. The magistrates had shown little interest in the cock and bull story that Dewar had spewed out, and sentenced him to twelve months in an approved school. Gregg had received a six-month sentence in an approved school.

'Well, yow might be happy with the sentences given out, but I'm willing to bet a fiver to a brass penny that if they stay on our patch, we'll be seeing them again and soon.'

Before Collins could respond, Ridley slipped into the seat beside Clark and said, 'Just the pair I wanted to see.'

'What for?' asked Collins fearing it was another police ball where Agnes would pull him onto the floor at every opportunity.'

'The Force's Quiz Night. Central have won it for the past three years and I reckon it's time we stuffed them.'

'Well, yow should have asked me sooner,' said Clark.

'I ain't interested in you two monkeys. I want the organ grinder Mrs Winters on the team. I reckon she knows more than the two of you put together. You two are the price I pay for getting me star.'

'Well me and the Mrs are in, said Clarkee.'

'Seeing as you asked so nicely, I'll ask Agnes. When's it on?'

'Saturday, October twelfth. A three-course meal is thrown in, so the entry fee is £8 for two.'

'Bloody hell, yow dain't give us much notice. Where's it being held?' asked Clark.

'Botanical Gardens, seven thirty kick off.'

The phone was ringing when Collins and Clark opened the CID door. Picking it up, Collins didn't have time to say anything before Rhodes asked, 'Mickey?'

'Yes.'

'I have to be quick. Two of our men in Liverpool followed James Charlton, father of Ronny Charlton, to a farm near

Birmingham this morning where he and his two sons met Ronny and Boyle.'

'Bloody hell.'

'Exactly what I thought. They followed Charlton and Boyle back to Birmingham. I've put four men on Charlton and a new team on Boyle.'

'Where did Boyle go?'

'To the hospital, where he spent half an hour talking to Martin Cunningham. Then he went back to his hotel.'

'OK. We need to watch him like a hawk.'

## Handsworth, 15.17hrs

Collins was at home when the phone rang. As he crossed the hall, Sheba stood in the kitchen doorway, tail wagging slowly. Collins picked up the phone, and before he could recite his number, he heard Steve Rhodes' familiar voice. 'Mickey, I've just got a message from our man at the farm. A truck just pulled up on the farm and within a couple of minutes it disappeared into the barn.'

Collins immediately recognised the potential importance of the information. The truck might be carrying the weapons Boyle had bought but they could just be building supplies. 'Did your man get a look at what the lorry is carrying?'

'No but he's going to slip in when the house quietens down.'

'Good. Let me know what he finds, no matter how late it is. I'll call Hicks, and make sure the Superintendent and the ACC know as well. If it is the guns, we'll need to meet to discuss what we're going to do.'

OK. You brief your people and let's provisionally agree that we'll meet at the station as soon as we know what's in the truck.'

'OK.'

The first call Collins made was to Clark, followed by Hicks, the Superintendent and ACC.

## Erdington, 18.47hrs

A smog of blue-grey cigarette smoke hung in the air. The room was full, with fourteen men standing and sitting around. All conversations were conducted in low voices while they waited for the Boss to arrive. Most of the men present were interested in seeing the new man whom Thorne had called in for the first time. Rumour had it that he was a vicious bastard who'd had been a trigger man for the Krays in London before he skipped out of Britain when the brothers were arrested.

The room fell silent as Reece's Jaguar pulled up on the gravel drive outside. Seconds later Reece, Thorne and a slim man of medium height with a bland, vacant, expressionless face entered the room. 'OK, lads,' said Thorne, 'grab a seat. You all know Mr Reece. The other gent is Mark. The reason we're all here is to plan how we take out Cunningham, Charlton, and his mates

'Why are we going after Cunningham?' asked a tall skinny man near the back of the room. 'I mean, they ain't never given us any trouble.'

'Until now. It was that lousy bastard that tried to kill me last week. That's why Mr Reece and me had to go into hiding while we found out who the hell were after us,' said Thorne.

'What the fuck is going on?' asked a small plump man near the front.

'As near as we can find out, Cunningham's accident was meant to keep him clear of what was going to happen. Ronny's boys were driving the car, but it went wrong, and Cunningham was left in a coma.'

'OK. I don't mind having a run in with Ronny's lads, but what about Cunningham's guys? Who the fuck are they and where the fuck do we find them'

'They are ex-IRA.' A murmur of disquiet ran through the group. Thorne ignored it and continued, 'I don't know where they are at the moment, but I know where they'll be tomorrow night at nine,' said Thorne and smiled.

## Thursday 10th October 1968

### Elm Farm, 02.33hrs

The two MI5 agents were cold, tired, hungry, and wet from the frequent light showers. The elder of the two, a chubby, red-faced man who looked more like a grocer than a spy, said, 'It's been an hour since the lights went out, so if they aren't asleep by now, then they must be a nervous lot. Come on, let's go take a shufti at what's in that lorry.'

His young partner nodded in agreement and they quickly walked the hundred or so yards to the barn. Staying in the shadows, they circled the barn checking doors and windows. All were locked tight. 'OK. I'll pick the lock on the back door.'

Less than a minute later the two men were standing in the barn beside the brown, two-ton Leyland lorry of the type used to carry metal and other heavy loads, registration EKG 601. Its flat back was covered by a dirty grey tarpaulin tied down securely by one-inch hemp rope. After finding where the rope had first been tied, the younger man undid the knot and pulled up a three-foot length of tarpaulin. Inside was a wooden box measuring two feet by three, with one of its planks already loose. Hitting it twice with the heel of his hand, the younger man raised the plank high enough to slip his hand into the box. At first all he felt were wooden packing shavings. Digging deeper, his fingers touched something round and metal, and he. worked his hand under it to lift it out. "It" was an US Army Mk 2 "pineapple" grenade and it looked brand new.

Holding it up, the older man nodded and said, 'Put it back and tie down the tarp while I go and have a look in the cab.' The cab was dirty and smelt of body odour. Several old newspapers, a rolled up chip paper and numerous wrappers from a wide variety of chocolate bars covered the cabin's floor.

Fortunately, an A to Z road map of Great Britain was in the door compartment, along with a list of roads starting in Liverpool and ending in Sheldon. The man smiled and made a note of the final road on the list.

Twelve minutes later both men were back in their car, and driving to the nearest telephone box. The older agent jumped out of the car and ran to the red box outside a closed fish and chip shop. He'd been in MI5 since he left the army in 1946, but this was the biggest find of his career. He quickly dialled Rhode's number, and as soon as the phone was answered he said, 'It's weapons and I know where they're headed.'

## Handsworth, 03.07hrs

Collins slept on the sofa in the lounge with the door open. The second ring of the phone woke him and the third had him jumping to his feet and running into the hall. 'Steve?' he asked.

'Yes. It's the whole bloody shipment.'

'You're sure?'

'As sure as the Mk 2 grenade that my men found.'

'Bloody hell.'

'Listen, do you know of any place in Sheldon, they might be delivering the load to?'

'Cunningham's yard is in Sheldon.'

'Well they'll be there at nine tonight. It will take Sir Aubrey three hours to get here, so let's meet at seven.'

'Fine.'

## Handsworth, 07.20hrs

Sir Aubrey and Rhodes arrived eighteen minutes late for the meeting. 'Sorry for our tardiness,' said Sir Aubrey, looking at his watch. 'An oil tanker turned over on the motorway. We were one of the first cars to be allowed through after they closed two lanes.'

'Well we're all here now, so let's make a start,' said ACC Knowles. 'To summarise what we know; the lorry at Elm Farm is carrying munitions, and they will be delivered to an address in Sheldon tonight between nine and ten. An address which we believe to be Cunningham's storage yard.'

'Do we have a plan of this builder's yard and surrounding area?' asked Sir Aubrey.

'Not yet, but we'll have one of the entire area by ten. DC Clark is at the planning department,' said Collins

'OK, then,' said the Superintendent, 'we should do some preliminary planning prior to Clark arriving.'

There was a murmur of agreement and for the next two hours various options were discussed, and most rejected. The biggest dispute arose over whether to involve the military in the operation or not. Despite his instructions to Collins and Clark that in matters of national security the police would follow MI5's lead, the ACC argued strongly against involving the military. However, Sir Aubrey wasn't to be budged. After nearly half an hour on the subject he finally said in exasperation, 'Look, we're not dealing with a criminal gang. This is the bloody IRA and they have a truck load of weapons and munitions at their disposal. We don't have the firepower to take them on by ourselves. We have to involve the Army.'

'All right, but can you keep the numbers down? I don't want a complete bloody platoon trying to hide in a confined area. They're bound to be spotted and we'll end up with the same bloody firefight you're trying to avoid,' said the ACC.

'This is not the first time I've been involved in something like this,' snapped Sir Aubrey. 'There will be no more than eight Army personnel on the mission, and they will be invisible. That I guarantee.'

'OK. You'd best get it organised then. Superintendent, can

you find a private room for Sir Aubrey to make his phone calls?'

'Yes, Sir. Collins, can you take Sir Aubrey to the CID office and clear the switchboard of personnel except for Sergeant Ridley?'

'Yes, Sir.'

Collins escorted Sir Aubrey to the CID room without saying a word, then went to clear the telephone exchange of everyone but Ridley. Ridley didn't argue with Collins. He knew that a meeting was going on and even if he didn't know the details, he knew it was important.

Returning to the CID room, Collins nodded at Sir Aubrey and said, 'All clear.'

The Deputy Head of MI5 made two calls. The first was to the Home Secretary, which lasted five minutes. The second was to an army base in Hereford which lasted a good deal longer.

By the time Collins and Sir Aubrey returned to the Superintendent's Office it was 9.40 and a break was called until Clark arrived with the plans.

When Clark arrived a little before ten, he was carrying a large sheaf of paper. Taking the plan from the top of the bundle he laid it out on the table. It showed Cunningham's yard and three substantial buildings within the compound.

He explained, 'This large building is used to store cement and other materials that could be damaged by rain. Next door to it is the delivery bay. I reckon that will be where the lorry will be unloaded, and the cargo carried through these doors into the storage room. All under cover. Across the yard this two-story block contains offices and a canteen. The rest of the yard is concreted over and part of is used as a car park. The rest is a storage area for all the regular building materials.'

'It looks pretty bare at the front of the yard. No cover there for us to get in without being seen,' said Rhodes.

'True enough,' said Clark with a smile. 'But the yard backs onto open land at the rear. An old bomb peck. Stored at the back is gravel, sand and timber. That's our way in,' said Clark with a smile.

'Not quite, Constable Clark. That will be the way in for six of the SAS men I've obtained for tonight's mission. The other two will remain outside the main gates acting as reserves and guards,' said Sir Aubrey.

'Well, thanks for telling me.'

'Sorry, but things have been moving fast this morning. What other buildings are there adjoining the yard or directly across the road from it?' asked Sir Aubrey.

'Directly opposite the main gate is this six-story office block,' said Clark and laid a second plan on the table. 'I reckon yow can see the entire yard, even the back wall, from the fourth or fifth floor.'

'Good,' said Sir Aubrey, we'll use that building as our HQ.' Looking at his watch he continued. 'It's now ten thirty-six. I suggest that we reconvene our meeting when the SAS arrive.'

## Handsworth, 11.07hrs

Back in the CID Room, neither Collins nor Clark found it easy to concentrate on anything but the night's raid. Collins read through the reports that had come in overnight and Clark jotted down how he thought the raid should be handled. Not that anyone was going to ask for his opinion. After all, he was only the most experienced man in the building on such matters.

A little before twelve Collins phone rang and Ridley said, 'Mickey you've got a visitor, Superintendent Patterson.'

'What the hell is he doing here?' Can you bring him around please?'

'No problem.'

Three minutes later Patterson and his latest bagman arrived. The new man was introduced as Joseph Penn, short and built like a middleweight, with dark brown hair, a broad nose, and a dimple in his chin.

'Do you want to grab lunch before we start or get stuck into it?' asked Collins.

'Let's get it done. From the look of all the Special Branch bods that are sitting around doing nothing you've got something big on.'

Collins smiled at Patterson, 'You're not wrong there, Sir.'

'Well, I just wanted to tell you I've now got a team of sixteen on the case. But from the report alone there is clear evidence of funds being dispersed to Robbins and Hill from the Golden Fashion Agency.'

'Well, they own it.'

'Yes, they do but there is also evidence that much of its profit is derived from prostitution. Therefore, they can be charged with living off immoral earnings. There are also numerous large payments made to them by Reece. But we'll need additional time to confirm this. There is also clear evidence that Reece used blackmail, threats of force, actual force, and bribery to obtain a number of contracts.'

'Did you find anything on Charlton?' asked Collins.

'Nothing significant. He seems to be clean, as does Cunningham. No, the corruption seems to centre on Reece, his mate Thorne, and Councillors Hill and Robbins. But I've only gone through the file once and there are a number of Council documents that I need to see. I'm certain that many more names will come tumbling out of the woodwork once we dig into the Council's records and interviewing whoever signed them. Four men on their own can't run a scheme as big as this one without a load of help. They'll have building managers, architects, surveyors, finance officers, solicitors and God knows who else on the payroll.

'One thing is for sure though, that auditor John Simpson

was a brave lad. Not many accountants would have kept digging like he did. Most of them would have done what the Chief Auditor Hastings did and cover up the whole bloody mess. It's a bloody shame the lad is dead,' said Patterson and paused before continuing 'I'll need to speak to Reece and Thorne.'

'Good luck with that,' said Clark. 'They disappeared over a week ago and we ain't been able to find them.'

'Did they get wind of your investigation?'

'Oh yeah. But it ain't us that scared them shitless. It were the IRA's appearance on the scene,' said Clark.

'Bloody hell. Is that what all the security bods are doing here?'

'Yep.'

## Handsworth, 15.13hrs

Nine men wearing black overalls climbed out of two specially adapted Land Rovers and started to unpack their gear from the rear of each vehicle in near silence. When this was complete, they ignored the front door of the police station and instead walked through the car park and into the station yard.

A new probationary constable seeing them thought they looked like trouble, and moved between them and the rear door. 'Can I help you lads?' he asked. His voice betrayed none of the nervousness he felt.

'You could show us the way to the Superintendent's office,' said a small man at the back of the group. His accent was middle England and very upper-class. The young copper relaxed.

'Of course. Follow me.'

As they walked past the canteen the small man stopped and said, 'OK lads, go and get a bite to eat and I'll join you after I've spoken to the Superintendent.'

Outside the Superintendents' office the young constable knocked on the door, waited for the instruction to come in and opened the door, 'You have a gentleman to see you Sir.'

'What gentleman? What's his bloody name?'

Stepping into the room the small man came to attention saluted and said, 'I'm with the Army, Sir. I understand you have a problem.'

The meeting with the SAS captain, MI5 and the police started at four fifteen, which gave everyone time to get some food inside them. The plan previously devised was basically sound and only a few minor changes were made to it. When the meeting finally broke up, Clark was found chatting to the eight men who had arrived with the Captain.

At twenty to seven five vehicles left Thornhill Road Station. The lead vehicle was driven by Collins and carried the senior police officers, ACC Knowles, Superintendent Thatcher, and Inspector Hicks. The second car was driven by Clark, and housed Sir Aubrey, the SAS captain and Rhodes. The two Land Rovers followed next and a vanload of twelve MI5 operatives tailed behind. Everyone knew their part in the plan but, as Clark and the SAS men knew only too well, once the shooting started, any plan would quickly become obsolete.

Once in Sheldon the two Land Rovers peeled off and headed for the back of Cunningham's compound. The van carrying the twelve MI5 agents parked near the entrance to the cul-de-sac, that wea Wagner's Road, ready to cut it off once the shooting started. The two unmarked police cars drove up to the six-story building opposite Cunningham's yard, and parked at the rear.

## Sheldon, 20.00hrs

At eight o'clock the two drivers boarded their lorry and slowly drove down the farm's dirt road to the exit. Every move they made was watched by a team of four MI5 agents. When they emerged from the farm track and turned right, the older agent contacted Rhodes by telephone and confirmed that the lorry was on its way.

'Good. Keep me informed of their movements every twenty minutes please.'

'Will do, sir.'

'They are on their way,' said Rhodes to those assembled on the fourth floor of the office block.

'Good,' said ACC Knowles.

'Is it all right, Sir, if Mickey and me head up to the sixth floor?' Clark asked the ACC.

'Yes, carry on.'

Collins and Clark were joined by Rhodes and they quickly picked up their kit and headed for the top floor. All three men were disappointed that they would have no part in the shooting match that they fully expected to start once the lorry arrived. However, they would have ringside seats to the action.

Looking down from their eyrie, the men took stock of the yard. Parked in front of the main offices were a grey 3.5 Rover, a black Jaguar E-Type and a dark Ford Zodiac. From the telephone messages received by Rhodes that meant that the Charltons and Boyle were on site.

At five to nine a flatbed lorry turned into Wagner's Road and drove slowly into Cunningham's yard.

'How long before the SAS start shooting?' asked Clark.

'The plan says they will wait until the lorry is inside the unloading dock, and then give them fifteen minutes to get the stuff off. If all goes to plan the whole op should be over within ten minutes of the first shot being fired.'

Almost immediately, the unloading dock doors were opened, and the lorry drove slowly inside. Before the vehicle had stopped moving, the heavy wooden doors were closed, and the door bolts engaged.

Collins looked at his watch and waited for fifteen minutes to elapse. His concentration was broken when a red lorry turned into the road and accelerated. It slowed only slightly before it swung into the wire and steel gates of Cunningham's compound.

'Who the bloody hell is that?' shouted Collins. He didn't have long to wait, as the truck came to a shuddering stop outside the loading bay and fourteen heavily armed men quickly disembarked from the rear. When the driver jumped out of the cab, Collins immediately recognised him as Christopher Thorne. Reaching back into the cab, Thorne took down two lengths of piping, each about thirty inches long, and snapped them together. 'What the hell is that? Collins asked.

'That, mate, is a bloody bazooka,' replied Clark.

Kneeling, Thorne lifted the tube onto his shoulder and Nugent loaded a rocket into the tube. Thorne pulled the trigger. At such close range the shell smashed through the wooden doors and exploded with an ear-bursting noise.

Collins was transfixed. He'd never experienced such a huge explosion as the rocket smashed through the wooden doors. Rhodes pulled him down an instant before the second explosion went off and the windows beside which he had been standing shattered into ten thousand pieces and covered him in glass.

If the first explosion had been huge, the second was like an earthquake. The building rocked from side to side. Doors were sent flying over the newly arrived lorry and across the compound, and the asbestos roof soared seventy feet into the air. Flames leaped from every window and door in the building. The explosions were quickly followed by the sound of individual grenades and packs of explosives exploding and bullets going off.

Collins looked at Clarkee who was shouting, but he couldn't hear what he was saying and lifting up his hands, he pointed at his ears. Clark knew what was wrong, pinched his nose and blew hard. Collins immediately followed suit, heard a loud pop in his ears and was able to hear Clark shouting, 'Who the fuck was in the lorry?'

'It was Thorne and a dozen or more men,' shouted Collins. Standing up, all three men looked at the devastation that the two explosions had caused. The goods inward warehouse was now nothing but a hole in the ground. No piece of the building larger than a yard in length remained. The lorry that Thorne and his heavies had arrived in was a smouldering mess of misshapen metal, and all thirteen men had been blown into pieces. Collins was able to spot arms, legs, torsos and heads in the flames that still burned in the receiving bays.

The dry goods warehouse next to the receiving bay had lost an entire wall and the roof was groaning and shifting. As Collins watched the roof collapsed, sending a cloud of dust into the air.

The administration building had lost every pane of glass and part of its roof. The front doors to the building had been blown into the lobby and lay on the floor. Pieces of metal were imbedded in the brickwork. Blood, patches of skin and shards of bone were smeared across the frontage. The three cars parked outside were just a jumble of scrap metal. The whole scene looked like something only H.P. Lovecraft could have envisaged.

## Friday 11th October 1968

### Sheldon, 01.46hrs

None of the SAS troops had been killed or injured. When they left at midnight, to head back to Hereford, they were still grumbling that they had not seen any action. Collins had spent the evening on site. No living person had been discovered on the entire compound and no body part bigger than a torso had been discovered.

Clark parked his car and walked the last six hundred yards to the compound. He'd been ordered by Chief inspector Hicks to go home, as he was still officially only on "sick duties", but he'd picked up his car and was now looking for Collins. Clark pushed his way past the press and TV cameras ,and kept walking and a minute later turned into what remained of Martin Cunningham's yard.

Collins saw him and trotted over. 'How you feeling?'

'I'm bosting,' said Clark, 'but yow look like something nasty that the cat dragged in. 'Have yow been able to identify the bodies?'

'Only the Charltons. All four of them were in the office at the rear of the building when the second explosion went off. The office collapsed and killed them all.'

'Have yow confirmed that Boyle were among the dead?'

'No. But his car was here so I think we can assume that the explosions or the fire did for him.'

'Well I just heard that Martin Cunningham were released from hospital yesterday. Fancy going to see him?'

'Why not?' Then, looking at his watch, 'Let's leave it until this afternoon. I'm knackered. I'm going home.'

## Handsworth, 11.03hrs

Collins came awake at three minutes past eleven and threw back the bedclothes.

He'd slept for seven hours without interruption and felt alive and ready to face the day.

A quick hot shower and a shave took ten minutes and he returned to his bedroom and dressed. When he walked into the kitchen Sheba rushed to greet him and Agnes smiled as he sat down in front of a full English breakfast. 'What time did you get in?' asked Agnes.

'About three.'

'Was it as bad as it looked on the TV?'

'The damage certainly was but there were no troops or police in the compound when it exploded. So, no casualties on our side.'

'But why such a big explosion?'

'Thorne fired a bazooka into the receiving bay doors. That would have been highly effective in normal circumstances, but what he didn't know was that there was a truckload of armaments and explosives inside. The resultant explosion killed everyone in the building plus Thorne and all his men.'

'Was Boyle among the casualties?'

Collins waited for a couple of seconds before he replied. 'I hope so, me darling, but there was no body. Clarkee and me are going to assume he got away.'

'Keep looking until you find proof one way or the other. If he's alive he'll come after you with everything he's got.'

Wrapping his arm around Agnes's waist, Collins replied, 'Sure, that's exactly what Clarkee said. But I doubt he's in any state to start trouble any time soon. Which means that you and I can go to the quiz tomorrow night without any worries.'

'What are you going to do today?'

'Clarkee and me are going to see Martin Cunningham.'

## Solihull, 13.48hrs

Collins rang the bell and waited. Yolande answered the door wearing a housecoat, her face serious. 'Ah, it's yourselves. I was wondering if I'd see you today. I've been watching the news. Is the yard as badly damaged as the TV makes it look?'

'Worse, I'm afraid,' said Collins.

'Well come on in,' she said and stood aside.

'We won't be long. We just need to have a quick chat with Martin, if that's possible.'

'You can but he had nothing to do with bringing arms into our yard. I can't believe I was so stupid as not to keep an eye on what Boyle was doing. I always felt uneasy about the man. But he was Martin's friend, so I ignored my concerns and put up with him. I'll show ya where Martin is,' she said and led them up the stairs and to the back bedroom. 'Are ya decent, Martin? I have Sergeant Collins and his mate to see you.'

'Bring them in.'

'In you go. I'll make a cup of tea and bring it up to you.'

'Many thanks,' said Collins.

Clarkee said, 'I'll give yow a hand,' and followed Yolande down the stairs.

Martin Cunningham was sitting up in bed with a bandage covering the top of his head. His eyes had dark rings under them and the animal strength which had been so evident when Collins had first met him had gone. When he lifted his arm to greet his visitor, Collins was reminded of how old men moved – slow and uncertain.

'Thanks for seeing me. How are you feeling?'

'Not too bad. Just weak and tired all the time. The doctors said it could take six months for that to go.'

'I need to ask you a few questions about Declan Boyle and what happened earlier. Are you up to that?'

'You'll know soon enough. When I fall asleep in the middle of our conversation it's a sure sign I've had enough,' Martin said, and tried to smile.

'Did you know that Boyle was in the country before he visited you in hospital?'

'No. I can't say I did. I thought he'd flown over until Yolande told me he'd been in Manchester.'

'Did you know he was an IRA member?'

'Sure, everyone in the village knew he was that. But he was booted out eight or nine years ago, or so we all thought until last tonight.'

Yolande opened the door and Clark walked in carrying a tray of tea and thick cut brack. 'Tea's up,' he said with a grin and placed the tray on the bedside cabinet.

'He never indicated to you that he was still active in the IRA?'

'No, by God. If I'd known, I'd have had nothing to do with the bastard.'

'Did you ever think it was him who arranged your accident?'

'Christ no. I've known him me whole life. No, it was Reece who did it, for sure.'

'Why do you say that?'

'Because he's a vicious, nasty bastard and probably thought I'd fingered him in your corruption investigation.'

'So straight revenge then?'

'Yeah. That and a warning to others,' said Martin with a yawn, his eye flickering open and shut.

Yolande stood up and said, 'I'm sorry, but he needs to sleep. You'll have to go.'

'That's all right. I hope you're feeling your old self soon,' said Collins and held out his hand. Martin took it but there was no pressure or strength in his grip.

As they walked down the stairs Yolande asked, 'Will you be working the whole weekend?'

It was Collins who replied.' Yeah, we will be working over the weekend but on Saturday night we're off to the Birmingham Police Quiz. Should be a good night. The Botanical Gardens always do a great meal.'

'Well I hope you enjoy yourselves. You deserve it.'

Walking back to the car, Clark asked, 'What do yow think?'

'If I was a respectable businessman who was doing something really dodgy and which could see me in jail for the rest of my life I might arrange to be run over by me mate. Two weeks in hospital would give me the perfect alibi.'

'That's just supposition. What did yow make of Martin?'

'Not once did he ask about Boyle. He wasn't interested in knowing if the man's body had been found or if he'd escaped from the explosion. And likewise, he didn't ask if Reece had been at the yard.'

'Yow mean he knows them are alive?'

'More than that. He's spoken with Boyle since the explosion. I'm sure of it,' said Collins.

'But how could Boyle have survived the explosion?'

'The Charltons' bodies were found in the back office. What if Boyle was lucky and had stepped out back to have a pee or make a cuppa? If he wasn't hit by a ton of bricks landing on his head, he could have climbed through the window and just walked away in all the confusion.

'I suppose that yow telling Yolande where wi'd be on Saturday was yowr way of getting Boyle to react and come after us while providing proof that Martin and Yolande were in on it all along?' said Clark.

'Yeah, if he does show up, we'll have the bastards. But I want one of your guns.'

'No problem. What are mates for?'

## Handsworth, 14.56hrs

The station was full of security service personnel and other people Collins didn't know. He slipped quietly away from the throng and found Clark and Hicks in the CID room.

'What time do yow call this, Sergeant?' demanded Clark.

'Three pm, Constable Clark. Why?'

'I was here an hour ago. What yow been doing?'

'Don't believe a word he says,' said Hicks. 'He got here about ten minutes before you.'

'Well what time did yow get here then, Sir?'

'I was here before ten this morning,' said Hicks with a grin and looked at both men to see if they would challenge him.

It was Clark who said under his breath, 'Lying sod.'

'What was that, Clark?'

'Just clearing me throat, Sir,' said Clark.

'Well, clear it on your way to the canteen, and get three teas and doughnuts,' said Hicks, holding a ten bob note in his hand.

'My pleasure, Sir,' said Clark.

The day continued in the same vein as it had started for Collins, Clark and Hicks. They had been on the periphery of events. What they had seen had been seen by everyone present and statements were taken only from the senior police officers present. At around half three Stephen St Clair Rhodes knocked and walked in. 'Just came to say goodbye. I'm off, back to London.'

Collins stood up and held out his hand, 'Thanks for all your help, Stephen. It's been a pleasure working with you.'

'He's never said it was a pleasure working with me,' said Clark, as he shook Stephen's hand.

'That's because it never has been.'

'Yow see what I have to put up with?'

'I'll pay for the tickets, if you'll take this pair with you to London,' said Hicks.

'No thanks, Sir. I don't think the security services would survive them.'

At four Hicks looked up from the report he was reading, checked his watch and said, 'Push off, lads. Nothing is going to happen today. I'll see you at the quiz tomorrow.'

Outside, Collins felt a cold shiver run down his spine and he stopped and said, 'Clarkee we need to go and see the Superintendent. Tell him that his hunch paid off. What do you say, we've got the time?'

Clark looked at his watch and finally said, 'OK.'

Mrs Wallace answered the door and it was obvious to both men that she had been crying. Collins said nothing but enfolded the small woman in a bear hug and said, 'I take it he's worse?'

'Yes. The doctor said he won't last the night.'

'I'm sorry to hear that,' said Clark, and following Collins' example, wrapped his arms around the grief-stricken woman. 'No-one could have done more for him than yow.'

Mrs Wallace dabbed her eyes with her hankie and waved them forward. 'Look who's come to see you, love. Sergeant Collins and Constable Clark.'

The Super's eyes came open and he blinked four or five times to focus on the two men. 'I was dreaming about you pair last night. I knew you'd ...' He started to cough, and he clutched his stomach with his right hand as the cramps grabbed hold of his gut. Mrs Wallace picked up a syringe but without a needle, filled with an opaque substance, and opening her husband's mouth, depressed the plunger and delivered a massive dose of opiates. Within seconds the drug began to work, and he relaxed back into the pillows.

'Sir, why don't you just lie there and relax. Me and Clarkee have one hell of a good story to tell you.'

'Yeah, yowr suspicions may have saved hundreds of lives,' said Clark.

For the next forty-five minutes Collins and Clark told the Superintendent of what had happened since their last visit on the tenth of September. When they had finished The Superintendent said nothing, nor did he smile, but his eyes were alive. He had always believed that there was corruption in Birmingham. Now, he knew that all the bastards who were responsible for it and still alive would pay for it. Scuppering the IRA'S plans was a bonus. They had lost a very valuable stock of weapons and explosives. He'd been right. He could die now. Finally he raised his head from the pillow and looking at Collins and Clark whispered, 'Thanks, lads.'

After Collins and Clark had left Mrs Wallace returned to her husband's makeshift bedroom and kissed his forehead. With what little strength he had left he said, 'Get the kids. It's time, love.'

Superintendent Wallace died that night at ten minutes past ten with his wife and three children by his bedside.

## Saturday 12th October 1968

### Edgbaston, 19.05hrs

'Does this look all right? It's not too young looking?' asked Agnes.

'Darling, you look gorgeous. I always like you in blue.'

'It's purple, not blue. A chimpanzee has a better colour sense than you.'

'The same chimp would tell you it's five past seven. We'll be late.'

'All right, then. Let's go.'

Collins' Capri was still at the compound while every ounce of evidence it contained was checked and double-checked. Agnes slipped into the driver's seat of her 3.5 Rover and Collins sat in the passenger seat. Agnes could drive as well as any man and better than most, but she was also a careful driver. The result was that she drove the whole distance to the Botanical Gardens in Edgbaston at three miles per hour over the speed limit. When they arrived, they found themselves joining a queue of cars blocking Westbourne Road for fifty yards. After a ten minute delay they were ushered into the car park and told in which bay to park by one of the Gardens' wardens. 'Just our luck. We're right at the end of the car park. It'll take us ages to get out tonight,' said Collins.

Once inside, they followed everyone else's example, dropped off their coats at the cloakroom and headed into the ballroom where nearly seventy tables were laid out for dinner. Clark and Ruth were already at their table and Clark rose as Agnes greeted him with a kiss on the cheek. 'I love your dress,' said Ruth. 'Did Michael choose it?'

Agnes looked at Collins and they both started to laugh. When they stopped Agnes told Ruth of their earlier exchange. Collins didn't fancy a fifteen minute discussion on men's poor style sense, and changed the subject. 'Where's the quiz going to take place?'

'Here,' said Clark. 'After dessert and during coffee. Then it's into the ballroom for a dance. I'll show you what a real rocker can do.'

'Have they got a band?'

'Nah. Just a DJ.'

The food was typical English fare, vegetable soup followed by roast beef, Yorkshire pudding and a choice of three vegetables. Although the menu looked uninspired, it had been cooked to perfection, and there were no complaints among the guests.

As the dinner plates were collected Sergeant Ridley made his way to the small stage at the end of the room and tapping the mike to check that it was working, said, 'Good evening, ladies and gentlemen. As many of you know, Chief Superintendent Wallace died last night after a long and brave struggle against cancer. We'll not see his like again. Would you all please stand for a minute's silence in memory of a great copper and an even better man.'

As everyone in the room stood up and bowed their heads. Collins looked at the crowd. Several of the women who had known the Superintendent and his wife well were crying, and many police officers' eyes were filled with tears.

After exactly one minute Ridley said, 'Thank you, ladies and gentlemen. Details of the Super's funeral will be sent to all stations when they are received. The Super always enjoyed a laugh and good food, so I'm certain he would want tonight's quiz to be a huge success. So, enjoy the rest of meal and remember that before we head into the dance we have the Birmingham City Police Quiz. For the last three years Steelhouse Lane have won the title of Quizmasters of Brum. But we may see new champions tonight.'

'No, you won't,' came the cry from the captain of the Steelhouse Lane Team, Chief Inspector West, his jowls bobbing up and down as he laughed at his own witticism.

'We'll have to wait and see,' said Ridley and continued, 'There are fifty questions each worth two points. Each table will submit just one answer on the piece of paper that you'll find ...'

The muffled sound of an explosion and the rattle of automatic gunfire drowned out whatever Ridley had to say. Clark was the first to react to the explosion and he rushed to the French windows. As he pushed them open, a hail of bullets ripped over his head and hit the chandelier, sending a shower of small shreds of crystal onto the heads and faces of guests below. Clark ducked down and ran to one of the large stone pots which were placed at the top of the steps. From there he was able to see that the bomb had destroyed a grey Rover at the end of the car park. Its bonnet and registration number had been blown fifty yards onto the grass outside the function room.

Retracing his steps, he shouted for quiet and slowly the noise died down. 'We're under attack by two, maybe three, heavily armed men. These men want Collins and me.'

'How do you know they're after you?' a voice from near the kitchen shouted.

'Because they just blew up the car Collins came in.'

Another voice asked, 'How do you know it's Collin's car?'

''Cos the number plate landed within ten feet of me.'

Hicks and Collins realised that Clark didn't want to spread panic among the crowd by mentioning the IRA, and it was Hicks who said, 'I suggest that all the women be escorted to the front exit. Officers will check if there is any sign of gunmen, and if not will lead the women out of the building and into the grounds of the Teachers' Training College over the road, then come back to help. Collins, Clark and I will deal with the shower outside. Now get going.'

Agnes looked at Collins and whispered, 'Its Boyle, isn't it?' Collins nodded yes. Agnes kissed Collins and said, 'Be careful.' Then taking Ruth by the elbow, she followed the crowd towards the exit.

The room emptied within ninety seconds, leaving just five people. Hicks, Collins, Clark, Inspector Archer, and Marie Bolding. Collins looked at Marie and said, 'You don't have to stay.'

'I know I don't, but I'm not letting some bastard try and kill my two favourite coppers, now am I?'

Another blast of machine gun fire raked across the restaurant, sending all five diving to the floor. Once the clip was empty there was a slight pause before a second automatic gun opened up.

'They're coming in,' said Clark. I've got two guns and a knife. Mickey and me will keep the guns. The rest of yow will have to find a weapon in the kitchen. So, get moving and stay down, for Christ's sake.'

All five scurried across the floor and into the kitchen. Four members of kitchen staff were hiding behind a large wooden table. Archer looked at them and shouted, 'Get the fuck out of here – now.' All four men ran out of the back door.

Hicks picked up a meat cleaver and a carving fork. Archer chose a rolling pin and a four-inch peeling knife. Marie picked up a large pot and stepped behind the door a second before it was pushed open and a balaclava-wearing man of medium build and height walked in. 'I've got them,' he shouted, and raising the sub-machine gun stepped into the room. As he did so Marie stepped from behind the door and hit him with the pot. There was a loud crack as the pot hit his skull, and he fell to the floor in a heap, blood pouring from a three-inch fracture to his skull.

Clark responded immediately, grabbing the machine gun from the man's hand and firing through the door. Collins grabbed the man's foot and dragged the body over to where he was crouching, leaving a six-inch wide blood smear on the granite floor. Quickly he searched the man's body and found two spare ammunition clips for the sub-machine gun, which he slid across the floor to Clark. The flick knife and a handful of pistol bullets he slipped into his jacket pocket. Only then did he check to see if the gun was fully loaded, and remove the safety catch. The revolver, that Clark had provided, he passed to Hicks.

'Well, you seem to be having all the luck tonight Collins. But it's about to run out for ya,' shouted Boyle as the door was kicked open and a grenade thrown in. Hicks and Archer both dived for cover behind the heavy wooden table. Collins threw himself on Marie, and Clark picked up the grenade and flung it through the kitchen window. The grenade blew up before it hit the ground, shattering every window in the kitchen.

Moments later two more men charged through the door firing from the hip. Clark was lying on the floor, about twelve feet away from them when he opened fire. Both men were thrown backwards as a barrage of bullets ripped their groins, stomachs and chest to shreds.

'Why don't you come in and finish us off, Boyle?' shouted Collins.

'Fuck you. You English-loving cunt. This isn't over.'

'Give me the gun,' said Collins. 'The bastard isn't getting away again.'

Clark slid the sub-machine gun and the two clips of ammunition across the floor and said, 'Leave your gun and ammo. I'll be right behind you.'

Collins picked up the sub-machine gun and opened the door slowly. No shots were fired. Flinging the door open, he ran for the French windows and as he did so he saw in the light of his burning car the tall skinny figure of Boyle running for the shrubbery area of the Gardens and the small ponds it contained. He set off at a near sprint trying to remember what lay beyond the boundaries of the Gardens. He thought that it was just sports grounds and playing fields, but he wasn't certain. If Boyle got into the sports grounds, he'd stand a very good chance of getting onto a road and finding a car he could steal or hijack. Collins increased his speed.

Running past the rock garden he saw Boyle head into the

shrubbery. Ten seconds later he followed. Then he stopped and listened. All he could hear was the sound of a large number of men shouting and mulling about near the car park. A smile crossed his face. Having got their wives and girlfriends to safety, they'd returned. He remembered what a Sergeant had said to the class during training. *If ever you're threatened by a gang, tell your Sergeant and you'll find out that we are the biggest gang in England.*

A shot rang out and Collins felt the air move as it missed his head by inches. Dropping to his knees behind a thick bush, he looked in the direction the shot had come from. It was off to his left. Boyle was heading for Cameron Path which ran along the boundary of the Gardens. He moved in the same direction. After about two minutes he heard the sound of a man moving quickly through the thick branches of the rhododendron bushes and saw the path just ten feet away. He made his way to the edge of the path and waited for Boyle to cross the road. One minute, two minutes, passed. *Has he already gone? No, he hasn't had time to cross without me seeing or hearing him.* It was then that he saw Boyle step from the tree line onto the path, still holding a gun.

Collins stepped onto the path and said, 'Hands up Boyle. I have a nice cosy cell waiting for you.'

Boyle dived for the grass verge and pulled the trigger of the sub-machine gun he was holding.

Collins threw himself onto the path and fired. But Boyle was rolling towards the bushes and Collins' shots missed their mark. Collins waited for a couple of seconds and only stood up when he heard Boyle running through the bushes and plants heading back towards the car park.

Clark saw Boyle sprinting up the hill followed by Collins thirty yards behind. Both men were shooting wildly. Clark shouted to the hundred plus police officers, 'Shut the fuck up and hide behind the cars. Don't let Boyle know we're here.'

The men did as they were told and silently took up positions behind the parked vehicles and waited.

Forty seconds later a breathless Boyle ran into the car park and turning, fired at Collins who once more threw himself to the ground and rolled away from the fire. After a two second burst there was a click from Boyle's sub-machine gun as his last clip of bullets ran out. Throwing the gun down Boyle raised his hands.

From behind the cars the police emerged and surrounded Boyle in a cordon four deep and thirty yards in circumference. Boyle looked at the silent coppers and smiled.

Collins arrived and Clark grinned at him, 'Yow got him Mickey. Well done.'

Collins looked at Boyle's eyes and could see they were filled with rage and hate. He could feel the anger of the man even from ten foot away. 'What's the matter, Boyle?' he said, 'Annoyed that a Dublin pipspeak, a traitor to old Ireland has caught you?'

'You're shit, Collins. It's you and your like that has helped Britain control Ireland for eight hundred years. But one day, and that day will be soon, you'll have to pay for your treachery.'

'Maybe but you won't be around to cheer when that day comes.'

'Why don't you and me finish it now man to man? Or do you need your small army to do the job for you?'

'Why not?' said Collins and handed his gun and jacket to Clark. 'Stay out of this, Clarkee, and keep the rest back. This is between him and me.' Then he remembered what Clark had said to him in a similar situation and he whispered, 'but if he kills me, kill the bastard.'

'OK, Mickey.'

Boyle grinned and crouched down. Collins moved forward. Boyle lashed out with a right hook which Collins ducked but was hit with the same fist when Boyle swung it backwards. It hit Collins full on the side of his nose and he immediately tasted the copper-like flavour of his own blood. Boyle smiled and closed in, swinging punches to the body. Collins tried to cover up, but Boyle was quick. As soon as Collins brought his fists down to protect his body Boyle switched the focus of his punching to Collins' face.

Collins backed away. Boyle knew how to box so a change of tactics was required. As Boyle moved after Collins, the younger man waited until he was just out of range and feinted to throw a left hook. Boyle moved closer to block the attack and as he did so, Collins raised his knee and flicked out a straight kick. It missed Boyle's testicles and landed full in the lower stomach and pushed him backwards. Collins followed up with a side kick to the stomach which caused Boyle to double over and Collins caught him on the side of the face with a roundhouse kick that sent him sprawling in the dirt. A huge cheer went up from the men present, and cries of 'Finish the bastard, Mickey,' and 'You've got him,' rang out.

Moving in, Collins stopped a yard away and said, 'Have you had enough?' Boyle raised his right hand and head as if in supplication, but his left hand slashed out and a six inch blade opened up a large gash on Collins' shin.

Collins backed away as Boyle jumped up and raced after him. The red-tipped blade slashed in arcs through the air. One of the crowd threw Collins a two foot length of branch. He caught it and it felt substantial in his hand, a bit like his old truncheon. Boyle backed off as Collins whirled the branch, almost hitting the hand which held the knife.

Boyle reached the edge of the circle which the men had created and was pushed in the back by Ridley, 'You ain't so fucking brave now are you, you Fenian bastard?'

Enraged, Boyle ran forward and was hit on the upper right arm and on the side of the face by the branch before he wrapped his arms around Collins and sent him crashing to the floor. Collins released the piece of wood and grabbed

Boyle's knife hand. Scrambling and cursing, Boyle worked his way on top of Collins, and grabbing the knife with both hands, he started to push it down towards Collins' neck.

Suddenly Clark shouted, 'Mickey,' and threw the knife Collins had acquired in the kitchen. Collins caught the knife in his left hand and stabbed Boyle in the side of his stomach, just below the ribcage, and pulled the knife upwards. A look of surprise and shock spread across Boyle's face. The pressure he had been exerting on his knife relaxed. Collins pushed him away, and scrambled to his feet.

Boyle lay on the floor, unmoving, his eyes growing dimmer and dimmer. Only Collins was close enough to hear the rebel's last words, 'This isn't over.'

## Sunday 13th October 1968

### Handsworth, 15.09hrs

Collins had spent four hours in the General Hospital's Accident and Emergency Department having his broken nose reset, stiches inserted in his gashed leg and a blood transfusion for loss of blood, before Agnes was allowed to take him home. He'd gone to bed immediately and had slept through the night and woken at three in the afternoon feeling stiff, sore and pleased. A large breakfast of toast, fried egg, bacon and two sausages added to his smile.

'That, darling, looks just the job.'

'Well, enjoy it while you can. You're getting slow and fat. You're on a diet from tomorrow.'

'Ah bejesus, you're a hard woman bullying the hero of the hour.'

'No, I'm not. I'm the women you're going to marry on February the ninth, and until then I'm going to do my best to keep you alive.'

'If I had the time, I'd take you to bed right now,' said Collins with a broad smile, 'But alas, Clark is picking me up in thirty-five minutes. We have to go and see a man about a horse.'

'Well if you can eat your breakfast in ten minutes, we'll still have twenty minutes free to enjoy ourselves.'

Collins started to shovel the food down his throat.

Clark parked outside the Cunninghams' palatial residence. 'How do yow want to play it?' asked Clark.

'Well I don't think we can use any rough stuff. Let's see if we can get him to make a slip.'

'How wem going to do that?'

'I have absolutely no bleeding idea.'

'Well that's good, 'cos most of yowr ideas never work out.'

'It's always motivating to hear what your staff think of you,' said Collins as he rang the bell.

Yolande opened the door and smiled, 'I didn't expect to see you pair today. Come on in.'

'We just wanted to give you and Martin the full story.'

'Sounds interesting. Go on up to Martin. I need to switch the iron off.'

As they ascended the stairs Collins turned to Clark and whispered. 'I'll do the questioning; you observe Cunningham see if he's shaken by anything I say.'

Clark nodded and knocked on the door and waited for Cunningham to say, 'Come in,' before opening it.

'It's you pair again. Did Yolande not tell you how many different coppers we've had in the house today?'

'No,' said Collins.'

'Well I counted seven who came to talk with me.'

'Well we just wanted to say how sorry we are that your friend Mr Boyle is dead. I know that you didn't support his IRA activities, but he was your friend.'

'He was me friend, but buying guns and explosives and trying to store them in my warehouse was the last straw. I'm now convinced that he was the one who arranged my little accident. The bastard. What I don't know, is did he intend to kill me or just keep me out of the way while he arranged shipment for his guns?'

'Sure, we'll never have an answer to that question. But personally, I don't think he was trying to kill you.'

'Why not.'

'It was a main road. Once you were hit the driver in the car couldn't reverse over you and make sure you were dead. There were too many witnesses. Plus, the most serious injury was your concussion which was caused by you hitting your head on the road. That was probably resulted from you jumping up moments before the car hit you.'

'Sure, that was down to my quick reactions. I've always had good reflexes.'

'Yes, I'm sure your reactions are as quick now as they were twenty years ago.'

'I wish they were, but they're still fairly good.'

Changing the subject Collins asked, 'Will you be going to Boyle's funeral?'

'No. I won't be able to travel on a plane for a few months yet. But Yolande will go. People would think it strange if neither of us went.'

'Yeah, funerals are great places to pick up information from.'

'You mean gossip?' asked Cunningham

'Yeah, I suppose I do. What will you do about your compound?'

'I've been thinking for a while now that it was bit small for me needs. I think I'll sell it off and move to bigger premises.'

'Well, good luck with the move.'

'Thanks.'

Walking back to Clark's car, Collins said, 'That was a disappointment. He's a smart one, that's for sure, but he's proud of his reflexes. Just what you need to avoid being run over.

'Yeah, I picked up on that. If a car's going to hit yow, yow jump up in the air. Which means that yow protect all yower vital organs. But that ain't enough to arrest the bastard. Yow'll need to watch yowr back. I've got a feeling that Martin Cunningham is far more dangerous than Boyle ever was. He's a man who will bide his time and strike when yow least expect it.'

'Well thanks for that pep talk. I feel a lot better now.'

'I think yow'll make it to Christmas.'

'Why so?'

'Cos Cunningham won't be on his feet for about two months. He can't arrange your death from his sick bed. He'll have to speak to people and he ain't going to phone them from his own home.'

'Maybe I'll hire a nice big car and run the bugger over. He can't escape death for a second time.'

'Na, you ain't a killer. Leave that to the guys who have been trained for it.'

Collins didn't reply.

## Thursday January 3rd, 1969

### Digbeth, 00.42hrs

Martin Cunningham had been drinking steadily for four hours in the Adam and Eve pub in Bradford Street, where most of the regulars were Irish. It had been a good night and the crack had been great. On leaving the pub he turned left and then took the next left heading for his car. This was the first night he'd gone out alone since the accident, and now he was going to drive home. He was sure he'd be all right as there was very little traffic on the road unlike the previous night. As he passed a doorway, he heard a man say, 'The Irish Sea is awful rough tonight.'

Martin stopped and replied. 'It will be calm tomorrow.'

The bullet hit Martin in the chest and exploded into his heart. The last thing he ever saw was the flash from the gun. He was dead by the time he hit the ground. The man removed the silencer from the gun and placed it and the gun in his overcoat pockets. Then he walked away into the night.

### Handsworth, 09.02hrs

Collins parked his new dark blue Mini Cooper in the station's car park. He'd never admit it to Clark, but he preferred the Mini to the Capri. It was better suited to city driving and just as fast as the Ford but was a damn sight easier to park. As he reached to turn off the radio he heard the Radio One newscaster announce that Martin Cunningham's body had been found in Digbeth in the early hours of the third of January and that the United Sons of Ulster, a previously unknown terrorist group in Northern Ireland, had claimed responsibility for his murder. He didn't hear the rest of the report and sat there stunned for nearly a minute before Clark rapped on the side window.

He wound the window down and Clark asked, 'Yow heard the news about Cunningham?'

'Just now. Who the fuck are the USU?'

'No idea. But one thing's sure, they done yow a favour.'

Collins looked at Clark and he remembered what the little man had said to him three months earlier about leaving killings to those that had been trained to do it. He would never know for sure but at that moment he believed Clark had killed Cunningham. 'Well at least he won't be bothering us again.'

'True. Very true. Fancy a cuppa and a bacon butty? To celebrate?

'On one condition, I buy them.'

'Yow'll get no argument from me.'

'Do you think that whoever killed Cunningham will ever be caught?

'If I were a betting man, I'd give you better odds on a snowball surviving the fires of hell,' said Clark with a grin.

Later that day, Clark left the police station and walked to Soho Road. Stepping into the familiar red telephone box, he waited until the door was shut, then dialled a London number from memory. The phone was answered on the fourth ring, 'Rhodes.'

'Steve, it's me. Just wanted to congratulate yow on the fine work yow do, and to say thanks. If ever I can repay the favour, yow only have to ask.'

'You're welcome. It was my pleasure. I'll see you around.'

'I hope so. Take care.'

# Epilogue

Chief Superintendent Wallace was buried on Monday 28th October. Men from adjacent divisions covered for the staff at Thornhill Road as they paid their respects to a great police officer. The Superintendent's wife and three children were comforted by the Chief Constable and the Lord Mayor of Birmingham. However, it was the kindness shown by the officers of Thornhill Road and the Superintendent's previous station, Perry Barr, which meant the most.

John Reece was arrested at Gatwick Airport as he tried to board a Thomas Cook package holiday jet to Spain, using a false passport. He was remanded in prison until his trial started on the 2nd September 1969. Charges against him included the murder of John Simpson, numerous assaults, blackmail, fraud, tax evasion and the bribery of nineteen local government officials. His trial lasted seven weeks and he was found guilty on all charges and sentenced to life in prison. The police continued to question Reece about the murders of Claire Lafferty and Christina Murray for nearly a year, but he continued to protest his innocence. The case remains open.

Superintendent Patterson only brought one charge against the City's Chief Auditor, Mr Hastings; the acceptance of a bribe while in a public office. His wife remained unaware of his infidelity and waited for his release from prison after eighteen months. Shortly afterwards they retired to Eastbourne.

Mrs Simpson received a public apology from the Birmingham City Police Force, read out by Inspector West at a press conference. She sold her house in Burntwood and moved in with Marjorie. The two women remain the best of friends although they don't always like the other's choice of men friends.

Clark's suit was delivered by Burtons in January and fitted him perfectly. The wedding of Agnes and Collins was well attended. In addition to friends and colleagues, Agnes and Collins had invited a select band of informants that had been of help to them over the years including Mary, Gloria and Upright Freddie, now known and respected as the Rev. Freddie Bartholomew. Michael Abraham Clark disgraced himself by crying loudly throughout most of the service, but no one seemed to mind and for the rest of the day he watched proceedings with a smile and giggled when tickled by every female in attendance.

In March 1969 Detective Chief Inspector Hicks, Detective Sergeant Collins and Detective Constable Clark were called to a meeting in Steelhouse Lane by ACC Knowles. There they were informed that the Chief Constable had given his approval for the creation of a small team of officers who would report directly to him. Their remit was to track, destabilise, break up and bring to trial criminal gangs in the Birmingham area. If the men agreed to join the Squad, they would each be promoted one rank on an acting basis.

In answer to Hicks' inquiry about how large the squad would be, he was informed that initially six officers would be allocated to the squad. The three additional officers would be chosen by Hicks.

The men asked if they could have twenty-four hours to consider the offer.

When Hicks phoned ACC Knowles the next day he said, 'The answer is yes from all three of us. With two requests, Sir. Firstly, we all want Constable Marie Bolding to be a member of the squad. Secondly we would like the squad to be situated at Thornhill Road.' Both requests were acceded to.

Jane Greggs and Andy Dewar were released from their approved schools within four months of each other. Their first act was to meet up and shag each other to within an inch of their lives. Their second was to move to Sheffield. Their third was to start fantasising about how they could abduct young boys and girls, murder them and dispose of their bodies without anyone ever finding them.

## The End

### Until A Death in Birmingham

# A Death in Birmingham

## By Jim McGrath

Barry Foster was a big man. Over six foot three inches he'd been the tallest and most powerful Marine in his platoon. He still smiled when he thought of his Royal Marines passing-out parade and the party he and his mates had held afterwards. They'd been happy days. Six months later the captain's seventeen-year-old daughter had got her claws into him and when they were caught naked in his bed she'd screamed rape. He'd spent four years in the cooler for indecent assault.

Now aged twenty-five he tramped the streets of Birmingham wearing an old checked suit, still older black brogues and a grimy white shirt. He had no overcoat, no money, no friends, no future and he hadn't eaten in two days. The winter of 1963 was setting records as the coldest on record and tonight the temperature was well below freezing. He didn't think he would survive. He didn't want to survive.

Turning into the alleyway behind the amusement arcade he stumbled towards the two wooden pallets leaning against the wall and the tea chest. They were just as he'd left them that morning. A torn plastic tablecloth pinned to the pallets give some protection against the snow and frozen rain. The ground between the pallets and wall was covered in two inches of old newspapers and cardboard. Kneeling he eased his way backwards into the gap between the wall and the pallets. When his feet were fully in the tea chest he lay down and rolled onto his back. Within seconds he was asleep.

An hour later the sound of voices woke Foster. 'Give us the money old man or I'll fucking cut you and take it.'

'Fuck off, you little shits. You have no idea who you're dealing with.'

Foster moved to where the plastic tablecloth was torn to check out what was going on. The old man was in his sixties and he had the look and confidence of a man who once upon a time was able to handle himself. Now he had a pot belly and white hair that only covered the sides of his head. The bigger of the lads swung a punch at the old man which hit him on the side of the face and sent him sprawling to the floor. The smaller lad then kicked the man in the belly.

Foster had seen enough. He stood up knocking the pallets over and shouted. 'Leave the bloke alone. You want a fight, try me.'

Both lads looked at the swaying tramp in front of them and started to laugh. 'Piss off and go back to your bottle of meths.'

Foster walked slowly towards the two lads. His legs were unsteady, and he really didn't feel well. The big lad marched up to him and then took a step back. 'Christ, you stink,' he said.

Foster didn't say anything, he just swung an uppercut into the youth's belly that lifted the yob two inches off the floor. Bent double, clutching his stomach, the young man had no chance to avoid the next punch, which connected with the side of his face and smashed his cheek. The lad dropped to the floor a low moan of pain – the only sound he made.

The smaller lad backed down the alley and Foster followed him. 'Why did you kick the old man when he was down?' he asked in a low voice.

'I dan't.'

'Yes, you did,' said Foster and landed a forearm smash in the boy's face which broke his nose and jaw.

Turning Foster returned to the old man who was now sitting up. Foster held out his hand and helped the man to his feet. 'Thanks, mate. I'm afraid me mouth keeps writing cheques that me body can't meet. I owe you.'

'Glad to help,' replied Foster as his knees collapsed beneath him and the ground came up to smash him in the face.

When he awoke Foster was sure he had died and gone to heaven. He was in a king size bed, in a room that was painted in a soft grey with a carpet to match. A drip was attached to his clean left hand and he felt incredibly hungry. A middle-aged nurse appeared at his bedside. 'How are you feeling?'

'Hungry,' he whispered his mouth as dry as an Irish pub after St. Patrick's Day.

'I'm not surprised. You've been unconscious for nearly three days. I'll rustle you up some food and tell Mr Summers you're awake.'

Foster waited until the nurse had left, then tried to sit up, but his head started to spin and he lay down and wondered how the hell he'd ended up here. The last thing he could remember was crawling into his bed between the pallets and wall.

He was too tired to think and lay still enjoying the feel of the Egyptian sheets on his naked body and the softness of the mattress beneath him. He started to drift off when the door opened, and Mr Summers entered. The sight of the older man, with a huge bruise covering the left side of his face, brought back memories of the fight in the alleyway. 'Thank God you are awake, lad. I was starting to think that you wouldn't make it.'

'What...? Where...?'

'Shush now. You've been sick and collapsed after sorting those two bastards out. I brought you home and called a doctor. You need to eat now and get your strength back. Then we can talk about your future. I owe you, and I always pay me debts. Just rest and eat for now.'

Foster felt his eyes start to close and he drifted off into sleep.

Mr Summers remained with him until a maid brought in a full English breakfast, woke Foster and started to feed him.

Outside the bedroom George was waiting for the Boss and immediately asked, 'How is he?'

'He's one strong bugger. He'll be fine once he's had some food and rest.'

'What you going to give him?'

'I'm not sure yet. I need to see if he has any brains to go with his bulk. Are the two lads awake?'

'Yes, Boss.'

'Well hose them down with cold water. I'll be down to see the bastards in half an hour.'

CPSIA information can be obtained
at www.ICGtesting.com
Printed in the USA
LVHW042053300620
659398LV00006B/888

9 781912 605675